A consignment of diamonds

is delivered to Montreal under cover of the
hectic confusi

plan an inger
million-dollar gems.

A Syndicate hit man

is in town to carry out a contract on one of the
thieves.

Olympic security forces

hear of plans for a political assassination.

As the games reach their ceremonial climax the
thieves, the Syndicate, the diamond merchants
and the security men collide explosively on the
Olympic site . . .

Pamela Ferguson (32) was born half American, half Cornish, in Chihuahua, Mexico. She started in journalism in Southern Africa after leaving the University of Cape Town, and arrived in London ten years ago with £50. Stateless for five years, she globe-trotted as a gipsy writer, in between anchor jobs on *Marketing*, *Adweek* and *The Times Business News*. She has lived and travelled extensively in the Middle East, using the research from various features to write two books, *The Palestine Problem* (1973) and *The Pipedream* (published by Everest in 1974). Early in 1975 she returned to Beirut on a special assignment for BBC TV. She's written for publications as diverse as the *People's News Service* and the *Financial Times*, London; *Worldview*, New York; *Palestine Affairs*, Beirut; *Financial Post*, and *Impetus* magazine, Toronto.

The idea for *The Olympic Mission* came out of a cover story she wrote on the Olympic stadia, in Montreal, for *Design*, London.

The Olympic Mission

PAMELA FERGUSON

EVEREST BOOKS LIMITED

4 Valentine Place, London, SE1

Published in Great Britain by Everest Books Ltd, 1976

ISBN 0903925 621 (Paperback)
ISBN 0903925 451 (Hardback)

Printed in Great Britain by
Richard Clay (The Chaucer Press), Ltd.,
Bungay, Suffolk

Dedicated to my parents –
Pan and Louis

CHAPTER ONE

'Is he dead yet?'

'No.'

'Jesus he's taking his time.'

The couple looked up instinctively as Tuesday's dawn began to throw grey spears across London's midsummer night sky. A man in a pair of soft thyme green pyjamas was draped languidly over an art nouveau sofa. In the grainy half light he looked as though he awaited the photographer from *Men in Vogue* instead of death. Behind him the view of the Regent's Canal was blurred by a rush mat blind pulled down over an expansive plate-glass window.

A series of frenzied shrieks and ka-peek ka-peek ka-peek ka-peeks split the sultry night air from Regent's Park Zoo. The couple glanced at one another.

'Say if he's not dead by sunrise?'

'Shut up. You make me nervous.'

'Can't we stick him in there now?'

'Are you mad? He'll suffocate!'

They hovered around the sofa alternately testing the man's pulse and listening at his chest.

'Are you sure you gave him a big enough overdose?'

'Almighty God. What do you think I am? Child playing with a chemistry set? After the liquor he put away *two* sleeping pills would have killed him.'

'Christ – he's moving.'

'He's dying, you bloody fool.' They bent over the sofa.

'Can you feel anything?'

'No.'

Swiftly they lifted the fresh corpse on to a fold-up stretcher and strapped it down securely. They carried it across the expensively furnished room to the kitchen, down a single flight of stairs leading to the basement and across to a deep freeze standing in the corner.

While one of them lifted the lid of the cabinet the other undid the straps on the stretcher. Gently they lifted the still-warm body into the deep freeze, made sure it was lying comfortably, closed the lid and locked it. They checked their watches. It was exactly twelve and a half minutes since the man died. Each second was important. Time of death would be established by the digested state of the man's stomach contents and that had to be suspended for a week until the early dawn of Tuesday August 3. Once the body was defrosted between twelve to twenty four hours depending on the temperature of the day, the evening scene could be recreated. In precise detail.

Remnants of an expensive meal.

Empty bottles of fruity red wine.

A quarter full bottle of Courvoisier left by the sofa.

Laughter and music replayed from a special recording.

And a bottle of barbiturates left empty in the bathroom where the man must have wandered drunkenly before falling asleep on the sofa.

The couple returned to the kitchen and quickly made sure they'd left everything in order.

'Do you have the cassette?'

'Course. I liked the way you stopped him watching the TV. Dancing around like that.'

'What else could I do? All we needed to ruin everything was the Olympics live from Montreal on the tape two day's after Sunday's finale.'

The couple returned to the basement and left the house by a back door. From there they crawled under a hedge at the side of the house to reach the Canal path. Beneath them the water lay syrupy and sluggish like an overfed beast trapped between two concrete banks. Dawn brought little air with it. By the time they'd reached the path leading back up to the road where their car was parked, the couple felt quite breathless.

London barely turned in its sleep.

*   *   *

Walter Moon stood and faced himself in a cloakroom at Heathrow Airport's terminal three. He had an hour to spare before his flight for Montreal was called at noon.

He looked wistfully at the dark auburn hair and beard so expertly trimmed close to his head, the bright blue eyes and full lips that had a mere seven days to go. It was a nice face. It had earned him a lot of money in his time. He patted it reassuringly and told himself that the plastic surgeon in Los

Angeles would give him one equally likeable.

Two million dollars was an expensive way to be changed out of one handsome body package into another, he thought grimly. He stepped back, wondering how it was medically possible to improve on the tall, finely tuned physique before him. The way his broad shoulders tapered down to his slender hips had once made him the most popular male prostitute along the Cote d'Azur.

The perfect image of himself in a black poster print shirt, honey coloured corded blouson and matching trousers suddenly shattered. The cloakroom door burst open and in rushed a group of thirty men wearing gaudy Olympic sweatshirts, bright green trousers and striped sneakers. They were one of countless groups of sports enthusiasts bound for the last five days of the Games.

Walter felt conspicuous. Hastily he returned to the departure lounge and searched among the crowds that crammed the terminal to find a seat giving him a reasonable view of passengers as they came through passport and customs control. His beard itched like crazy when he was nervous but he fought against the temptation to scratch it. Nothing was more irritating and noisy. To distract himself he put on a pair of tinted glasses and rustled a copy of *Die Zeit*, wondering what the hell he'd do if Air Canada Flight 801 were called before the man he awaited appeared.

He read through the arts pages twice, glancing up every now and then until he spotted a Franciscan monk walking slowly out of passport control. He started to giggle and then quickly controlled himself. The monk's mop of flaxen white hair looked like a thatched roof hanging down almost as far as a Woody Woodpecker beak-like nose. His long brown habit was neatly tied at the waist with a length of rope and his open-toe black sandals squeaked on the vinyl floor. Walter wondered if other lapsed Catholics watched monks with the same feeling of amusement and guilt. The Franciscan paused and then made his way to the news stand. He carried nothing but a cheap looking black briefcase that bulged with what appeared to be a solid box.

A group of people flooded out of passport control followed by an agitated tour operator carrying a load of airline tickets. For a moment the monk was lost in the midst of them. Walter saw the thatched hair bobbing up and down and decided how

9

easy it would have been to arrange for an expert pick-pocket to do the job there. Trip the monk over his skirts and run off with the black briefcase with its $20 million worth of Vatican diamonds *en route* to Montreal.

But Walter had not spent five months planning anything so crude. His theft would take years to reveal itself. By then Walter Moon would not exist. He sat and watched as the flaxen head emerged out of the group and thought back bitterly to the chilly February day that had turned five months into an obsessive plan to escape.

The gnome from Zurich had joined the Paris branch of Walter's health and pleasure centres to learn the Tai Chi Chuen blend of physical and spiritual discipline. He relaxed afterwards with a young Italian boy in a pure silk kaftan before flying back to his wife and family. Late one afternoon he made an appointment to see Walter, and bustled into his office fresh from the sauna.

Walter had been pleased to see him. He enjoyed exchanging views with his clients at his centres in Paris, London and Vienna.

'Can I offer you a cognac, Herr Borg?'

The man nodded enthusiastically and glanced approvingly at the Art Deco items that cluttered Walter's office. He drew a table lamp of two women holding a globe between them towards him and stroked their arched naked backs sensuously.

'I found it in London,' said Walter, pouring cognacs for them both, 'at a junk shop in Camden Town – years before they discovered the word antiques. *Servus*.'

Borg smiled and returned the toast. 'I'd like to take young Eduardo away with me,' he said, holding his glass to the light.

'My team isn't for sale. Did he tell you where I found him? He was a barman in a hotel in Jamaica – imagine that, a boy with those looks.'

'How do you choose your "teams"?' asked Borg, cupping his hands under the cognac and swilling it around.

'Europe, West, East Africa, Japan, the West Indies. Anywhere. Could be a campus here or a martial arts centre there or a waterfront bar or a hot-dog stand. Doesn't matter. I know as soon as I see a man or woman. It's not just looks.' Walter sipped his cognac thoughtfully.

Borg took his hand off the lamp ladies and smiled. 'I brought you something,' he said handing Walter a soft white leather folder with the shy air of someone passing over an unexpected gift.

Walter looked at him and turned on the lamp. He opened the folder and took out five large white envelopes. The first was neatly addressed to the British Prime Minister and contained explicit photographs of opposition members of parliament with the same girl at Walter's London club. Walter couldn't help smiling. He let his computer work out an intricate traffic flow to prevent the MPs from finding out they both shared the same fleshily built Finnish girl.

The second envelope contained photographs of an American food tycoon's twin sons busy at either end of one girl. A third envelope contained photographs of a world famous conductor, nude, in the Yoga headstand and other positions, engaged in *soixante-neuf* with a heftily built boy dressed in billowing chiffon.

Walter paused and sipped his drink. He opened the fourth envelope. Out came the wife of a former French cabinet minister in a finely embroidered Victorian blouse, making love to a young woman sitting astride her. The final envelope held the secret of one of Britain's most famous chairmen. He wore a gym slip.

The photographer had taken exceptional care to include details of Walter's three centres to prove the setting of each subject. The background of pine panelled walls, huge cushions covered with rich oriental silks, deep pile carpets, original paintings and exotic potted plants appeared in each. Walter replaced them neatly in their envelopes. He hadn't uttered a sound and hoped his eyes looked expressionless. He handed the white leather folder back to the man sitting opposite him.

'You don't *look* as though you need money,' he said sarcastically.

'Very perceptive, Herr Moon. My colleagues are reasonable men. We have no wish to destroy either your reputation or that of your club members.' Borg's fresh face looked lined with concern.

'Colleagues?' Walter frowned, feeling a quiet rage pull at the corners of his mouth.

'We have various business interests in Europe and North America. We know there are ways your enterprise and our own could be made more compatible.' Borg nodded intimately and took out a packet of king-size slim cigarettes from his pocket. He offered one to Walter.

Walter refused. 'So why the fancy photographs?'

Borg laughed lightly and lit his cigarette with a gold Dunhill lighter. 'In this inflationary age,' he began, 'the essence of successful development lies in seeking out men with a creative flair, like yourself, who have proved themselves. We're not interested in risky innovation.' He blew out an energetic cloud of smoke.

Walter sensed the man knew he hated people smoking in his office.

'We think long term,' Borg continued. 'We admire the way you have built up these centres. You were a good prostitute yourself once, Herr Moon. It was wise of you to use your considerable earnings to take degrees in the sexual and business sciences before – establishing yourself?'

'You *are* complimentary.' Walter hardly moved.

'We don't want to buy you out,' assured Borg, leaning forward in his chair. 'You'll run the centres and we'll provide the necessary capital to help you expand in North America. I know your centres turn over ten million dollars a year after, how many years is it? Five? Yes, well, we can't see how you can expand on the scale we envisage without our assistance.'

'Expand? Who says I want to expand?'

Borg's eyes crinkled at the corners. 'Would you like to hear our innovations?' He sounded excited.

'Why don't you just buy me out?'

'Waste of capital. We want *you* to run the centres.'

Walter sat back and drained his cognac.

Borg replaced the folder in his briefcase. 'We aren't unreasonable, we know it takes time for businessmen like yourself to make up their minds. It's the third of February today so we'll finalize everything on the third of August.' He clapped his hands and prepared to go. 'You can review your books, prepare detailed financial statements – oh – and it would be helpful to have outlines of five-year development plans with the necessary financial projections.'

Walter stared as Borg's three-inch-long ash fell on to the top of his highly polished desk. Neither man attempted to sweep it away.

Borg paused and replied to the heavy silence. 'I don't have

to say that you won't have much left of this' – he gestured around the office – 'if we show these photographs about, do I?'

Walter started to get up.

Borg stubbed out his cigarette on the base of the Art Deco lamp and turned to go, then he drew in his breath as if remembering something.

'There isn't much in your own life we don't know about,' he said, silently hoping for a response from Moon. 'For example –' he took out a flat leather diary from his inside pocket. 'A day in the life of Walter Moon. How about July the sixteenth last year?' He dampened his fingers and turned over a number of pages with speed and accuracy. 'Yes. You flew non-stop to Vancouver, spent the night with one Staki Lin at the Bayshore Inn. We took photographs of you both from a helicopter hovering over the marina opposite your suite. Ms Lin's family would be interested in these, wouldn't they?' He looked up, waiting for a response. There wasn't one. He shrugged and continued, 'Now let's see. On the nineteenth of July you flew from Vancouver to Montreal to be with your lifelong friends the Greek prostitute Boubolina Melas, and a black radical, Sole Dubois.' He made it sound like a snippet from 'This is Your Life'. He paused and smiled warmly. 'Shall I go on?'

'You've made your point.' Walter stood his ground.

Borg patted his silk tie neatly down and turned to the door. 'You have my various telephone numbers on your files of course. You can leave recorded messages on any of them.' He opened the door and glanced back. 'I must hurry. Eduardo is waiting at the airport for me.'

Walter waited until the door closed and then picked up the Art Deco lamp and flung it across the room. It exploded against a wall spraying the air with millions of tiny pieces of glass.

There was another half an hour to kill before Flight 801 was called. Walter looked up angrily at the flight information TV and felt himself sweating profusely at the thought of the February day. He moved across to the airport bar, ordered a Campari and sat where he could keep the monk in view. He spooned several lumps of ice into his drink and stirred it vigorously, remembering all too vividly how he had reacted to Borg's visit. He spent his life beating obstacles but this one

13

had caught him off guard.

He was getting soft. That hurt the most. He had kicked his way out of a slum using a technique of feet fighting that made him the most feared kid on the block. He screwed his way into the bank balances of the idle and frustrated rich with a sexual dexterity fired more by revenge than desire.

He fought viciously to hide his vulnerability. And as soon as he stopped fighting he was exposed. In one hour Borg turned him from the sophisticated, cultivated Moon he had fought to become, back into the lanky slum kid with the killer feet he'd fought to forget.

There was only one thing he could do. Disappear. This was a part of his life no multi-million dollar network of organized crime would pin down. The day after Borg had visited him, he caught the first direct flight from Paris to New York. Driven by a paradoxical mix of intense anger and Yoga-trained discipline he spent a few days zig-zagging his way across the States to California to the one man in the world who could help him.

From Kennedy Airport he had taken the short milk run to Lebanon, New Hampshire, hired a car at the airport and drove to Rutland, Vermont. It had been snowing heavily. He could hardly see the banks on either side of the road and was sorely tempted to hop back on a plane and to hell with it fly straight to LA. But the sight of a metallic blue Chevelle glued to his mirror like a kid's transfer made up his mind. He ditched his car in Rutland and walked to the Greyhound Terminal where a bus was just loosening up its engine before heading for Woodstock along route 4. He sat near the front and asked the driver to drop him off just by a road sign that read REST, FISH, ENJOY, the come-hither of a motel at the base of Bridgewater Hill.

As he got out he paused briefly to sniff the mixture of maple, pine and spruce. The bus pulled away and the Chevelle shot past at high speed. Within minutes Walter checked into the motel and stayed there just long enough to shower, shave off his beard, change from a business suit to one of the three outfits he took with him – heavyknit fisherman's sweater and fleece lined jeans.

He reversed his overcoat and reappeared on the road in time to catch the next bus for Woodstock, where he hired another

14

car at the terminal.

From Woodstock he drove like a man possessed, stopping only half a dozen times for gas, hamburgers and coffee, determined to pass through Albany, Binghamton, Cleveland, Toledo and Gary, to reach Chicago before the following night. Nobody tailing him would believe anyone could take such an insane route to California.

He drove to the outskirts of Chicago where he pulled off the road at the first motel and persuaded the owner's son to drive him to Midway Airport – O'Hare was too obvious – and drop the car at the U Drive Office.

At the airport he bought a single ticket for Denver and as he had twenty minutes to spare, ordered a steak at the cafeteria. Later he took a timetable on the flight and decided to catch the next flight out of Denver for Phoenix.

It was midnight by the time he arrived in Phoenix so he dozed for a couple of hours stretched out on a seat in the lounge, before changing into a safari jacket and trousers, and hiring a car from a sleepy Hertz attendant at the airport. From Phoenix he drove solidly up towards the Hoover Dam on the border of California and Nevada.

A dot on the road turned into a shape huddled under a blanket in the early dawn. It clutched a massive cardboard notice. LAS VEGAS OR I'LL EXPIRE.

Walter skidded up next to it and opened the passenger seat door. 'Jump in.'

'Thanks, pal.' The hitch-hiker climbed in next to him and the blanket fell from his shoulders revealing a youthful, peeling face, jeans faded white by the sun, and shoulder length hair. He clutched a crumpled canvas sunhat and kitbag.

'How long you been on the road, kid?'

'Coupla hours. Guy in a delivery truck got mad at me and threw me out. Fuckin' cold out there.'

'Why did he throw you out?' Walter stretched into the back seat, took a flask of whisky out of his bag and handed it to the boy.

'Thanks. I dunno.' he took a long swig.

Walter restarted the car. 'Going to gamble away your fortune in Vegas?'

'Naw. They're advertising for bar staff at the "Water Lily".'

'Where you from?'

15

'Louisville.'

Walter whistled. 'Like to earn some bread?'

The boy looked at him quickly.

Walter laughed. 'That's not what I meant. Trade your jeans for my clothes plus a hundred bucks?'

'*Hundred* bucks? Are you kidding? These jeans took me two years to wear in!' He looked scornfully at Walter's outfit and took another swig of whisky.

'Listen, kid. This isn't just crap I'm offering. Cost me over five hundred bucks and this is only the second time I've worn it.'

'Mister, I don't give a sheeit. I wouldn't sell these jeans for that.'

'How much you got on you?'

'Ten bucks.'

'Okay. I'll give you seventy times that.'

'Nuts.' He looked at Walter in disgust.

Walter slowed down and pulled off the highway. He took out a wallet, opened it and removed a rubber band from a pile of notes. He glanced briefly in the rear window as a cloud of dust on the horizon quickly turned into a Pontiac that was beyond them in seconds.

'You drive?'

'Sure.'

'Okay, here's seven hundred bucks. Change clothes with me, drive into Vegas, turn the car in for me and you'll earn another hundred.'

The hitch-hiker didn't say a word. He took the money, placed it on the floor with the flask, unzipped his jeans and pulled a sweatshirt off his head. 'You're out of your tree mister.' He winced as Walter handed him his own outfit.

'Do I have to wear that?'

'Just until you drop the car.'

'Whew! They must want you bad.'

'No questions.'

After he changed into the boy's damp, clinging clothes and pulled on the canvas hat, Walter hopped out of the car and ran around to the passenger seat. A Ford pick-up truck rattled by. The hitch-hiker waited a minute and then started up the car. Walter slouched in the seat and turned on the radio. The final bars of Dolly Parton's 'Jolene' filled the morning air. He drifted off peacefully until the boy woke him at the first road-sign for Las Vegas.

'Okay, this'll do. Hey, one last thing. Swap your kitbag for mine – just the kitbag and I'll throw in another hundred with the whisky flask. Here's three hundred. Don't forget to turn in the car.'

The boy shrugged, took the notes and placed them wordlessly in his pocket. He picked up the flask, made the final exchange and Walter stepped out on to the road. 'Take care of my jeans,' he said dryly. He grinned, half waved, accelerated noisily and kicked up a sweep of dust with his back wheels.

Walter watched him disappear down the road. The sun was climbing steadily in the sky but six cars drove by at top speed without so much as a glance at the figure by the roadside. By the time a bus came Walter would have bought it to make it stop. He took it all the way to Bakersfield California. He reached the outskirts by dusk and hopped off at the first motel in what seemed like an endless line of them stretching along the highway.

He had checked into one under a false name and gave a woman with a mouth like Jeanne Moreau a fifty dollar bill not to disturb him until seven the next morning. In the privacy of his room he had called Los Angeles direct and confirmed his appointment for 11 a.m. with one of the best plastic surgeons in the world.

Walter finished his Campari and ordered another. The monk sat at a near-by table quietly sipping a cup of tea. The terminal lounge was uncomfortably close. Walter removed his blouson, aware that his black shirt was clinging to him like a second skin. For one wild moment he thanked Borg, for forcing him back on his raw impulses. There was something stimulating about planning your own disappearance.

There was something equally stimulating about planning a multi-million dollar robbery under the nose of the most advanced security precautions taken at any Olympic Games to date.

He knew and everybody knew that no amount of jaw about the Olympic spiritual ideal could paper over the cracks of acute political grievances between participating nations. But the International Olympic Committee, determined that no trigger-happy elements from the left or the right should destroy 1976, had invested heavily against a second Munich.

17

They had employed Big Brother to fake the appearance of the cosy Brotherhood of Man in the same way that a tobacco company might employ a fancy public relations company to persuade everybody that smoking was healthy.

Walter thought back wryly over each of the previous five months and how his own plan to disappear had been helped by the three people closest to him and most threatened by Borg the Zurich gnome. Staki Lin, a Chinese-Canadian air-hostess, was at that moment preparing for the intensive security check for Flight 801. Sole Dubois and Boubolina Melas were waiting for him in Montreal.

Walter's beard began to itch again. Frantically. Okay, in a few weeks it wouldn't be there. He'd have to find something else to scratch. He wondered if McGlure was sharpening his knives in Los Angeles. Their first meeting had been weird after his hell run from New York.

'Come in, Mr Moon. Dr McGlure won't keep you a minute.' The pretty receptionist stood back to let him into the front porch of 1475A Winchester Boulevard, a double-fronted mansion backed by acres of rolling lawns the size of a mini golf course. 'Can I offer you some coffee? Juice? Coke?' She took him into a spacious waiting room that was coolly empty except for a few comfortable chairs and a highly polished table half covered with magazines in six languages.

'Coke will do fine.'

'While you're waiting, could you complete the form on the table?' She pointed and smiled.

'Oh, sure.' Walter watched her approvingly as she left the room. He sat down and drew the form towards him. He was relieved to find it asked only general details about background, education and health.

McGlure's was one of those names he made a point of collecting on his travels. Names of men and women all over the world with different skills, who could be called upon in an emergency. He heard about McGlure from a talkative client in an Estoril hotel during the summer of 1971.

'Mr Moon?'

Walter turned around quickly. A man stood at an open door behind him. He looked like a freshly baked Groucho Marx. Walter blinked in surprise and stood up to take the doctor's outstretched hand. McGlure was much younger than he ex-

18

pected. He wore lightweight tartan trousers, a crisply laundered pale lime clinical top neatly buttoned across one shoulder and canvas loafers.

'Come in!'

Walter moved into a room that looked more like a hunting lodge than an examination room. A massive bearskin lay on the floor with its leering head lifted slightly against the edge of a large yellow-wood desk. The walls were covered with a variety of different skins.

'I see you're an avid ecologist, Doctor,' said Walter, nodding at the floor and walls.

McGlure chuckled. 'That was how my granddaddy made his living. Fiercest thing I ever shot was a racoon.' He gestured towards an examination area that was discreetly hidden behind folding Japanese screens. Aided by the receptionist who returned wearing a bright yellow uniform, the doctor deftly put Walter through a detailed physical. Forty-five minutes later Walter sat in front of him doing up his cuffs.

'Mr Moon, you're in excellent health. Normally I have to tell my patients to spend six months shaping up before I'll touch them. But I could start on you tomorrow!' The doctor rinsed his hands at a small basin and dried them energetically. His nurse smiled at them both and quietly left the room. McGlure smoothed down his bristly moustache, and took out a slim pen from his pocket. 'What do you do? Work-out in a gym each week?'

'Sure, alternating with Yoga, depending on my mood.'

'Uh huh? Now then,' began McGlure, sitting down and getting straight to the point. 'If you want to disappear successfully, you can't just depend on a change of hair, a new nose and contact lenses to make your eyes look different. That's theatre. Not modern medicine. That's not our ball game. Nor do we believe we can change people overnight. Before I go into details, you do understand that our fees buy you total confidentiality?'

Walter nodded.

'We work only on recommendation,' McGlure continued. 'Once a patient leaves these walls there is no record here of their previous identity. None. Can I offer you some coffee? Or no –' the doctor grinned boyishly. 'I've discovered that one of my girls makes the best malts in California!' He kissed his fingers and buzzed the intercom. 'Chocolate or banana?'

'Chocolate.' Walter watched the doctor curiously.

'Carrie – coupla those chocolate malts?' The doctor sat back. 'Mr Moon – say, can I call you Walter? I'm Don. Uh – Walter, our process doesn't just make a man or woman taller or shorter, fatter or thinner, older or younger. With our reconstructive surgery we change *nationality* and *race*. But that doesn't happen with surgery alone. No sir. Our pre- and post-operative therapy changes *inner* man. Completely!' He paused as a girl in jeans and a halter top breezed into the room with two huge glasses frothing over with chocolate malt.

'Carrie, meet Walter!'

'Hi, Walter, nice to know you. It's not everybody that gets malts here. You must be real special.' She winked at McGlure, stretched out her arms to place the glasses in front of the two men, and walked out from patio doors.

'Nice kid. Works in our library.'

'Library?' Walter picked up a wide straw and plunged it into the dark bubbles.

'Yep. The pulse of our re-educating process. Boy. You ever taste a malt like that? You see, this isn't just a matter of making occidental eyes look oriental. We teach you a new language and thought pattern. By various processes we *de*-culturize you and then *re*culturize you so that you *are* your new identity.'

'Doesn't that take a helluva long time?' Walter sounded faintly panic stricken.

'A month at the most.' The doctor dismissed the point with a casual sweep of the hand. 'We use modern hypnotic methods and we have innovated special crash courses in the adopted culture. You live here, attend classes and therapy sessions, and while you sleep we continue working on your subconscious – tapes and so on.'

Walter shuddered visibly.

The doctor laughed heartily. 'All my patients do that in the beginning. Then they start thinking it's all a new adventure, like packing a suitcase and taking a ticket anywhere. We arrange a new family tree, a hometown, school, college or whatever. Sure, some of our patients want to go so far that we arrange for them to cut out totally all details of their previous self – reactions when they bump into people they know and so on – man, oh man, these malts!' He looked down lovingly into

20

his glass. 'You needn't be afraid that what we do will in any way break you psychologically. We look for the "new you" inside the old you. We're all parts of different people, you know. Here we wake up the dormant stranger within you.' The doctor sucked deeply through his straws.

Walter replaced his own glass uncertainly on the desk. His beard itched and for once he scratched it noisily.

'Now on the *medical* and surgical side,' added McGlure undaunted, 'you know of course that war injuries have been the real incentive behind reconstructive surgery? There was a time when substitute parts were taken from other areas of the body – but today we use synthetic substances acceptable to the body.'

Walter wondered if he'd ever stop.

'I spent four years as a field surgeon in 'Nam. I learned how to remake a boy's face out of layers of pulp and nothing to guide me but an ID photograph.' The doctor shook his head rapidly.

'Nice malt. Thanks.' Walter wiped his mouth on the back of his hand.

'Warned ya didn't I? Now. Let me show you what I mean about changing a person.' McGlure swung his chair around to a waist-high filing cabinet and took out an album. 'These are composite pictures, Walter – naturally we can't show you actual cases – but these will give you an idea of what we can do.' He began flicking through the pages. 'Okay Chicano to Negro. Russian to Puerto Rican. Korean to Spanish. Negro to Moroccan. Japanese to Indian. Indian to Japanese! Irish to Lebanese. Ah – and one of my prizes – Swedish to Malay and Chinese to Danish!' The doctor sat back with a flourish, downed the remnants of his malt and wiped his moustache with a Kleenex.

Walter studied the photographs closely and clucked in amazement.

'We get even fancier,' said McGlure and swung around in his chair to take out a second album. 'See here – Scottish male to Oriental female. Russian female to American Anglo male. Kenyan male to Algerian female.'

Walter hissed through his teeth. 'You mean people go *that* far? Why, for God's sake?'

The doctor chuckled and half his moustache disappeared up his nose. 'Exiled kings or rulers or political leaders go that far.

Superspies. Generals or leading scientists east of Budapest seeking asylum in the West. You name it.'

'I guess others go that far too? How about wealthy fugitives? Assassins? Guys collecting life assurance?'

'Oh, you're quite a joker, Walter – we're going to have a lot of fun together!' The doctor giggled naughtily, deliberately avoiding the innuendo. 'Now here's a case who doesn't mind being shown in person –' He showed Walter two photographs. 'Fella with a Dorian Gray complex. We took thirty years off him. Thirty years! Boy. You should have seen what we did with his balls.' The doctor shook his head with self approval and snapped the album shut.

Walter pushed his own form tentatively towards him.

'Hm. I see you were born in Vienna in 1938 but your family moved to Montreal when you were a month old. Jewish?'

'No. My parents were members of the Communist Party.'

The doctor glanced up at him quickly. 'How did that affect your upbringing?'

'My parents split up after the war. Mother returned to Vienna and they spent the next fifteen years scratching together enough to import and export me across the Atlantic a couple of times until my mother died. My father died in 1961 and I left Montreal for –'

'No no. I meant how did their *politics* influence you?'

'Oh, ah.' Walter paused. 'Well, I think most kids rebel against their parents' political beliefs, don't they? If mine had been greedy capitalists I'd be an anarchist at Berkeley. Anyway, I grew up mainly on Montreal's East Side and that breeds two kinds. Those that fight thirty hours a day to liberate themselves and their families. Those that fight thirty hours a day to liberate the slum.'

The doctor took in Walter's peach coloured soft suede shirt in a single glance. 'No need to ask which way this fighter went, eh?'

Walter frowned. He hated the way people always tried to make him feel guilty about it. Why was it that kids from the slums were expected to do more for society than anyone else?

The doctor cleared his throat. 'What happened after 1961?'

'I went to pieces,' Walter snapped. 'A pal of mine suggested I work on a health farm near Nice for a while to help get me back into shape. After a summer I realized I could earn more with my dick in a few months than most families cleared in a

22

lifetime.'

McGlure moved uncomfortably in his chair. 'Yes, well, ah, when did you change your name to Moon?'

Walter continued to stare him out. 'My father changed it soon after we arrived in Montreal owning nothing but what we stood in. He thought "Moon" sounded pure.'

McGlure scribbled down a few notes for diversion. 'Of course we'll need to talk a lot more – but with your background you could select any one of a number of identities. You're most fortunate. You've lived in Vienna, Paris, London, Montreal, New York, Cannes – and speak quite a few languages too, I see. That solves half our problem.' He beamed warmly but his eyes avoided Walter's gaze. 'Now then, you could become a German farmer from Australia? Or a French speaking mulatto? An Algerian? A second-generation Greek from the Bronx? I'll make out a long list of probables and you can ring the top three of your choice. We'll whittle it down from there. With your dark auburn hair you could go *real* dark, or very blond. Very fortunate!'

Two hours later Walter sat with his list in a rented car at the foot of McGlure's driveway. He decided to find the nearest motel with a pool and cut out for the rest of the day. Then he'd fly back to winter in Paris and figure out how the hell he'd get the two million dollars McGlure required to grant him his freedom.

Freedom?

Walter hooked his feet around Heathrow's bar stool and wondered what it was going to feel like when he emerged out of McGlure's process plant as 'Georgio Stavropoulos' from the Bronx.

CHAPTER TWO

Flight 801 was eventually called at noon.

Walter moved to the edge of the bridge and waited until the tall figure of the Franciscan swept by. The monk was taller than he expected. He'd been studying his life story for a few months, but always at a distance.

At the departure gate each passenger was subject to slow and intimate frisking. Walter was interested to note that the Franciscan got his share of crotch slapping along with all the other men. The IRA had certainly taught British Airport Authorities a thing or two by using priests or comrades dressed as priests to ferry explosives across the Irish Sea.

Everybody's hand luggage was passed through a newly designed German-made X-ray machine that would show up a paperclip if it was sewn into the seam of a suitcase. No metal of any kind went by undetected. As the Franciscan placed his briefcase on the conveyor belt Walter hung over to look, pretending to be absorbed by the technology of the machine. He saw the outline of a large shoebox containing four neat parcels that looked like cabbage rolls. When the briefcase reappeared on the other side of the machine Staki was there as chief hostess to make spot checks. She carried a passenger list on a clipboard.

'Is this your briefcase here?' She swung it off the conveyor belt.

The Franciscan nodded wordlessly.

'Would you come to the end, please?' He followed her to the end of a long trestle table that looked like a good day at a rummage sale. Staki unzipped the case and took out the contents. Apart from the box there were three buff folders, a shaving kit, a few packets of mints, copies of *Le Monde* and the *Financial Times*.

'Keeping track of your shares, Brother?'

The Franciscan smiled weakly. He handed her a customs clearance form. 'Sweets for the Sisters of the *Sacre Coeur*,' he explained nodding at the shoebox.

Staki undid the crumpled brown paper and lifted the lid.

24

She examined the rolls and then replaced them. 'Thank you.' She looked up and smiled briefly, then turned to make other spot checks.

Walter watched her with a feeling of pride, aware of the flattering remarks the men behind him were making about her generously proportioned body and shapely legs. As agreed previously they made no sign of recognition. He walked by her to the two transit buses that waited to take passengers to the aircraft. Airport security was so tight that the authorities instructed all planes bound for Canada to take off about half a mile from the departure gates.

On board the aircraft Walter was relieved to see that Staki had arranged for him to sit across the aisle from the Franciscan in the few rows reserved for non-smokers. As the plane filled up gradually a child travelling alone was placed in the window seat next to Walter. A businessman in a fawn linen suit settled himself and his wife in the seats next to the monk.

Staki busied herself with the passengers, lifting down pillows for a young couple, helping an old lady with her seat belt and making sure hand luggage was put away neatly beneath the seats. She ignored the lewd comments coming from the back of the plane where four Australians sprawled out, purple-faced from too much beer and too little sleep. They ordered drinks before the plane started to taxi along the runway.

Walter helped the little boy next to him with his seat belt and glanced up briefly as Staki handed around a basket full of candies and chewing gum. When she came to him she moved her hand slightly over two strips of juicy fruit gum. He took them and flashed her a smile. Instead of throwing away the wrappers he folded them carefully and left them in his pocket until the plane was off the ground. While the other passengers were undoing their seat belts and lighting up cigarettes in the split second of relief at being airborne, Walter excused himself to his fellow traveller and headed for the toilets. He locked the door, took out the gum wrappers, smoothed them out and read them in the trembling neon light above the basin.

Staki's neat printing was easy to decipher. 'Package between two to three kilos. Box from size twelve Clarks men's sandals. Four separate parcels with hundreds of tiny envelopes in heavy white tissue paper sealed with 1"-wide off-white masking tape. Take care. See you Sunday.'

Walter smiled and kissed the bits of paper with a flourish.

He set them alight with a pocket lighter, flushed the pieces away in the pan and scattered around drops of *Eau Savage* from a bottle he always carried with him. He sniffed the air sensuously, remembering how he used to soak himself in expensive colognes to prove to everybody he could afford them.

Back in his seat he noticed the monk dozing quietly before lunch, so decided to play cards with his young companion. He had several hours ahead to acquaint himself with the Franciscan's idiosyncracies. One of them would offer a clue to help Walter when he switched the twenty million dollars worth of diamonds in Montreal.

*   *   *

In Rome Cardinal Vincente Zerelli, head of the Prefecture for the Economic Affairs of the Holy See, glanced about his book-lined office in the Vatican and absent-mindedly fingered the heavy crucifix hanging on his chest. He picked up a minute antique clock. The journalist from *24 Ore* was expected at one fifteen, which gave him exactly ten minutes to phone Montreal. Word had reached him from London that the courier was safely aboard Flight 801. He looked up the long dialling code, made a careful note of it, and satisfied himself that eight five was early enough for the Apostolic Delegate in Montreal to have the courier's arrival confirmed.

He dialled and waited for the various clicks that progressed his connection through the five-hour time difference. The phone rang once at the other end. The Cardinal said exactly three words before replacing his receiver.

'Zerelli. Octingenti unus.'

The various high officers of the Church required the minimum of words with one another. Monosyllabic courtesy was the currency in which the Vatican's day-to-day economic affairs were handled, as the journalist from *24 Ore* was soon to discover. His arrival was announced at exactly one fifteen, and that pleased the Cardinal. He loathed unnecessary delay. The young man walked towards him in a well cut blazer and light grey slacks, and dutifully kissed the ring on the hand stretched out to greet him.

'Your Eminence,' he asked of the Vatican's finance minister, 'is it true that the assets handled by the five financial departments and the bank for over a thousand religious orders, the Institute of Religious Works, may be worth as much as six billion to twelve billion lire?' The journalist was eager to show he'd done his homework.

'That's a nonsensical figure.'

The journalist looked crushed. 'Say if I suggested something like three hundred thousand million lire?' He referred quickly to a sheaf of notes.

'I can tell you,' began the Cardinal with studied patience, 'that the Holy See's productive assets are worth far less than a third of the amount you estimate.'

'Can you give me an accurate figure?'

'I am not authorized to do that. The assets include property, real estate and movables – stocks and bonds. Much of the real estate is used for offices, and is an item of expenditure rather than a source of income. Other properties are leased at low rents to those employed by the Holy See. The income from these is small – especially in Italy where the Holy See must obey rent control regulations.'

The journalist took down every word in impeccable shorthand. 'Why is it that a few years ago investments were transferred out of Italy to countries abroad, like the United States? Are you afraid of the increasing power of the Communist Party in Italy?'

'Not all our assets were transferred. But like any administration we have to invest in areas where the returns are better and taxation is lighter.' He ignored the second half of the question.

'Your Eminence, in the United States you have investments in telecommunications, insurance and banking, and I understand you have shares in certain armaments manufacturers.'

'Don't believe everything you read about the Vatican's finances.' The Cardinal glanced at his antique clock.

'With due respect, Your Eminence, would you not say that your investments in –'

'I am not able to discuss details of our investments. Much of what is said about the Vatican is based on the gossip of ill-informed people. Now, if you will forgive me, I have a lunch appointment with the Cardinal of Westminster.'

*   *   *

The hostesses aboard Flight 801 wore bright candy striped dresses in the five Olympic colours, black, red, yellow, green and blue. They bustled about handing out lunch trays and bottles of French-Canadian wines with the compliments of the airline. The labels carried the simply designed logo of the Montreal Olympics, white in a solid red background for red wine, red in a white background for white wine.

The businessman sitting next to the Franciscan held his bottle out at arm's length and nodded approvingly. 'Nice clean piece of design, don't you think, my dear?'

His wife glanced at it. 'Not really. I thought Munich's had more impact.'

'On the drawing board in a well-lit studio perhaps,' he said turning the bottle around slowly, 'but it was certainly not as successful as this when reprinted by thousands of different little men the world over. Were you at Munich, Brother?'

'No,' replied the Franciscan; and that was the only word he said to them throughout the entire flight.

Walter was disappointed. He hoped to learn more about the oddly silent man in the brown habit. But the monk had done nothing but read through his newspapers from cover to cover, catnap and eat his lunch.

Walter glanced about restlessly. His young companion slept blissfully by his side. He looked towards the back of the plane and caught sight of Staki carrying a trayload of beer cans to the four Australians. They wolf-whistled and cat-called as she left the tray and walked towards the front of the plane. Walter giggled to himself and wished he was in bed with her. It was quite a unique feeling for him. Like a man who discovers wine after working in a vineyard all his life.

They had known one another nearly eighteen months. He remembered what appealed to him most when he first met her on a non-stop London to Toronto flight when the plane was half empty. She treated him with indifference. It made such a contrast to the men and women who usually fawned over him. He remembered being fascinated by her eye-catchingly interesting looks that straddled east and west, the result of being born Chinese and brought up North American. She was a powerful lady who made love with certainty and command. He liked that in women. Too many of them suffered from inhibitions imposed first by their mothers, who brainwashed them into thinking there was something not quite nice about enjoying some lusty sex, and secondly by inadequate lovers or husbands who felt menaced by an active woman in bed.

Sure, she was good to look at. The combination of honey-coloured skin, and waist-length hair wound around her head made Walter understand Gaugin. But there was something else he liked. One day she was superhostess Staki, at ease in Hong Kong, Tokyo, Manila, Paris or Stockholm. On the next day at home in Vancouver with its second biggest Chinatown in North America after San Francisco, she became the shy little ex-convent girl. She still stood in trembling fear of her grandmother, who ruled her parents, her father's import business and her three younger sisters with an iron hand.

It was also Staki who had given him the idea about switching the gems. They had known one another a year at the time, and it was a few weeks after the meeting with Borg from Zurich. Walter was so obsessed with the need to raise the necessary two million dollars for McGlure's fee, that he broke a strict rule – that of telling a lover his troubles.

They were in his London apartment. He had just told her about the meeting and his subsequent hell drive to Los Angeles. She wandered around nude, contemplating what he had told her, and pausing briefly to study each of the three George Grosz satirical sketches that hung on his walls. The first was entitled *Rape and murder in the Ackerstrasse 1916* with a freshly decapitated woman lying on a bed. The second, *Happy people, rue Blondel 1925* was a subject of six bloated and distorted faces. The third *The Pimps of Death 1919* showed three grimacing generals standing together against a backdrop of skeletons going about their work in the city.

'Walter?'

'Hm.'

'Why don't you get some cheerful paintings?'

He sat up on his elbow and stared at her blankly. 'Hm? Oh Grosz. My father's idol. He felt they were two men against bourgeois hypocrisy and the slavering warmongers. Difference was Grosz had talent. All my father could do was run a corner store, so badly he died with a mountain of debts. Those prints are all I have left of him.' He lay back again and then sat up quickly, rippling his circular waterbed. 'Is that all you have to say after what I've just told you?'

She turned back to the sketches and began, idly, to plait her long thick black hair. 'The Vatican plans to send a courier to Montreal during the Olympic Games with a parcel of twenty million dollars worth of diamonds,' she said flatly.

'So?' he said sourly.

'So steal them.'

'You're crazy, Staki. How the hell could I do that? Anyhow, where d'you get that kind of information? Is that the sort of thing the nuns twitter about at your school reunions?'

'I'm serious.' She turned and faced him, untwining her hair.

Walter propped himself on his elbows again and looked at her. She was standing under a sloping skylight. 'Come here,' he said, enjoying the way her thighs moved towards him. She lay down beside him and he began to caress her absentmindedly.

'Walter don't. I'm serious.'

He began to tickle his own nipples.

'Walter *please*!'

'All right, all right! I'll hold everything for two minutes.' He made a great show of putting his hands under the duvet.

She ignored him. 'A few months ago I was serving lunch in first class,' she said staring at the ceiling, 'and I happened to hear two cardinals discussing these diamonds.'

Walter lay back and laughed. 'Oh, that's beautiful. Two sons of God sitting on a plane full of people, talking about diamonds. Was that between the caesar salad and the grilled smoked salmon or, let me see now, between the canape and the chateaubriand?'

'There were only five people in first class that day,' she continued, 'so Jim the blue-haired steward and I had an easy trip. Who cares about a bit of eavesdropping?'

Walter stretched vigorously on the bed, deliberately rocking the water under them. 'Boy, do I need a work-out. You haven't seen the gym and sauna I installed in Paris, have you?'

Staki said nothing but waited patiently until the bed was smooth again. 'Nobody would discuss something like the transfer of millions of dollars worth of diamonds publicly,' she persisted as if addressing a room full of schoolchildren. 'But then cardinals of different nationalities talk in Latin to one another.'

'*Latin?*' Walter sat up quickly.

'Sure, smartass,' she snapped. 'You forget your Staki spent fifteen years at a convent school and majored in Latin. But the sons of God look at me, see slit eyes and a yellow face and think all I know is pidgin English and how to say "*Tiǎr hěn hǎo tong zhī*".'

30

'What the hell's that?'

'It's lovely weather comrade, in Mandarin.'

'Oh. Go on.'

'Okay, they discuss the best ways to get the stones across the Atlantic and then decide that the two weeks of the Olympics would be the best time. Nobody's going to take notice of a priest with a box of glass among those thousands of people.' She began to stroke his chest.

'But they must know the city will be crawling with police and security men?'

'So? That's one form of protection they don't have to pay for. Also,' she added, bending over to bite his nipples, 'they said the gems were going to be stored under the stock exchange and sold gradually over several years.'

Walter moved her gently off his chest, jumped out of bed and walked over to a triangular desk built to fit a corner exactly. He opened the top, took out a cassette player and slipped in a tape of Jack Elliott doing Woody Guthrie's *Talking Dustbowl Blues*.

Staki shook her head. 'Why, for God's sake? Depressing drawings, depressing music. Boy, do you need a shrink!'

'I'm nervous about bugs. I'll beat that Borg and his crawling friends every way they turn.'

'You've been reading too many Watergate stories. Anyhow, why do we have to hear about Oklahoma in the Depression?'

'Guthrie's good for my adrenalin. Okay, butterfly you're in the plane and the Cardinals are talking. Now take your time, think back. Try to remember everything they said in detail — everything.' He walked back to the bed.

Staki threw back the covers and pulled him towards her. She began kissing the back of his neck. 'Well,' she said, running her finger around the base of his hairline, 'the courier is a monk called Mark Land.'

'How d'you work that one out?' He turned around, stroked her breasts with his face, grazing them gently with his beard.

'Hey, that's no way to treat a nice girl from Chinatown!'

'How d'you find out the courier's name?'

'Who? Oh *yes*, just like that — don't rush me baby — make me wait —'

'Staki, you said they spoke in Latin. Hey. Just feel you. Give me your hand.'

'Wait, baby, wait. Latin. Yeah, wait, Jesus, that feels mar-

31

vellous. Bit more to the left, down a bit, yes, right there.'

'Staki, how do you know the courier's *name*?'

'– Wait – make me wait. They said Marcus Terra. That's Latin for – wait – for – *oh yes*, oh God yes, again, quickly this time – yes!'

Walter looked up embarrassed.

'Would you like a drink sir?' The hostess repeated for the third time, getting slightly annoyed.

He blinked. 'Drink?'

'Yes, you know, drinkies? Drinky drinkies?'

'Oh.' Walter flushed and glanced around at the sea of amused faces. 'Oh, well, uh, do you have any beer?'

'Oh, I think so, sir. We had several dozen cans back there last time I looked.'

*　　*　　*

Cardinal Vincente Zerelli had personally selected the lunch menu for the Cardinal of Westminster in his private dining room, concentrating on his friend's favourites. Chicken done simply but expertly in oil and lemon on a bed of tagliatelle, a salad of crisp lettuce, celery, green peppers and olives, newly baked bread, a Vatican estate bottled white wine, and a sharp country cheese to follow.

But the Italian cardinal had arranged the lunch during Westminster's monthly visit to Rome for more than just a frivolous chat about the recent recital of Monteverdi vespers or the value of pop music at mass.

When the meal was nearly over he sliced a piece of cheese and sniffed it delicately. 'Our concern is growing,' he began, sweeping crumbs off the finely crocheted tablecloth, 'about the number of priests who feel it is their duty to become involved in international groups of a somewhat "radical" nature.'

The Cardinal of Westminster raised his eyebrows. 'Radical?'

'Allow me to be more specific. The Church's name has been involved with gun running for the IRA, with anti-government groups in South Korea and with the Basque militants.' He paused, adding: 'We speak between ourselves of course. We have always been open with one another. I can tell you freely that the political aspect of these activities is somebody else's worry. Not mine. What bothers me most is the way church

32

funds are being diverted.'

'I understand. But surely you m—'

'Such activities must be stopped,' the Italian Cardinal butted in. 'Naturally we are unable to supervise every move, mass or confession. Never let it be said that the Church is run like a dictatorship. But I do feel that tighter control of parish budgets is what is required in these sensitive areas.'

Westminster replaced a slice of cheese that was poised at his lips.

'Of course,' added Zerelli, busying himself with the coffee tray, 'I am not suggesting that we should plant spies, merely that the activities of suspect priests in Northern Ireland and of course the United Kingdom should be subjected to closer scrutiny.'

'And Eire?' Westminster shifted uncomfortably in his chair. The main reason for the lunch was now quite clear.

'Ah, Eire I will deal with separately, as of course I'll deal in turn with Spain and South Korea. Black or white?'

'Black, please.'

'At this moment it is your territory that concerns me, not that of others.'

Westminster knew by the tone of Zerelli's voice, quiet, kindly, words selected with precision, that the remark was both a warning and a criticism.

'I have a solution in mind,' continued the Italian Cardinal, 'a little *creme de menthe* with your coffee? No? Ah well. I have just the priest to roam around the parishes, build up local confidence, keep in touch with grass root activities.'

'You do mean *spy*.'

Zerelli shook his head. 'Mark Land is the one to carry out the task – as soon as he returns from Montreal. He's on an errand for us.' Zerelli emptied some salt on the tablecloth to soak up a minute drop of coffee.

'*Land?* But it's only a year since you removed him from the Franciscans and sent him to London!'

'Where he's proved to be outstanding. He manages our interests in the City admirably. That was a wise move on our part. He was too brilliant, too restless for the Franciscans.'

'You mean he was a troublemaker,' snapped Westminster.

'On the contrary. Any man in an incompatible environment will become abrasive. We have learned how to handle our rebel priests. Move them. Quickly. Before they define their personal

33

source of discontent and influence others.'

'Land has hardly done that in the City of London.'

'No. True. But he finds it difficult to avoid temptation. Anyway his choppy nature is well suited to change. His tendency to criticize all that we do here in Rome will, I believe, make him more acceptable to the rebel priests of Ulster. He's back in his brown habit again after a year in pinstripe. I wonder how it feels.' Zerelli's voice drifted off into the distance.

'How do you think he'll like the idea of being a spy?'

'I have no idea, Your Eminence.' Zerelli smiled and rang a tiny silver bell for the table to be cleared. 'Because it is up to *you* to brief him when he returns from Montreal next week.'

CHAPTER THREE

'Good day, ladies and gentlemen. This is your Captain speaking. It looks as though the temperature in Montreal is hovering between eighty-five and ninety degrees. I must say I'd rather be flying up here than running a mile down there trying to win a gold medal for Canada, heh-heh-heh-heh-heh. Local time in Montreal is precisely eleven forty-seven, and our estimated landing time is around two forty-five. *Bonjour mesdames et messieurs –*'

Staki stood in the tiny metal-lined kitchen at the rear of the plane and started to prepare tea trays. She glanced down the full length of the aircraft and noticed that Walter was fast asleep. So much for his planned vigil, she thought dryly. She admired his confidence. He always said it was something to do with being brought up poor, but when she reminded him that she was too, he dismissed this briskly.

'You're the sort of person who never learns from being poor. You know why?' he had asked one day as they strolled along a cobbled street in Vancouver's trendy Gastown. 'It's because you're all ruled by that shrivelled walnut of a grandma which means you've never broken free. And you *still* live in ghettos, call them Chinatowns or whatever. You may as well go back to mainland China. Jesus. Your mother hardly speaks English!'

'What's so big deal about speaking English?'

'All you remember about your childhood,' Walter persisted, 'is living in a funny apartment over a shop with dark red chickens hanging up in the window. Neon lights flashing in your eyes at night, and you cringing to a convent each day.'

'I'm pleased to learn so much about my childhood. Buy me some white chocolate in that pretty candy store and stop talking *mǎ pi jing*.'

They turned off the street into an arcade, bought the chocolate and walked on to an open air cafe opposite a leather and soapstone store.

'Staki? What's "*mǎ pi jing*"?'

'In your lingo, shit. In mine, essence of horse fart.'

35

Walter ignored her. 'When my parents left Vienna and ended up in Montreal, they didn't stick around gloomy little cafes weeping into cups of filtered coffee. We lived with Italians on one side, Greeks on the other, Poles across the road, poor French-Canadians next to them, Puerto Ricans above them, and Latvians on the ground floor. And us kids? We played, fought and fucked in *all* the languages.'

'Hey, who's boresville of the month?' A boy in a leather vest and beads turned full round from the next table and pulled out a chair for Staki.

'It's okay friend,' she said grimly, 'it's only because he couldn't get it up last night.'

All heads turned as she rose angrily and walked away from the table. She jumped into the first roving cab and asked him to drive her straight to the airport. There was no point in arguing with Walter's occidental logic. He really had no idea what it was like to grow up on a diet of street gangs shouting, 'Chinky chinky chinaman sitting on a rail, looking like a monkey hanging by his tail. Hey chinky! Does your mother have a slit pussy?'

Hăo. Hăo. Okay, okay, she reflected at the back of Flight 801. Insults from the street she learned to cope with. But what she couldn't square up were the insults from the pasty faced nuns. 'Staki Lin and the other Chinese are to wash before school,' they'd say piously every morning because Mother Superior had been brought up to believe Orientals were dirty. If anybody reported a theft it was always the Chinese kids who were pulled up first. All this in the name of the Catholic Church. She was in her teens before she stopped feeling the convent had saved her from some terrifying Oriental fate nobody would ever mention.

So helping Walter to switch the Vatican's gems was her own private way of getting even. Completely. But she'd had to work for it.

She thought back cynically to one icy March day.

Walter had just collected her from Heathrow. She'd flown in from Hong Kong and was shivering violently from the cold. He turned up the heating in his Jensen Healey and swung behind the queue on the M4 motorway. 'We've discovered that Mark Land's a bit of a weirdo,' he said squinting at the road.

'Weirdo?' She couldn't care less.

'Sure. After you found out where Land operated from that helpful Vatican travel agent in Rome – that was a stroke of genius – I had two of the London centre's private dicks watch him for a couple of weeks.'

'Oh.'

'Ever since friend Land swapped incense for investments he's been living it up.'

'How? *He!* Getta load of this weather!' She stared gloomily at the countryside, barely visible through a blanket of rain that swept the motorway.

'I'll tell you how. He has a male secretary, fella called Peter Turtle-Shit Smith or something. One of those public school types all mouth and ass and nothing else. Smith has a fancy apartment in that lousy Barbican complex in the City, and that's where most of the action takes place. He brings girls there, arranges parties and so on, and then Land arrives, I'm told. Very cosy. Land lives in a Vatican house a few miles away but keeps his private life locked up at Turtle-Shit Smith's place in the Barbican.'

'Fascinating.'

'Staki, c'mon, c'mon.' Walter snapped his fingers briskly. 'Apart from that, Land seems to keep to himself. So, the vital key to his inner, whatever, is via Peter –'

'Turtle-Shit Smith.'

'Right on. Now T-S drinks in the Mermaid bar down on the Thames at lunchtimes, the boys tell me. At night he spends an hour or so at a Cheapside pub near to their office.'

'With a girl?'

'No. This is what the boys can't work out. All he seems to do is pick up chicks to take *back* to his apartment for Land's little parties.' He slowed down for the lights on the Cromwell Road, turned and grinned at her.

'So?'

'So –' the lights turned green. 'We need an "in", right?'

'Oh, screaming Jesus, Walter, that's just what I feel like, playing bar-girl after flying out from Hong Kong.'

'Oh, I wasn't thinking of tonight, butterfly. Tomorrow will do!'

She took a blanket from the back, curled herself up in it and turned her back on him. Walter took the hint and slipped a cassette into the player. Warm strains of Brahms' lovely Double

37

Concerto filled the car through three stereo speakers. By the time it finished he was driving through Hyde Park a few minutes away from his apartment, and Staki was sleeping soundly.

'Staki, you okay?' The air-hostess looked at her anxiously. 'You look like you'll burst any minute. What's with these tea trays huh?'

'God, I'm sorry, Belinda. I've lost thirty-six hours in the last few days and I —'

'C'mon Stak,' Belinda winked broadly. 'You've been flying too long to pull that one. Go on up front. I'll finish these trays.'

Several seats away from them Walter awoke from his sleep feeling refreshed and relaxed. He stretched comfortably and glanced about at the various states of disarray that characterized the long-distance air traveller. He was pleased to hear the familiar clatter of the tea trays.

He was aware of relaxing properly for the first time in months.

By late March he had begun to feel the heavy strain of keeping up an outer pretence of total normality for the benefit of his tails, and finding unobtrusive ways to further the Olympic mission behind the scenes. He allowed plans to go ahead for a health food bar in his centre in Vienna. Once, the thought of his own design taking shape had appealed to him. But he viewed the flagstone floors, bare brick walls, scrubbed pine tables and chairs with raw cynicism.

He knew that among his full time staff of fifteen in London, twelve in Paris and ten in Vienna, with as many again as part-timers, some must be on Borg's payroll. The young Italian boy Eduardo had disappeared completely. Walter didn't have the inclination to spend paranoic hours checking the others. He coped by removing himself from the front line. He allowed his managers to take over, and excused himself on the pretence of working out projections with his accountant.

As soon as Staki told him about the Vatican mission, there were two things he had to do. The first was to learn as much about diamonds as he could. The second was to find a buyer who was untraceable.

The first part had been easy. Walter hung around waiting for the monthly phone call that came from his jeweller in

Hatton Garden, London. Saul Greenberg was the son of a diamond cutter, but avoided labels of any kind for himself. He despised the pomp and flashy neon-lit satin-lined cases of the upmarket jeweller, preferring to work on an exclusive basis for a handful of customers. His shop measured seven metres by nine metres. He ran it alone from a glass cage at the back where a casual customer off the street was lucky to see the top of his head and one eye covered by a magnifier. Those put off by the gruff 'Yes?', and the general clutter and chaos, weren't the sort of customers he wanted anyway.

But those who saw something more to Greenberg than a collarless striped shirt and an act that seemed as though he didn't want to part with anything in the shop, were hooked for life. Because Greenberg was a master craftsman. Beyond his own work he constantly sought out items, both antique and from the workbenches of the new experimental breed of silversmiths and jewellers. He had an eye for finding the exact piece for his customers. They accepted his judgement unquestioningly.

He called Walter regularly each month if he found a finely engraved choker, bracelet or unusual ring. The pieces had to be exclusive and unobtrusive.

'Moon? Greenberg. It won't start a world war but this choker is nice. Clean. Square links in soft silver. I'll send it registered post?'

'No, Greenberg. I'll be in London tomorrow.'

The visit gave Walter the excuse he needed to pick Greenberg's brains.

'Why diamonds?' The old man perched on a high stool and examined the inside of a Victorian fob watch. He kept murmuring appreciatively. 'Mmm, beautiful work. Diamonds? Not for you, Moon. Silver's for you. Clean. Personal. With diamonds people talk value, value, value. I have a customer who walks in and says: "Greenberg, this ring for a thousand pounds. If I buy it for my wife today, in six years I can sell it for four thousand five hundred? That bracelet at eight thousand seven hundred and fifty – will it buy us a twelve roomed house when we retire?" Bleh!' Greenberg pushed the magnifier to the top of his head in disgust. 'You want tea, or you want to buy a diamond?'

'I don't want to buy a diamond. I just want to know about them.'

'Nobody asks about diamonds unless they want to buy one. Now, you want tea or do I have to run out to buy you coffee?'

'Tea will do fine.'

Liquid the colour of burnt wood spattered into two mugs from a large brown pot with a cracked spout.

'First you must understand,' Greenberg began, handing Walter a mug, 'that the diamond business is one of the biggest cartels you'll ever see. The selling of some eighty per cent of all the world's diamonds is handled by the Central Selling Organization. The CSO also fixes prices. It is part of the Oppenheimer empire that includes De Beers and the biggest single concentration of diamond mines and production in the world.' Greenberg slurped his tea noisily. 'I'm telling you, Moon, those diamonds sold by the CSO – say over a thousand million sterling worth a year – are sold to a handful of up to two hundred and fifty special customers. These are invited down the road to Eleven Charterhouse Street less than a dozen times a year. So you see, no outsider gets into that club.'

Walter nodded slowly and sipped his tea thoughtfully.

'So at the one end,' Greenberg continued, 'you have this mountain controlling every centimetre of the business. At the other end you have thousands of scattered workshops of diamond cutters and polishers – Antwerp, Tel Aviv, Amsterdam – fathers teaching their sons, sons their sons and grandsons. Families who share crusts in a depression while a six thousand pound value stone sits on the bench waiting to be cut.' Greenberg moved off his stool and poured himself more tea. 'What's a matter? Don't you like my tea? Help yourself.'

Walter swilled the brew in his cup and added hot water from an electric kettle attached to the wall socket with bare wires. 'Hypothetical question, Greenberg. Say if you stumbled over a parcel in the street and discovered it contained a few million dollars worth of diamonds and you wanted to get rid of them fast?'

'Within the system or outside of it?' Greenberg scratched around in a drawer for a half empty packet of digestive biscuits. 'Want to dunk one?'

'Thanks, no. Let's say outside the system.'

'Find a jeweller that doesn't ask questions.'

'I'm talking about several million dollars worth.'

'You think jewellers don't have money?'

'Let's say the diamonds should pass out of circulation for a

40

while, huh?'

Greenberg dunked a biscuit and sucked it pensively. 'For that you need a buyer with itchy millions panting around for sound long term investments.'

'Exactly.' Walter snapped his fingers.

Greenberg looked at him in amazement. 'Today, buyers like that only come from the Gulf.'

Walter pursed his lips.

'I'll tell you something,' added the old man, scratching the back of his head noisily. 'You know Israel has one of the largest diamond cutting centres in the world? So there are chains of cowboys who run from the *bourse* outside Tel Aviv to a plane for Athens and from Athens to Beirut where they sell some of them, and then on to the Gulf where the rest are sold. No problem. This is how the nationalists on both sides smother their revolutionaries. "Capital".' He rustled disgustedly in the packet for another biscuit. 'Boycott shmoycott. Don't believe the *shyss* you read in the *Jewish Chronicle*.'

Walter studied his shoes for a full minute and then glanced out at London's leaden grey skies. 'Not surprising they call March suicide month, is it?'

'Moon. *February* is suicide month.' The jeweller turned to a shelf behind him and took down a long thin box. 'Don't forget your choker or you'll say Greenberg's getting senile. You want to pay in sterling or dollars?'

Three days after he returned to Paris Walter received a call on his private line. Less than a dozen people had access to the line. Although his club in Paris was just off the Avenue de l'Opera, a short walk from the Louvre on one side, and a longer walk to the Opera House on the other, the phone number was not of the relevant district. It could be traced only to a derelict warehouse near the airport. He managed this, ironically, through one of the clients depicted so graphically in Borg's blackmail photographs: the wife of a former French cabinet minister.

'Mr Moon? How do you do, sir. Julius Hammond speaking from Teheran.' He spoke as though the entire world knew who he was. 'I'll be passing through Paris on my way to a board meeting in London tomorrow. I hoped we could lunch together.'

Walter arranged to have him met at the airport. As soon as the line died he direct-dialled a contact at a merchant bank in the City of London.

'Julius Hammond? Surprised you haven't heard about him, old boy. Great-grandson of the original Julius Hammond. Old established steamship company that used to transport slaves one way and spices the other – you know the sort of concern. By the time slavery was abolished they had a stake in God knows how many sugar plantations and trading stations. The group now has subsidiary companies in shipping, insurance, property, you name it. But young Julius – he's in his early thirties – got bored when he came down from Cambridge. So he pads around the world as a superduper investment adviser. Believe he only takes on millionaires.'

'Hmm. What's his specialty?'

'Ah,' the voice hesitated. 'He's earned the reputation of knowing about a *coup d'etat* or revolution or war before anybody else spots the dust on the horizon. Beats me how he finds out. But he knows exactly when to advise people to sell out – property in Portugal before the 1974 coup for example – property in Malta before the British withdrawal. That sort of thing. Some of my colleagues in the City play a "spot the Hammond" game and start getting interested when he's seen somewhere. Oh yes, and, ah,' the voice faltered, 'you didn't get this from me, but he sometimes acts as middleman for countries wanting to buy and sell napalm. That way both sides keep their tracks covered.'

'Jesus. He sounds like a nice guy,' Walter commented hollowly.

'Oh, he's a charmer. Where did he phone you from?'

'Teheran.'

'Teheran, eh? So that explains it. He was part of the Shah's entourage of friends and advisers on the slopes of St Moritz in January.'

Walter rose early the next morning and peered casually out of his window overlooking a fountain on the Rue de Molière. The car he noticed the previous night was still parked outside. He drew the curtains, took an icy shower and ordered black coffee from the kitchen.

He could hear a man grunting at regular intervals and reminded himself to get the floor below insulated. He picked up the intercom and asked for his head of security to join him for coffee.

Within minutes a curly headed athletic young man popped

his head around the door and smiled.

Walter turned his back on him and parted the curtain. 'Yves, why didn't you tell me about this small Fiat outside? It's been there over twelve hours.'

'The Fiat? Oh, that's the bodyguard of the Norwegian *chargé d'affairés*.' Yves walked towards the coffee tray.

'Who told you?'

'He did.'

'You checked his papers?'

'I didn't need to. The *chargé d'affairés* has been here all night. Listen to him! Eh – *pas mal m'sieu, pas mal!*'

A series of delighted shrieks rang out and then the building fell silent. The two men glanced at one another and moved to the window. A large black Volvo edged its way down the narrow road and stopped just behind the Fiat. The drivers made no sign of acknowledgement. The front door opened and a short fat man stepped gingerly into the street, tiptoed over to the Volvo and crouched down in the back seat. The driver nodded once and reversed the car smoothly up the road. The Fiat didn't move.

Walter struck Yves sharply across the face. '*Du ferdammder ideod!*'

Yves staggered back in surprise. Walter only used 'Viennese' when he was really angry. He swept out of the room, ran down the three flights of stairs to the ground floor and paused briefly before walking nonchalantly into the street. He turned left and headed for the bread shop. The smell of freshly baked loaves hung pungently in the crisp morning air although the shop was at least two blocks away. Walter turned at the first corner and waited against the wall.

Footsteps moved hesitantly towards him. Walter flattened himself. For a split second the two men blinked at one another and then Walter kicked him viciously in the crotch. The man doubled over and a camera rolled into the street. Walter jumped on it and smashed it to pieces. He picked the man up and kicked him again. 'Where's the other film?'

The man grovelled in agony and tried to grope inside his jacket. Walter kicked his hands away, knelt astride him and went through his pockets. The man was wearing a tiny pearl handled pistol in a holster under his armpit. Walter pulled it out and looked at it in disgust. He stood up and kicked the man repeatedly in the kidneys.

43

'You tell your boss not to insult me!' He pulled out the cartridges and flung the pistol in the man's face. 'Okay, the film. Quick.'

The man began to spit blood. Walter hauled him over, went through his back pockets and took out three rolls of film. He kicked the man over to the side of the road, turned, and walked back to his club.

Yves waited nervously at the front door.

'Find out who owns that Fiat and then see it is smashed up. *Immediately.*'

Yves nodded unhappily and looked guiltily at the small car parked by the fountain.

A few hours later Walter personally collected Julius Hammond from the airport and drove like a madman, collecting two traffic tickets *en route*, until he reached the Georges V Hotel.

He dumped his car, tipped the doorman a fifty dollar bill to take care of it, and whistled down a taxi. He hustled Hammond in to it and barked directions to the driver in a heavy Algerian accent. The taxi, a late fifties Peugeot, rattled and backfired its way to Les Deux Saules Cafe, Les Halles. Walter satisfied himself they hadn't been followed, jumped out of the car and led Hammond straight through the cafe to a discreet table at the back. He removed a black leather cap, unzipped an elastic waisted leather jacket and held out his hand. 'Walter Moon.'

'I know. Congratulations. First class piece of driving.'

Hammond was tall, spare, prematurely greying, and quite unruffled. He wore an expensively cut cocoa brown suit flared at the waist, a cream silk shirt and Liberty print necktie in richly blended autumn shades. Exactly as Walter pictured him. 'I *say*,' he said, admiring the colourfully painted tiles on the cafe walls, 'a workman's caff in Art Nouveau. What fun!'

Walter put his fingers to his lips and whistled. A boy in a snow-white T-shirt and bell-bottomed red trousers swung around. At the sight of Walter he flung out his arms. 'Hey, Rumbaba!' He came up and squeezed Walter's cheeks between his fingertips. 'Rumbaba, *Ça va bien? Qu'est que tu veux aujourd'hui?*'

Walter ruffled the boy's hair affectionately and ordered the cafe's speciality, *pommes frites*, salad, sausages and a yard of bread with a carafe of house wine.

Hammond smiled broadly, but his ice-blue eyes darted apprehensively around the cafe. 'I hear you sell pretty glass Mr Moon?' he asked as the wine was placed on the table.

'Among other things, yes.' Walter poured glasses for them both.

Hammond glanced at him briefly. 'I have clients who appreciate glass. What are you selling?'

'Oh – a good parcel. Around twenty million dollars worth. There'll be a fine selection of the larger stones, I'm told. There was a run on them a few years ago, you know, but nobody was buying them last year, so the larger stones come with a discount. Excellent long term investment.' Walter crossed his fingers, blessed Greenberg in his heart and raised his glass in a toast. *'Servus!'*

'I thought you Americans said "here's mud in your brown eyes" or something!'

'I'm a Viennese Montrealer.'

'Oh yes, of course. Forgive me. Will it be possible to view the stones this week?'

'I don't think so. I have two other buyers who're interested. And I don't expect to take delivery of the complete parcel for a few months yet. It takes time to select such gems.'

Hammond looked slightly annoyed.

Two plates of food were slapped down in front of them on the table. *'Voici mes amis. Bon appétit!'*

'Merci Michel. Mr Hammond, I guarantee you won't taste french fries like these anywhere else in the world!'

'Mm. Delicious. Quaint little place. Where would you suggest we meet?'

'I'll let you know. By the way, I insist on cash. Untraceable dollars.'

Hammond stopped chewing and raised a glass of wine to his lips. 'This is somewhat irregular. Don't you have a numbered account in Switzerland?'

'I do.' Walter didn't feel obliged to offer an explanation. He broke off a piece of bread and dipped it in his food.

'Where can I reach you? At the number I used yesterday?'

'No, because it'll change next week. I'd prefer to keep in touch with you.'

Hammond said nothing but dipped a slice of sausage in some mustard. 'Excellent sausage.'

'Who's your client?' Walter asked casually, rubbing the

45

edge of his plate with a piece of bread.

Hammond laughed. 'Twenty million dollars is the sort of pin money he'd keep in a safe in his library. Your good health.' He raised his glass.

'Is the Shah feathering his nest in case he's overthrown some day?'

Hammond ignored him. 'Can you give me some idea of a date?'

'Okay. 1 August.' Walter glanced around nervously as the cafe filled with people.

'Where?'

'I'll let you know.'

'I'll have to bring my glass expert along with me, naturally and make you an offer.'

'Naturally.'

'Where?'

'I'll let you know.'

'Oh come now, Mr Moon. My appointments take me up to 1979!'

'I'm impressed. All right. Montreal.'

Hammond took out a pocket *Economist* diary. 'That will suit me nicely. I have a meeting in Chicago on the twenty-ninth so I'll fly straight up.' He took out a slim gold pen and filled in the date in minute handwriting. 'Good Lord. That's the last week of the Olympics, isn't it?'

'It certainly is.'

'But the city will be impossibly crowded! Weren't you there for Expo 1967?'

'I'll find a keyhole for us. Coffee?'

'Love some. Where in Montreal?'

'I still have to arrange that.' Walter looked across at the bar and raised two fingers to the waiter. 'Are you ever in Vienna?'

'No. But I can easily stop over there between Teheran and London.'

'Good. Tuesday 21 July at 11 a.m. Could you meet me at the Kunsthistorisches Museum? By Pieter Bruegel's *The Peasant Dance*?'

'Done.' Hammond dutifully scribbled this down in his diary. 'Ah, here's coffee.'

'Cream?' said Walter, stretching to the far side of the table.

'Please.' Hammond toyed thoughtfully with his spoon. 'Would you mind if I asked an impertinent question?'

46

'No. Go ahead.' Walter asked for the bill.

'How on earth did you get the name Rumbaba?'

Walter chuckled to himself on the plane, and quickly turned it into an embarrassed cough. He often wondered how Hammond had reacted at the suggested meeting place, because Walter had had no intention of keeping the appointment in person. He wasn't even in Vienna at the time.

Hammond had arrived on the first flight from Teheran on the morning of 20 July, and taken a taxi straight from the airport as far as the Hofburg. It was a long time since he'd strolled in Vienna and he intended enjoying the summer morning.

He wandered leisurely under the arches of the Hofburg, pausing briefly as the horses from the Spanish riding school trotted out for their daily exercise in the courtyard. Tourists who couldn't afford the price of a ticket to see the performance clamoured to watch it *gratis*. Hammond glanced idly through the window of a small art shop and then crossed over the road to a cafe for an espresso before walking briskly to the museum.

He arrived at exactly three minutes to eleven and inquired at the desk to find out where he could see Bruegel's *The Peasant Dance*. As it was the height of the tourist season the galleries were lined with people, faces upturned in rapture. Hammond glanced about quickly but there was no sign of Moon. He glued himself to the painting and after five solid minutes decided that peasants looked the same the world over. Such red noses.

'Herr Hammond?' A short attendant in a neat uniform stood behind him and smiled inquiringly.

'Indeed.'

'Ich habe einen brief für sie.'

'Ah –'

The attendant handed him an envelope.

'Thank you. That's most kind of you.' Hammond reached for his wallet, but the attendant stepped backwards, shook his head and walked away insulted.

Hammond shrugged. He moved away from the clutch of people who were trying to study the painting and slit open the envelope. Inside were two tickets for the last two days of the Olympics. They were wrapped in a piece of paper that read, simply, '1 August, 8 p.m. Fountain at back of Velodrome

47

cycling stadium. Dress as popcorn men.'

Hammond replaced the tickets and note in the envelope and turned to leave the museum. He'd been asked to do stranger things in his time.

Walter's stomach protested as the plane lost height. He craned his neck to look through the porthole, and saw the office towers of Montreal. The pilot tilted a wing and the aircraft banked into a turn.

Walter touched the shoulder of the sleeping youngster beside him. Irrationally, he felt protective towards the unaccompanied boy. 'Time to wake up,' he said gently. 'We have arrived.'

CHAPTER FOUR

Boubolina Melas sat rocking gently to and fro in front of a window overlooking *Le Jardin Crêperie* on Montreal's Place Jacques Cartier. It was early and the square was practically deserted except for sweepers and an old tramp feeding the birds. Beneath her the crêperie owner, Philippe, walked around his garden inserting colourful umbrellas into the table tops. People would fill the square later, at midday, as they flocked to sit and drink at the open balconies of the hotels.

Whatever the time of day Montreal's very own smell, a sensuous mingling of Gauloises and charbroiled hamburgers, clung to the air as the inescapable standard bearer of French North America.

Any stranger walking the streets who happened to glance up at Boubolina's window would think she cradled a large baby in her arms, from the outline of her silhouette. But no Montrealer would make that mistake. Because 'La Boube', as she was affectionately called, was reputed to have the largest breasts in Canada. They were known from Newfoundland to Vancouver, and from Nova Scotia to Niagara. But now she was sixty, and the men rushed to her no longer. Once they had talked about her, on salmon fishing trips off the Pacific coast, in the plane-loads of hockey enthusiasts pouring into the city for the game. The truck drivers had dreamed of her as they drove savagely through an Alaskan winter, making enough in a month to keep them for a year. The little door-to-door Fuller Brushman from Moose Jaw, Saskatchewan, had longed for her as he smoothed back his hair and brushed the breakfast crumbs off his necktie before reversing his Plymouth sedan out of the driveway.

But their dreams had aged. La Boube's body was her own once again. She was tired. Deeply tired. Not a tiredness that a few early nights could soothe, but a tiredness that came solely from years of knowing in her sad moments that she was merely 'La Boube' to the world, to the bulging arms and eager crotches of Canada, the spurting ejaculations that had covered her breasts time after time after time.

Because Boubolina could do things with her breasts that

49

made them the most hunted game in Canada. And gave them a life that was alien to her own.

The ritual was always the same. Boubolina sat in a chair at one end of the room with her customer before her. She had a way of kneading her nipples with her fingertips to make them swell out like the lush plums of summer. The effect of lifting a single breast with one hand and sliding the other hand underneath in slow rhythmic movements made men squeeze their thighs together in anticipation.

There were those men who would watch, pay up and leave. There were men who sat and waited until she came across to them, caressing her nipples with the palms of her open hands, before bending over to slap their cheeks tantalizingly with one breast then the other. Then she would move to her bed and wait for them to join her. She would kneel before them and rub oil into her breasts until her handsome brown Mediterranean skin glowed like the moon on the sea. She would lift her man's legs on to her shoulders, cross them behind her head, then clasp her breasts on either side to grip, roll, push and pull him between two mountains of oiled womanhood.

Some men became violent and lunged for her. One screamed 'Mama' as he spurted into the tight, deep cavern between her bosoms. Another tore at her with his fingernails until she screamed and then retreated from the world for weeks. Some wept softly with relief. Others left sullenly.

Her only respite was a few days each month when premenstrually her breasts would swell and the weight became unbearable. The swelling started under her arms and pulled her skin so taut she feared it would tear. Then she'd ignore the incessant noise at her front door:

'Nous désirons La Boube. Où est-elle? s'il vous plâit, c'est très important.'

But the black-eyed woman from the Greek island of Hydra would open her door to no one.

From the age of eleven her shape made men stand in wonder and talk among themselves while the old women would cluck their tongues, shake their heads and draw black shawls across their faces. Many sighed with relief when, at fifteen, she left the island on one of the cattleboats that took thousands of poor Greek and Italian immigrants to the east coast of North America.

Twenty-five years later it was rumoured that half the men

in Canada had paid to see her naked. At forty she wasn't yet at her peak. With her thick dark hair already attractively grey and worn close to her head, she kept Montreal warm when winter winds sent Antarctica to the city.

Two young boys visited her along with the stream of men. One was Black, brooding, stocky and painfully shy. The other was auburn-haired and so skinny he wore his trousers twisted several times around his waist Both came to hide their early adolescence and nestle between her breasts out of a mixture of youthful ardour and a need for comfort. They arrived, hair slicked back with vile smelling creams, pimples shaved off in a desperate bid to look mature, wearing shirts with singed and half ironed collars. Then they walked into her room with a swagger achieved after hours of practice in front of a full length mirror.

But the hours of preparation were swept aside the instant Boubolina started to undo her blouse, gazing at them with a mixture of amusement and concern. A second and the humiliation was complete as the semen made a mockery of their freshly laundered underpants.

Walter Moon and Sole Dubois did not know of each other until they came face to face on Boubolina's front porch. The intense strain of preparation and the late July sun that beat down mercilessly made the boys leap at one another savagely and roll off the iron stairway into the gutter. Egged on by whistles and catcalls from the crowds gathering in the road they nearly killed one another until Boubolina screamed from the top of the stairway. She ran down, yanked them both to their feet and ordered them up to her kitchen. Inside she bathed two bleeding noses, a bulging eye and badly cut lips.

'Boys. Yah! Why I waste my time with you? *Je suis* crazy!'

But she showed more anxiety than anger in her own blend of Greek, English and French. After half an hour the boys sat at opposite ends of her large kitchen table looking dejected and forlorn, their entire world of rice-paper thin maturity shattered for ever.

It didn't take long for Boubolina to realize that neither boy wanted to go. She clapped her hands loudly and pulled up a chair between them. '*Páme*. Come boys. No more fights. Okay boys? Sole, shake hands with Walter. Walter, shake hands with Sole. From today no more fights. From today you see me

51

together. *Endaksi* boys?'

She slapped some Greek bread, *feta* goat's milk cheese and some black olives on the table and turned to make coffee. 'Hey. You boys ever eaten a proper Greek meal?'

Both shook their heads.

'No? *Yeti?* Why? And you live on east side? Fantastic! *Kala.* Good. Tonight I cook for you. *Lipon*, so, some *taramasalata* to start with, then *dolmades* and salad.'

The meal was to be the first lesson for the boys in Greek cooking, the Greek language, life, love and anything else Boubolina taught them in a close relationship that had lasted over twenty years.

'Boys, I tell you,' she used to say in the mid-fifties. 'When you make love to girls don't make like bulls rushing to a fence and remember your snotty school friends are wrong when they think a girl just wants to be poked ratta-tatta-tatta-tatta-tatta-tatta-ta and then whoosh bang bang over and out and you lie snoring like a pig as she stares at the ceiling wondering where's the poetry. And remember boys, each woman is built differently. Each likes to be touched in a different way. Some are like sea anenomes that want to suck you in and hold you. Some are difficult to find between so many folds. They need to be encouraged, gently. Others are full, defiant, like tiny rosebuds. And when a woman has had a baby she changes there –'

She stopped short as both boys looked at her with quizzical expressions. 'Eh. Men for money. Women for love. *Tin-Kanimé?* So what?'

* * *

'Boubo? You want to come with me to the airport to meet Walter in a couple of hours?'

'*Oichi efcheristo*, Sole. I want to shop for food for us all. Make sure he comes here tonight, huh?'

'Mm hmm.'

Sole withdrew his head from the window and did up the metal clasps on his snow-white dungarees. The contrast with his supple mahogany skin was good and he knew it. He wore the dungarees without a shirt to emphasize his muscular physique.

He sprawled on his bed and reached out for a copy of *Moustique* that had just been delivered from the printers. He had started the underground paper in his room in Boubolina's home. It was guaranteed to worry and sting the hell out of the establishment. It followed no party line. Neither did Sole. He was Sole, the anarchist, his own one-party man. *Moustique* was hawked from street corners in the summer and at points in Montreal's subterranean city in the winter, from kiosks to *brasserie*s to taxi ranks, and anywhere else in La Belle Province where the gossip, exposés, intrigue and backchat found a responsive ear.

'*Tabernacle*,' he swore loudly, noticing a mistake and using one of a string of liturgical curses that typified French Canadians. This was one issue he wanted to be perfect. He'd arranged for it to be distributed on the press stand at the main Olympic stadia, along the two metro lines taking spectators to the site, and at focal points at the Olympic Village.

The issue concentrated on a single subject: the CIA and its notorious use of the Olympic Games as a massive recruiting exercise. *Moustique* let a double-page spread cartoon do all the work, showing CIA men in various guises at an Olympic reception for athletes and managers.

One was dressed as a rubber plant trying to pick-up a muscular lady shot putt from Leningrad. 'I'm telling you lady wid your physique and my brains ...' Another cartoon showed an officer swinging upside down in a chandelier hopelessly entangled in recording equipment. In a third strip an officer, dressed as a maid with hairy little legs sticking out of a black miniskirt, batted his false eyelashes at a Zambian athlete. A fourth cartoon showed a bullet-headed cigar-chewing tank of a man surrounded by a ring of Chinese gymnasts over the caption, 'Course, 'ole Mao and I were at college together and my momma used to fix him club sandwiches like you never saw ...'

Another cartoon had a line of officers bulkily dressed in tracksuits talking to members of the Russian delegation. 'Say, fellas, why not let your hurdler champ defect and we'll bring him back to you for Moscow's Olympics in 1980?'

Sole chuckled. His co-editor had hamburger for brains but even Sole had to admit he was a damned good cartoonist. He swung his legs off the bed and walked over to tap out a quick note on a rickety typewriter, before changing into his part-time role as a taxi driver. For that he fluffed out his Afro hairdo, put on masses of beads, and shoved a pouched cap over his eyes. It went down well with the tourists, none of whom expected to see a Black face in Montreal.

53

'Oh, I just drive a taxi part-time,' he'd tell them. 'Rest of the time I'm a clown in a circus. That's when I paint my face white.' Then, depending on the reaction – raucous laughter or stony silence – he knew if he had pals and potential subscribers to *Moustique* behind him, or just a bunch of honkeys. Sole didn't believe in hiding his grudges. His father had been beaten to death by a bunch of five bible-thumping vigilantes in his home town in Florida when they heard that the nigger from the local gas station was returning to Montreal to marry some pretty white girl he'd knocked up. His mother heard about it a month before Sole was born.

That was thirty-five years in the past. Emmanuelle Dubois had no will to live and Sole could still remember how, when he was eight, the waters of the St Lawrence turned his sad-faced slip of a mother into a bloated monster streaked with oil from the dockyards. His grandparents took the strange, wild-eyed little boy into their home a few yards from the main railway line. He soon learned that there wasn't much difference between a poor French-Canadian and a poor Black.

On one side of the railway line he stood and watched the plush trains go by. The clusters of indifferent faces showed no reaction to the contrast between the exquisite meals and service they were about to enjoy, and the rows of crumbling shacks that slumped against the railway line outside. Sole shared his grandparent's large brass bed, mud floor, and a life that was nothing more than a statistic on a welfare list until he left school at fourteen. He started working at the age of ten delivering newspapers to the wealthy parts of the town. Westmount. Mount Royal. Hampstead.

In the afternoons he worked for a shoemaker and earned the nickname 'Sole' that soon replaced 'Jean-Claude'. He taught himself English by listening to the radio, and keeping his eyes shut during American movies to avoid reading the subtitles. By the age of nineteen after two years at night school he won a place at McGill University but was kicked out after a term. He publicly accused an eminent professor of teaching history with a racist bias. The incident put guts into his political thinking and later shaped his adult life.

Sole was aware that *Moustique* existed only just within the law. Sure, his scruffy bedroom/office was raided from time to time when the Separatists got lively in the city. There was no way the police were going to forget his role in organizing a taxi drivers' revolt against the monopoly taxi company sharks in the town, or his arrest with hundreds of political activists when members of the Front de Libération du Québec kidnapped British diplomat James Cross and French cabinet minister Pierre Laporte in 1970.

His paper campaigned bitterly against the Quebec farmers who slaughtered hundreds of young calves during the fall of 1974 to protest against inadequate subsidies. Other Canadian farmers who dumped eggs and milk at the same time suddenly found themselves and their families blazoned across the front pages of *Moustique*.

But the authorities, although they kept a beady eye on Sole, considered him more of a nuisance than a serious threat. He played up to the misconception, clowning in public, festooning his taxi with winking dolls and gadgets and attaching cheeky slogans to his aerial. *Moustique*'s needs gave him an excellent excuse to roam around where and when he pleased and make frequent trips to the United States for discussions with Black-power leaders.

Sole liked to play it all ways.

In Montreal he was part of the fury of those French-Canadians who resented being second-class citizens in their own province where well over half of industry was owned by American corporations and much of the rest controlled by English-Canadians. The combination of consistently higher-than-average unemployment and some of the worst slum conditions in North America brought a unique type of violence to the streets of French Canada in the seventies.

As a result bi-lingualism became a self-conscious catchword throughout Canada. In Quebec French was magnanimously made the official language of the French speaking majority. But Bill 22 and all it implied wasn't enough for people like Sole. The linguistic acceptance had a note of patronage about it that went skin deep. French words on a packet of rubbers didn't rehabilitate the bums on the street corners. Nor did it shake the fact that Quebec was still dominated by American capital, rich English-Canadians and a few wealthy French-Canadian families of whom the Prime Minister was a product.

As soon as Sole started thinking along these lines he decided the local problem wasn't merely a matter of getting uptight when the English refused to speak French to a Montreal or Quebec City taxi driver. So he hustled his way into the offices and political meetings of Black-power leaders across the border and worked on their increasing influence among Caribbean immigrants in Montreal. He didn't stop there. He got involved with the Indian caravan that crossed Canada from British Columbia to Ottawa during the fall of 1974 collecting radical sympathizers *en route* to swell the numbers of demonstrators outside the Houses of Parliament, demanding equal rights, better housing and educational facilities for Indians. That drew him into another dimension of political thinking and convinced him that French-Canadian separatism didn't go far enough. A tight link was needed between all the groups that shared fundamentally similar grievances against the establishment and business corporations.

America had Canada and its vast resources by the balls and it was time all Canadians did something about it. Not just a few radicals from Simon Fraser University at one end of the country, some demonstrating Indians here and groups of French-Canadian hotheads there. Forging everybody together in cells across the country, across the massive dimensions of Canada, required money. Mobility. Sole's shares of the Vatican gems. The thought of stealing them from the Church gave him a profound sense of triumph.

It was one way of returning money to the people who'd been milked by the Church for generations.

* * *

'Hi, Sole.'

'Hi, Baby.'

Sole swung Walter's suitcase into the boot of his bright green Buick taxi, narrowly missing a group of people that flooded out of the airport and climbed excitedly into a line of buses covered with Olympic symbols.

'Good to see you, Baby.'

'You too.'

Walter lifted up a newspaper to pretend he was reading in the back seat. The airport was crawling with security men and there was no point in making them think that he was other than a casual pick-up outside the airport. Walter had visited Montreal four times in the previous year but was too nervous of Sole's political reputation to meet him openly. He had depended on a series of discreet meals in different kebab houses, brasseries, crêperies, bars and steak houses all over

56

town. Both knew that after Munich, Montreal's security arrangements started way before the first block of turf was turned to lay the foundations of the main Olympic stadia at the Maisonneuve Park.

The two spoke a strange mixture of the local *patois* and good old fashioned east-coast slang.

Briefly Sole filled Walter in on some of the work he'd been doing in the city. 'Your courier isn't staying with the Apostolic Delegate like you thought.'

'How d'ya find that out?' Walter glanced wearily at the strangely formal line of double storey houses on one side of the road that led into the industrial areas on the outskirts of the city.

Sole flung back an envelope containing photographed pages from the Apostolic Delegate's diary. 'He's an old friend of Boubolina's so she arranged a little dinner *chez nous* and I spent those hours at his house going through his desk diary as you can see.'

'Jesus Christ. I thought I said Boubo wasn't to be involved!' Walter rustled the papers angrily.

'Have you ever known her to earn money without working for it? *Merde*. She doesn't take two million bucks like some fucking welfare handout.'

—'You're right. I'm sorry. So where's the courier staying?'

'Hampstead. Fancy house called St Dominique's. It's a kind of stop-off for visiting priests on Vatican business or priests they don't know what to do with.'

'Mm. Who's there now?'

'Four priests live there. One's pensioned off and doesn't hear too good. Sort of papa to the rest. There's a mick in a black suit, square glasses, never out of his collar, y'know the sort. The fella who runs the place, late middle aged and French-Canadian of the old kind – large family – shoved into the priesthood while he still thought his *moine* was only something to piss through –'

'Okay. Who else?'

'The fourth priest is just pussy – golden curls and cupid bow lips –' Sole batted his long eyelashes in the driver's mirror. 'I think he's there until they decide what to do with him.'

'That's all?' Walter squinted into the mid-afternoon sun,

57

beginning to feel the first waves of a jet lag he rarely experienced.

'Yea. And there's a kid who does the cooking. He answers the phone and so on.'

'How did you find all this out? Leave Boubo on loan to St Dominique for a week?'

Sole chuckled. 'Baby, what's bitin' your ass? I did a deal with a kid from McGill who was delivering their laundry and delivered it myself for two months. There isn't much about St Dominique I don't know.'

Walter sighed, opened the envelope behind his newspaper and flicked through the contents. 'Who's this Monseigneur Lancey expected tomorrow for a supper meeting at St Dominique's?'

'This is gonna freak you. He's a jeweller from New York. He's no more a Monseigneur than my asshole – *calice* these drivers!' A bus whistled past leaving an inch of air between itself and Sole's taxi.

'A *jeweller*? Shit. That screws up the deal if he buys something!'

'Nuh-uh,' Sole shook his head firmly. 'Big jelly bean like that doesn't buy rocks second hand. He'd get them from the same source as the Vatican. Nope. He's going to St Dominique's tomorrow night around eight to make sure the courier's brought healthy rocks with him.'

'And then?' Walter sounded unconvinced.

'At 1 a.m. a car calls at St Dominique's to drive them to the stock exchange!'

'Uh huh.'

'Jesus, you're a miserable bastard.' Sole flung another envelope into the back seat. 'I photographed St Dominique's diary too. *Merde!*' He pulled up suddenly at a red light. 'Hey,' he snapped his fingers. 'You know the Vatican owns the stock exchange site? – not the building – but did a deal to get part of the basement. They flew out a team of engineers from Rome to design a system of safes. You can't even see them. One's behind a pump here another's in the ceiling under the floor of the john. I found out from a Martinique guy who helped carry some of the equipment down. They figured because he's Black he's dumb.'

'Hmm. Good thing I didn't decide to bust a safe.'

'I'll – pheuwweeee – look at that ass!' Sole hung out of his taxi as he was about to turn left into Sherbrooke Avenue. The lights changed just in time. A tall Black girl moved across the road like an Alvin Ailey dancer wearing skin-tight jeans with a large red butterfly stitched provocatively around the inside of her left thigh. 'Whowee – move it, *belle cuisse*!' He rolled down his window and was about to call out when the lights changed and Montreal's downtown peak hour traffic began parp-parp-parping on their horns. He shook his head and the car shrieked around the corner.

Walter rubbed his eyes. 'How did you find out the jeweller's a jeweller?'

'Easy. After watching St Dominique's I discovered that curly cupid lips runs errands for the Apostolic Delegate during the day, and picks himself up a piece of male pigeon on "*rue de la tapette*" at night.'

'So?' Walter scratched his beard and longed to shower.

'So I paid our friend Mic-Mac – you remember Mic-Mac – to –'

'*Black*mail him?' Walter looked angrily in the mirror.

'Nah. Grease him up a little – get him talking intimate about Lancey, wondering if he's the Lancey Mic-Mac remembers from his days at Jesuit College. Cupido fell for the line and told him Lancey was a jeweller.'

'Great. Now how do I play happy families at St Dominique's?'

'I fixed you up a little date with cupido!'

'Oh *Jezuz*, Sole!' Noticing they were a block away from the Maple Inn where he'd booked a room, Walter added irritably, 'Keep driving around the block.' He stared glumly out of the window at the crowds that packed the street, Montrealers leaving work mingling with thousands of visitors pouring out of the metro after a day at the Games. Montreal's city population of nearly one and a half million had turned out every spare room, dog kennel and shoebox to accommodate those visitors unable to find hotel rooms. They were used to it after Expo 1967.

'Tomorrow night the kid I told you about is off duty from the kitchen, so I figured a way of getting you into St Dominique's. They've – hey, Pierre!' Sole hung out and banged on the window of the taxi in the next lane. 'Pierre! *Ça va bien, mon chum?*'

A grizzly face turned and beamed at them both and started

to make frantic signs with his hands, inviting them both for a drink.

'Sole, for Chrissake!' shouted Walter angrily.

'Okay baby,' he shrugged and shook his head at Pierre who pulled away into the next lane. 'I'm dropping you off now. Godamn shower and do your manicure and walk around to Boubo's in a coupla hours. I'll take the story from there.' His taxi whined on to the rubberized driveway of the Maple Inn and the doorman stepped forward automatically. 'Tip him well baby,' Sole growled as he waited for Walter to get out before pulling away.

* * *

Saxon Forth had a simple brief. Keep the 1976 Olympics clean.

He hung over the ticker tape, read through a coded message from the American embassy in Paris and swore crudely. Tuesday and the Games were two thirds over. Why did a hit man and a creep like Toni Carbetti suddenly decide to fly to Montreal?

Forth looked more like a dumpy second-rate boxing promoter than one of the CIA's top electronics experts. He had helped design reconnaissance satellites, worked out ways of bugging the private conversations of a rebel general planning a counter coup in Chile, and helped build up intimate dossiers on organizations in the West known to be working for the Palestine revolution.

And he wasn't going to be outwitted by some punk wop with a greasy dick. He picked up a private phone on his desk and pushed a button for airport security.

'*Oui?*'

'Robert?'

'*Oui.*'

'Top priority. Get your boys working on the passenger lists of every flight from Europe today. There's a hit man on one of them – from Paris or London. An Italian called Toni Carbetti, but he could be travelling under one of fifty names. I'm passing his photographs and other data to you on the wires now.' Forth slammed down the phone and signalled to his secretary to get the relevant information from Washington on the computer.

They both sat at desks at one end of a long narrow room

fitted out as a replica of the US State Department's computer-ized anti-guerrilla nerve centre set up in Washington after the Munich Olympics. Fed by daily reports from the CIA, FBI and various wire services, the centre kept tabs on guerrilla groups, activities, attacks, political meetings, existing and potential sympathizers worldwide. Forth was seconded to Montreal at the end of 1972 to set up a local centre on the advice of the State Department to both the Canadian Prime Minister, and the International Olympic Committee.

Montreal was nervous. The events at the end of 1970 were too fresh, too vivid. The kidnappings of James Cross, and Pierre Laporte who was subsequently killed, caused the Prime Minister to bring in the stringent War Measures Act. And the people didn't like it. Cells from the FLQ had out-radicalized the radical premier. 'Watch me,' he warned, and watch the people of Montreal did, as the Quebec police chief was put in charge of five thousand combat troops and twelve thousand policemen. Seventeen thousand men against – as it was later discovered – only nine kidnappers.

Forth's centre had immediate access to information stored by, and supplied hourly to, the computer bank in Washington. The local footwork in Montreal was done by Squad O, a hand-picked bunch of men with intensive security and paramilitary training, from the CIA, Canada's various police and armed forces, and the FBI. Squad O was suitably and deliberately polyethnic. This way its officers both infiltrated Montreal's ethnic communities, and kept tabs on foreigners moving in and out of the city by air, road or via the St Lawrence Seaway. During the Games, Squad O officers became ticket collectors, ice-cream sellers, balloon men, reporters, hosts in red blazers, time keepers, cloakroom attendants and chefs. They were dotted like flies around the main Olympic stadium, mast, swimming pool and Velodrome cycling rink. They were also dotted about the twenty-three other indoor and outdoor Olym-pic sites all over town, and hung around strategic points during the yacht racing at Kingston.

To keep Squad O on an international level for diplomatic reasons, it was agreed that the officers should report directly to Forth. But Squad O was tightly linked to the security chiefs of the Montreal Police Department, the Quebec Provincial Police and the federal Royal Canadian Mounted Police.

Montreal 1970 and Munich 1972 were years Canadians

61

didn't want repeated in Olympic City 1976.

Forth glanced around the operations room, took a thick cigar out of his top pocket, spat out the butt and lit it with a foot-long flame from a Zippo lighter.

Apart from a cluster of computer programmers, telex operators and analysts there were three men from Squad O in the room examining an electronic wall chart detailing each Olympic site. On the opposite side of the room a member of the Israeli secret service, the Shin Beth, and a man from the German secret police stood in front of a massive world map covered with flags and blinking lights. If a plane was hijacked anywhere in the world the information was processed by the computer within seconds and electronic impulses charted the course of the flight along the map.

'Okay, you fellas,' barked Forth. 'Nobody goes home tonight so warn the ladies now. I don't want those lines crammed later with sweet talk.'

The men didn't even glance in his direction. They'd had a gutfull of false alarms.

Forth left his cigar in an ashtray and walked across to the john unzipping himself *en route*. Damn job he thought wryly. Gave him nothing but a splintered marriage and a sackload of foul memories. He faced the urinal and pissed along the cracks between the tiles. The concentration helped him think. He felt self-conscious. There was nobody for him to call but he didn't want the whole operations room to see that.

He turned from the urinal, glanced at himself in the mirror and pulled in the paunch that strained against his shirt buttons. Fiddling around always gave him the necessary diversion before he could get stuck into anything tough. He smoothed down his grey hair and curly sideburns and grunted hopelessly at the heavy bags under his eyes. He wasn't even fifty.

Back in the operations room he looked casually at the data his secretary placed before him, but knew most of it from his time in Rome. He turned to a board behind his desk and clipped on a photograph of Carbetti that had just come through on the wires from Washington.

'Gentlemen –'

The men looked up and stared blankly at the photograph.

'Antonio Carbetti.' Forth paused to relight his cigar. 'These dark pointed features and small bones have let him run around like a cockroach disguised as fifty different men across the

Mediterranean and Middle East. He's been known as Francisco de Sousa from Oporto. Mustafa Mustafa from Istanbul. Dimitri Vlachos from Limassol. He started off throwing knives at a Marseilles fairground but don't let that kid you. He'd have your wang off and you'd hardly notice the tear in your pants. Now he only uses knives or guns when he's caught. His speciality – the technological "accident" – politics? Nil. His minimum charge is $50,000 so it's whoever can afford that kind of greenery.'

Forth lit his cigar for the third time. Several pairs of eyes measured the length of the flame.

'Last July,' he continued, 'Carbetti eliminated a Black strike leader at an Italian car plant in Pietermaritzburg South Africa. The Special Branch hired him for that because they knew if the strike leader's followers suspected them there'd be a riot on their hands. The plant chairman co-operated and footed the bill. It was cheap at the price. Carbetti worked at the plant for a month as Carlo Vitti, went beserk one day and let a car drop on the troublemaker and six mechanics. Exit Vitti for shrink treatment in Italy. Two months later he was hired by a wealthy Portuguese family to protect their interests in Luanda. Three mulatto student leaders died in a plane crash as a result. Later, several dozen guerrillas and villagers died in an explosion at the base of the border of this family's ranch. This we know for sure. Then there's the coincidences to play with. Carbetti was in Teheran last year when the American embassy got blown up. He was in London when –'

'Sounds as though he was employed by the CIA,' commented the Shin Beth officer dryly.

Forth ignored him. '– he was in London when two directors of a tea group got smashed up in a car "accident" two days after a report came out about the slave wages they were paying in Ceylon. Latest report says Carbetti's been acting bodyguard to some financier in Zurich. I'll have more on that soon as the bureau moves its Swiss ass –'

Forth snapped his fingers impatiently at his secretary, Simma. A slender woman in her mid-thirties, with frizzed out ash-blonde hair and owlish spectacles, casually moved off a table at the far side of the room and walked towards him. She communicated with Forth via sign language and monosyllables, and knew the guts of his work as well as he did.

'So Carbetti moves about,' added Forth, 'left, right, back,

forward. It makes no difference. He might be arranging a pretty accident to wipe out the Ugandan team. Or perhaps he's been hired by the Ku-Klux-Klan to shoot every Black athlete in sight. Maybe there's an anti-Mrs Ghandi group out there planning some action at the Games to coincide with a *coup* back home. Or maybe somebody wants to show the Portuguese guys that Socialism's not nice. Remember the politics mean nothing. It's fifty thousand bucks per head.' Forth paused and looked at Carbetti's photograph. 'He's bright coming in at the end of the Games. He thinks we're getting sluggish.'

The groups of faces around him remained expressionless.

'Yvon?' Forth turned to a French-Canadian member of Squad O. 'I want a run down on events at the site tonight through Sunday. Find out from the boys at the Olympic Village if there's been any jealousy or rivalry that could cause some athlete high on sweat to mash up his opponent.'

Yvon Benoit, a slight, serious looking young Laval University graduate, seconded from the RCMP's plain clothes department, nodded and left the room.

'Pete?' Forth turned to the English-Canadian. 'I want you to look at the same list – work out which nation's teams are involved and which aren't. See if there's any beef or conflict. Politically.'

Pete Taylor, a gangly officer seconded from the army's anti-guerrilla unit, strapped on a shoulder holster and picked up a file.

'The rest of you can start shaking up your contacts in the city,' said Forth pointing around the room. 'Carbetti'll have a dancing partner in town who'll supply the juice, plastic or hardware. Check if anything's been reported missing, army supplies, building sites, use your imaginations –' he broke off as Simma handed him the phone.

'It's Robert.'

'Yes Robert?' Forth frowned at the mouthpiece.

'Carbetti. He has shoulder length hair and a long thin moustache hanging down to his chin. Very clever. He's on an Israeli passport, using the name Shimon Ben-Or. Checked into the Maple Inn. He arrived on Flight 801 from London.'

CHAPTER FIVE

'Carbetti?'

The couple sat down behind the Italian in a Gay strip club on Montreal's east side. Two powerfully built young men in G strings did an energetic front-to-front snake dance on a tiny platform in the centre of the room. Carbetti leaned backwards as if enraptured. It was the only way of hearing the couple behind him over the beat of half a dozen drums.

The place was packed. Quietly dressed businessmen mingled self-consciously with men in drag, boys in white baggy jeans and striped tops, and muscular characters clad from head to foot in close-fitting leather. Two boys dressed identically in candy striped bermuda shorts sat entwined at the bar. Three Olympic gold medallists enjoying an afternoon out after the event, glanced around the room in expectation, half hoping they'd be recognized, half hoping they wouldn't.

'Word's come through from Zurich. The old man wants you to stick with Moon. Make sure nothing happens to him.'

Carbetti scowled. 'I thought –'

'Forget that. Meet one of us on Wednesday night – say seven thirty at *La Bergerie*. Do you know it?'

Carbetti shook his head once.

'Corner La Montagne and St-Catherine. Underneath the *Rive Gauche* store. You can't miss it. All aluminium bars and glass. If we're not there we'll leave a message.'

The drums beat towards a climax. Disco lights turned the club into a pulsating kaleidoscope. The two men on the platform thrust their hips at one another and locked in a scissor dance. Carbetti blinked and half turned. But the couple had gone.

*   *   *

Boubolina Melas stepped out of the noisy *taverna* two blocks from her home. She threw back her head and sang lustily about the Greek sponge divers sailing around the Asia Minor coastline. A block later she tried out her own version of a song immortalized by Maria Farandouri from Theodorakis'

Antigone. By the time she turned into Place Jacques Cartier she was singing soulfully:

'*Stroseee to stromaaa sou gia dio* ... Prepare your mattress for two –'

She stopped. Somebody behind her made a lewd comment followed by a series of lusty kissing noises. She turned around angrily and screamed a string of abuses in all the languages she knew. '*Mange la merde – na fas skata –* eat shit!'

But there was something faintly familiar about the tall outline. She paused, gasped, and broke into shouts of laughter. 'Waltaki! *Pethikamou*!' She flung her arms around his neck and kissed him on both cheeks.

'*Yasou Boubo yasou* ... *poupas? Poupas?* Where are you going?' He took her face between his hands and kissed her warmly before clasping one arm around her ample shoulder and turning her in the direction of her home. It was only six months since she'd seen him, but six months, six days, six minutes, it made little difference. They walked down the square like a honeymoon couple, cuddling and kissing until they reached the crêperie. Walter waved gaily over a dozen heads at the proprietor, and shouted '*Vive le Québec!*'

Philippe kissed his fingers and made a victory sign.

Bouboulina's front door was next to the crêperie. They walked in, past Sole's room, and went straight up to the kitchen where they both knew he'd be waiting for them. Sole sat at the table surrounded by blown up photographs of the main Olympic site, and his own detailed layout of the interior of St Dominique's. Bouboulina took one look at her kitchen table and shrieked, 'Sole *malakàsmene* – we're going to eat paper huh?'

Sole stood up obediently and began pulling the photographs towards him. As Bouboulina heaved a large bottle of Greek wine on to a cleared space he slapped her noisily on the behind. 'Mama – give us half an hour downstairs together and call us then. Okay?'

'*A sto diavolo* – go to hell both of you!'

Walter laughed and kissed her before following Sole downstairs to his room.

Sole pushed open the door and kicked aside a pile of page proofs. He walked over to the windows and pulled down the blinds blocking out the inquisitive faces in the crêperie garden outside, before turning on the lights.

Walter swept a series of rolled up political posters on to the floor and rubbed the dust off the table top with his sleeve. 'Jesus, Sole, these posters were lying there the last time I was here!'

'Tough.'

'Hey, whose underwear is that hanging over the coffee cups?' Walter pointed to a line of frillies suspended on a piece of string.

'Chick from New Orleans,' said Sole spreading the photographs and diagrams on the table.

'Is she still here?'

'I dunno. Have you looked in the bed?' Sole dived for it, tore back the covers and searched about frantically. 'Naw,' he said, and then, in a reedy falsetto, 'they take what they want and then drop you. They're all the same!'

Walter nudged the posters under the bed playfully and then hooked out chairs for them both with his heel. 'What have you got for me, joker?'

Sole switched on a radio and winked at him. 'St Dominique's. I deliver laundry around seven forty-five tomorrow. The Apostolic Delegate and Lancey are expected at eight. Remember I told you that the kid who works in the kitchen is off duty? So I put you into the closet there with the laundry.'

Walter rolled his eyes and examined the diagram Sole had drawn of St Dominique's.

'Man,' added Sole, 'this is a *big* closet. See this instrument? You'll be able to hear everything that's going on in St Dominique's.' He showed Walter something that looked like a pocket calculator with two identical dials on it. Attached to it was a small pair of earphones. 'This is a "Hero",' he explained. 'It works like a light meter on a camera, except it doesn't record light, but sound *dimension*.' Sole stood up to demonstrate it, taking care to detach the earphones.

Walter took the instrument and held it gingerly.

'The Hero registers dimension electronically,' Sole began, 'for example if I press this button it'll make a reading of my room. Watch the needle. So. 14.267X. Now if I go to another room in the house – any room – and set this other dial on 14.267X, attach my stethoscope and press the button on the back, I can listen to everything that's going on in *this* room!'

'You bastard. Where the hell did you pick up this toy?' Walter looked at it in disbelief.

'Baby, when Rockefeller's boys started doing a CIA on the CIA last year those guys who play both sides got jumpy. So my buddies 'cross the border put the screws on the known agency stool pigeons. Rockefeller's gorillas were paying high prices for info on leaks within the agency. To keep quiet we asked for the agency's latest eavesdropping gadgets. This Hero makes Watergate bugging seem like something out of the ark.'

'So I sit in the closet with this for four hours?'

'Sure. Think of the masses you can recite. I've taken readings from every room in St Dominique's – even the johns – so you can dial into anyone's conversation. You'll be able to hear Lancey's comments when he looks at the stones tomorrow night.'

'And walk in cross legged from sitting in the closet, ask them cutely if I can switch the gems, and walk out again?'

'I'll come to that.' Sole turned abruptly to his diagram. 'Here's a list of readings from the different rooms, and a layout with the Hero readings in the various rooms. So, Walter sitting here in the closet,' – he tapped a smudged X on the diagram – 'can tell exactly where Lancey is just by running through the different readings until you hear somebody talking about gems. Then you check the layout, see how far you are in your closet from the gems. See here. I've timed the distances from the closet to the different rooms.'

'Hmmmm.'

'*Merde!* Don't sound so ecstatic! Go on. Dial 27.903Y and listen through the stethoscope.'

Walter set it, plugged in the stethoscope, pressed the appropriate button and listened. 'Hey –' he looked at Sole and beamed, 'I can hear Boubolina singing, ah, um, I guess that's a kettle boiling, and chopping, say, celery being chopped on wood?'

Sole took the Hero and listened through the stethoscope himself. 'Right on!' He pulled it out of his ears. 'You see? Just like a radio set, but instead of dialling a station, you dial a *room*. The Hero registers dimension when the room is quiet. Then when you dial into the disturbance – guys talking or scraping chairs or balling – the sound is picked up and transmitted back.'

'And no bugs in the room?' Walter fiddled with the dial.

'Bugs went out with God, short stuff. People are getting

wise to them. They can be knocked out if some pain-in-the-ass puts a book in the wrong place. Or they can screw up if somebody puts a record on. But with this method there's no aggro.'

'Wid diss mettid dere's no aggro, huh?' repeated Walter in an exaggerated French-Canadian accent.

'*Sacrement*. I haven't spoken like that for years.'

'C'mon boys!' bellowed a familiar voice from the top of the stairs. 'Come, let's eat. *Na famé*.'

*   *   *

'Car 46 to Forth.'

Forth ran to the buzzing speaker on his desk. 'Yuh.'

'Sir. We're sticking by Carbetti. After he left the fruit pick-up joint a coupla hours ago he returned to Place Jacques Cartier and he's sitting on a hotel balcony drinking beer opposite the same house we saw him in before he went to the fruit disco.'

'Who owns the house?'

'La Boube.'

'Who the hell's that?'

'A fat Greek whore with boobs like pillows.'

'Yeah? So he picks fruit in the afternoon and tits at night?'

'Well. He was in the whore house when La Boube was out today. Can't make that out. We figured he was watching some athletes in the fruit joint this afternoon.'

'Athletes?' Forth frowned at the speaker.

'Yea. Three of them. All gold medallists, and get the combination – Yossi Telz from Israel, Dwajan Kahn from Iran and Ho Kwan-Ho from mainland China.'

'Jesus fucking Christ.' Forth stood up and stared down the full length of the room.

'That's what we thought. Pete Taylor's checking them out now.'

'Find out how the hell those guys slipped their security nets.'

'Right away.'

'Ah, see if there's any tie-up with this boob woman. Carbetti could be doing some blackmail on the side. Stick with him. Like I said before. I want a twenty-four hour surveillance on him and the places he visits.'

'Ten four.'

Forth switched off the speaker and sat down slowly. He didn't even notice he was out of cigars.

* * *

'Sit, Sole, *parakolo*, please. Walter here. Like old times, huh, boys?'

Boubolina walked around the table putting down a dish of lemons, a large bottle of olive oil, a wooden bowl with noodles, black olives and salad, dishes of radishes, chillies and tomatoes, and a long narrow dish with several skewers of lamb and pork. 'Nowhere in Montreal you get kebabs like in Boubolina's kitchen, eh Waltaki? Eh Sole?' Greek music played incessantly in the background and nobody made the slightest attempt to turn it down.

'Walter – why do you not bring Silki?'

'Silki? Oh *Staki*. Mama, I've told you why.' Walter rolled an olive around in his mouth and spat the pip into his cupped palm. 'I keep my lives separate.'

'*Asiktir*.'

'Don't be crude – here, drink more wine. Sole where the hell's your glass long stuff?'

'Short stuff. Long stuff. You tell *me* not to be crude?' she said biting into a chilli and waving her hand in front of her mouth to cool it.

'*Yamas* everybody,' said Sole clinking glasses around the table.

'You ashamed of Boubolina, Waltaki?' she persisted, bouncing her breasts playfully against the salad bowl. 'You see, Sole, with his presidents and bank chairmen and movie stars, he can't tell them about *putana* Boubo here –'

'Don't be crazy, Mama.' Sole crunched radishes loudly. 'He's nothing but a *putanos* himself. Look at you in your yellow and black windcheater, yellow jeans and striped hot-shot sneakers. What're you after now, Walter? Bumble bees?'

'Oh c'mon c'mon,' Walter protested, 'my whoring's in the past. I've done more for cleaning up the streets than twelve vice squads. One day I'll get my hands on Montreal – those pathetic whores with their fat thighs bulging out of stockings at the mercy of every two bit pimp in town. All that's going now. You should see what I've done in Vienna. My prostitutes are protected, pension schemes, free medical services, mort –'

'What the hell are you on about?' butted in Sole, helping

himself to a load of salad. 'Only the rich can afford *your* guys 'n dolls.'

'Right now that's true but later on it won't be. Once only the rich could afford vacuum cleaners and colour TV. Today everybody has them.'

Sole snorted and picked his teeth. Boubolina pulled meat off two skewers neatly and expertly. She had heard the conversation a hundred times before.

'Look at Boubolina,' Sole said suddenly, 'you talk pension schemes. Shit. Where's her pension? You think she's been living on your fancy duty free perfume these last five years? Do y—'

'Shaddup, Sole –' Boubolina slammed a saucepan menacingly on the table.

'It's okay, Mama!' Walter squeezed lemon over his kebabs. 'He's just mad 'cause he couldn't pimp for you successfully.'

'Yea – you would have let all the crap in town jerk-off on her for a buck!'

'*Shaddup – gamo ti pragmatotita sou!*' cursed Boubolina, banging the table violently with his fists.

But Sole's blood was up. 'Pension rights, you patronizing bastard. You drag your stinking "rights" around Europe satisfying every pussy and assole that can afford them. Soon you'll supermarketize everything – cut price pussy here. Assole and pussy combined there for the price of one. Fifteen-inch hard on there for whoever has a thousand bucks to see it. Come see da lady being see-sawed one man up in front one behind. Come see da contortionist who can suck himself off. Watch a brother and sister screw. See there a father with his son. What's in it for you, you lying crud? Huh?'

Walter smiled and continued eating.

'I'll tell you what's in it,' persisted Sole, 'not pensions for your circus performers you pump with fancy talk about sexology and college degrees – it's cold hard cash for you. Okay, brother, what you do is your own affair. But don't come over this half-assed crap about fucking pensions and health schemes and mortgages and keeping the streets clear for your bourgeois conscience. When Boubolina had a breast removed five years ago and couldn't work I drove my taxi twenty hours a day to keep us alive. What happened? Didn't she qualify for your welfare?'

Boubolina switched off the radio and the room went deathly quiet.

Walter looked at her. 'Why didn't you tell me – ?'

'Because she wouldn't let me,' Sole hissed. 'You want to know why? She thought you'd be ashamed of her. *You!*'

* * *

'Saxon Forth to Car 46.'

'46.'

'What's the latest on Carbetti?'

'He's still drinking beer on the balcony. One helluva row's going on in the house across the road. But he seems to be waiting for somebody.'

'Call me when he moves.' Forth flung a full packet of sandwiches into his wastepaper basket and bellowed at his secretary to send out for a hamburger. He walked over to a cabinet, took out a bottle of rye and poured himself a double shot.

Pete Taylor from Squad O walked through the door. He wore his blond hair long and had carefully cultivated a bushy moustache, hallmarks he believed were a necessary part of political spying. 'Could be pay dirt or zilch,' he said, eyeing Forth's drink, 'but that Iranian horseman who was in the Gay disco this afternoon isn't just a gold medallist. He's the son of Iran's Minister of Police.'

'Nuts,' Forth snapped. 'Minister of Police is called Ramshid.'

'I know. The kid's from a former marriage and uses his mother's name.' Taylor glanced around the operations room but nobody was listening to him apart from Forth.

'Shit. Is the kid competing again?'

'Tomorrow and Sunday, I think. He won a gold medal at individual jumping today.'

'So that gives him licence to get careless?' Forth looked up angrily at a wall chart detailing the Olympic programme for the rest of the week. 'Sunday, Sunday – team jumping. Okay, Taylor, I want the kid moved to the special security wing at the Olympic Village tonight, and double up security on the rest of the team. Only tell the manager as much as he needs to know. Put a coupla guys from Squad O into the stables where the team's horses are being kept.'

Taylor bit his lip. 'What makes you think it's the Iranian kid Carbetti's after? Why not the Israeli kid? After all, Carbetti came in on an Israeli passport and that seems to me like a perfect cover for anybody planning another Munich.'

Forth looked at him pityingly. 'Weren't you listening this afternoon? Didn't I tell you Carbetti helped blow up the American embassy in Teheran?'

'But you said there was no proof!'

'Don't worry. I'll get proof.' Forth downed his rye. He shouted at his secretary who just disappeared into the Ladies. 'Simma – get the hell outa there. I need data from Iran urgently.'

The speaker buzzed sharply on his desk. He stretched over and pressed down the switch. 'Yea?'

'Car 46 sir, guy with a beard just walked out of La Boube's. He looks mad as hell. Heading for Notre Dame. Carbetti's just spotted him. Seems like he's waiting for the other guy to walk on a bit. Yes, he's starting to make a move –'

'Stick with them. If they've arranged a meeting they aren't going to let you know about it. If they go to a hotel I want every call and message taped.'

*　　*　　*

'Sole?' Walter sounded embarrassed.

'Uh-huh.'

Long silence.

'Feel like coming over for a night cap?'

'No.'

'We need to talk about tomorrow and Sunday.'

'Maybe.'

'For Christ's sake, can't we spike what happened today until after Sunday? How can I say I'm sorry?'

Long silence.

'Sole?'

'You tell Boubolina you intend disappearing when it's all over?'

'How the hell can I?'

'Maudit Christ en Tabernacle!'

'Sole, if I don't speak to you you'll be driving a taxi for the rest of your life. It's for her sake as well as for ours.'

'Okay. Noon, usual place.'

'Can you bring something with you?'

'What.'

'Boubolina's kitchen scales?'

73

There was an inaudible sound on the phone and the line went dead.

Saxon Forth listened to the recording again and shook his head. He squinted up at the list for the following day and read them out loud. 'Wednesday 28 July. Athletics. Basketball. Canoeing. Cycling. No, damn, not cycling. Equestrian sports. Fencing. Handball. Hockey. Judo. Wrestling. Hmmm. So the only tie-up we have with Sunday is "equestrian" where the kid's concerned. It's the only event that'll take place on both days. Simma? Where's the equestrian event being held to-morrow?'

She glanced up and said, 'St Helen's Island – and it's dres-sage.'

Forth nodded and switched through to the Olympic Village. 'Get me Yvon.'

'Yvon speaking.'

'Find out if the Iranian kid is in the dressage tomorrow on St Helens island.'

'Sure he is. He's getting his gear together.'

'Can he hear what I'm saying to you?' Forth gestured at his secretary to pour him another drink.

'No.'

'Is he co-operating? Thanks, Simma.'

'Perfectly.'

'I want fifty of the best shots covering those horses to-morrow. See the kid leaves the Village by chopper.' Forth switched him off and buzzed car 46.

'46.'

'What's happened to Carbetti?'

'Still in his hotel room. He ordered a meal and the other guy Moon ordered a bottle of Irish whiskey. But they haven't made contact. We've placed a guy opposite them and we're covering the foyer.'

Forth grunted and switched him off. Taylor walked slowly towards him from the far end of the operations room, absorbed by a full colour magazine entitled 'Alice and her Alsatian'. He whistled and folded back a double page spread captioned 'position 180'. 'Hey, fellas – you ever think this could work?' He held it up to half a dozen computer programmers.

'Taylor,' Forth bellowed. 'Put down your pretty postcards and move your ass. There's a kinky set-up down Jack Carter square. What do you know about a cat called "Sole"? Find

74

out if he's had anything to do with any anti-Iranian groups. Also this godamn boob woman. And Walter Moon, this guy Carbetti was following. He travels on a Canadian passport. Get through to Ottawa and see if there's anything on him. Simma? Any chance of some coffee? Say – what happened to that guy from the Shin Beth who was here a couple of hours ago?'

'He went to check on the Israeli athlete,' Simma replied, picking up an empty Cona. 'He said it was impossible for the athlete to be in the fruit disco because he'd seen him with a girlfriend this morning –'

Forth exhaled loudly and lifted himself off the chair to shift his crotch into a more comfortable position. 'Moshe Ben-Butch huh?'

'Something like that.'

'Simma, play the recording of that phone conversation between Moon and Sole to Pete before he leaves. See if he makes anything of it.'

Taylor propped himself on the edge of Forth's desk and listened carefully. *'Kitchen scales?'*

Forth shrugged. 'Perhaps it's their cutey cutey way of saying equal amounts of plastic explosive?'

'Saxon!' Simma shouted at him from the Cona machine, 'report coming through on the wires from Teheran.'

Forth and Taylor jumped up quickly, and ran to the telex pointed out by Simma. They stood and waited as the machine clacked out its message:

XL MONTREAL FROM G TEHERAN STOP POLICE MINISTER RAMSHID REPORTED MISSING THREE HOURS AGO STOP INFORMED SOURCES SUSPECT LEFT WING REPERCUSSIONS TO RECENT EXECUTIONS OF TWELVE STUDENTS STOP SENDING HALF HOURLY BULLETINS STOP

'Shit.' Forth tore off the message.

'Shall we bring in Carbetti and the others?'

'On what grounds, Taylor? For talking about kitchen scales?'

Taylor looked at him and at Simma in turn.

Forth returned to his desk. 'If Ramshid's been kidnapped there'll be demands in a few hours. Taylor – call up Williams from downstairs, he's had enough beauty sleep. Get him to help you. Check out details of any anti-Iranian demos here in

Montreal in the past three years, do a run down on the organisers, see what the second generation Iranian-Canadians are up to, what student groups they belong to and who hangs around with them. Come up with names and faces. Fast.'

CHAPTER SIX

Cardinal Zerelli felt tired and a little peevish. He'd sat up far too late the night before watching the Games on the portable TV set at the foot of his bed, and that always left him a bit jaded the next morning. It was annoying being five hours ahead of Montreal.

It was too late to cancel his eleven thirty appointment so he sat and thought about the curses he'd utter if he wasn't a Cardinal. He had to see Gino Pavone, one of his investment advisers attached to the Rome office of an international bank. Pavone was the son of a well-known Milanese family and the Cardinal always regretted he'd chosen business rather than the Church. The Vatican's financial hierarchy could do with Pavone's flair to shake it up from within occasionally, the Cardinal thought wryly.

A buzzer jarred his thoughts, followed quickly by a knock on the door.

'Come in, Gino.'

'Your Eminence.' Pavone walked briskly across the carpet and the two men clasped hands briefly. Ring kissing was unnecessary during business discussions. Pavone was casually dressed in a pale blue linen suit, cheesecloth shirt and David Hockney print necktie. He wore his curly black hair in a modern bob.

The Cardinal watched him unzip a crocodile skin briefcase. 'Gino,' he began, 'the diamond buyer you found for us did an excellent job over the past months. The appreciative value of the gems should prove highly satisfactory over the next ten years.'

Pavone nodded and opened a report.

'There's a lot of work to be done in Canada,' the Cardinal began. Briefly he voiced his anxieties about the way the 'quiet revolution' of the sixties had loosened the power of the Church in Quebec, greatly reducing the number of men and women in orders, and church attendance.

Pavone sat and listened in silence, trying to look attentive.

'Today Gino, Montrealers drive visitors around and show

them Vatican-owned apartment blocks and business complexes and sneer when they see Bingo notices outside the churches! We face a crisis in Quebec and must find a way of solving it.'

'What do you mean?'

'We cannot risk being seen to get involved in projects of a delicate nature.'

'Delicate?' Pavone frowned.

'You recall the James Bay hydro-electric project and the row that caused with the local Indian population and their ancestral rights or whatever it was. That is precisely the kind of project we must avoid. We mustn't seem to be at variance with the people.'

Pavone snorted impatiently. 'But we've drawn up a list of projects for you. It's impossible to foresee another James Bay incident. Do you want to take a timid line with your investments? You don't need my services for that, you can leave it to some pensioned-off bishop with badly fitting dentures.' Pavone snapped his report shut and replaced it in his briefcase.

The Cardinal toyed with an ivory paperknife. 'I'm just suggesting that we must be better informed on site. Quebec has had appalling troubles in its construction industry. The sort of strikes, showdowns and lockouts that very nearly prevented the Olympic site from being ready on time have been put down to a mixture of organized crime stooges infiltrating the unions and holding employers to ransom, and good old fashioned corruption at local level.'

'Quebec is no different from any other province or state,' interrupted Pavone irritably, 'only the North Americans are particularly good at exposing their moral diseases in public.'

The Cardinal ignored his remark. 'Our returns on Vatican owned properties in Quebec are among the highest in the world. We can't risk expensive delays caused by either political action or any other. Clearly we need to make attractive offers to those union leaders or find new ones with which to negotiate.'

'So, you believe we should buy out union leaders who are on the payroll of the organized crime bosses?'

'Yes.'

'I'll look into it.' Pavone made a move to go.

The Cardinal waved his hand. 'There's another important issue about Quebec I'd like you to examine,' he took out a box of lemon sweets and slid them across the desk. 'Some of my

78

colleagues think the way back to the people would be through eccentrically modern cathedrals to outdo some of those grand designs favoured by the mayor of Montreal. But that's such superficial thinking. The growing Marxist inclinations of the young people of Quebec are what we must concern ourselves with.'

Pavone loosened his necktie. The Cardinal's air conditioner had broken down that morning and his office was stifling. He sucked on a lemon sweet and nodded.

'I'd like to set up a special institution for Third World studies – independently of our own institutions and those of the province of course. We can think up a suitable philanthropic fund – perhaps your own family would be good enough to lend its name? We'll give scholarships, employ the finest political analysts from the Left, invite revolutionary leaders as guest lecturers and so on. Its independence of the establishment will give it the appeal we need.'

Pavone reflected on the idea for a minute. 'Why Canada?'

'Because Montreal is taut with political fervour, and Canada likes to think it maintains good relations with the Third World. I'd like you to find out how much such a centre would cost.'

'You intend getting grants from various countries?'

'Of course. The centre has to be self financed after our initial injection of capital released from the sale of some of the diamonds.' The Cardinal crunched noisily on a lemon sweet.

'I take it the purpose of such a centre is to provide you with more than merely a detailed bank of information about the Third World?'

The cardinal reflected for a minute, looking beyond Pavone at an original Dürer.

'We need a platform for a new branch of enterprises in the Third World. On one side we'll research varieties of wheat that can be grown in the tropics for example. And behind the scenes we can maintain a closer vigil over certain trouble spots, and over our rebel priests.'

'What about the return in lire?' Pavone stood up to go.

'Ah.' The Cardinal stood up with him. 'This is where the project becomes creative and where I'll need your help to make the necessary contacts. Once the multi-national companies realize our sympathies, our work in the Third World will become invaluable to them.' He paused at the door and

79

stretched out his hand. 'They will pay handsomely to work through us.'

*   *   *

Walter gasped when the alarm call came through at 7 a.m.

He glanced miserably at the quarter full bottle of whiskey standing open by his bedside. Instinctively he lay back and made every muscle in his body go taut before allowing himself to relax, piece by piece: first his toes, then his feet, calves, thighs, buttocks, waist, fingertips, arms, shoulders and finally his scalp. He closed his eyes and concentrated hard on the point between his nose.

Finally he climbed out of bed, sat on the floor, drew up his feet into the lotus position and remained like that for ten minutes, before unlocking his legs, swinging them around, clasping his hands over his forehead, and leaning over to go very naturally and easily into the headstand position. His breathing was full and profound.

As he lowered himself slowly and gradually to the floor his beard began to itch desperately. He was dismayed at his lack of concentration. He held himself quite still in mid air. When the itching stopped he lowered his legs gradually to the carpet.

He lay flat for five minutes before springing up to reach out for the phone to call room service. He felt hungry and thought guiltily about the half completed meal he'd left at Boubolina's the night before. After a quick glance at the breakfast menu he selected fruit juice, black coffee, griddle cakes, bacon and syrup. He gave the order and then decided to take a quick shower.

Although the room was pleasingly cool thanks to a humming air conditioner he knew the heat outside would soon start climbing towards ninety degrees.

The water had the force of an enthusiastic firing squad. Walter idly wondered if the victim's sensation was the same in the split second that switched life to death. He philosophized on it while washing his hair and beard in a soft lemon shampoo. He was dabbing the same brand of cologne around his body when he heard a breakfast trolley being wheeled into the room, and the discreet sound of a door closing.

Hotel life was nice, he decided, watching himself in the bathroom mirror as he put on a pair of hand tailored bright green cotton jeans and a matching shirt. He slotted a white canvas belt around his waist, and carefully fastened on the choker of square silver links he'd bought from Greenberg in London.

Walter ate his breakfast while his hair was drying and jotted down a list of the things he had to do before he could meet Sole at noon.

He was out of the hotel by eight thirty and made his way through groups of people dangling with cameras and binoculars, who were waiting for a coach to take them to the big events of the day. Walter turned left down Sherbrooke Avenue, south into University Avenue, and walked for several blocks until the turning on the right for the Place Bonaventure. Built at the end of the sixties as a massive commercial complex, it combined convention, exhibition and hotel facilities with brightly designed trade, retail and shopping arcades, and its own metro stop. It was the liveliest way Walter could imagine of buying everything he needed under one roof.

He pottered about the boutiques that faced one another across wide, brightly-lit stone corridors built on several storeys to resemble indoor streets. Colourful Olympic flags were festooned overhead. Each store had selected a different theme from the Games and improvised to effect in window displays. Everybody from the sweater manufacturer to the ice-cream maker, the button seller to candy store had variations on the Olympic logo.

Walter went into a stationer's first and bought a roll of off-white masking tape, two rolls of soft white tissue paper, and dozens of tiny envelopes, the sort used for buttons or pins. He paid the cashier and decided to try the next floor up for shoes. *En route* he passed a silversmith and some bracelets in rolled silver caught his eye. He bought one for himself that fitted neatly over his wristbone, and a heavier, chunkier variety for Staki.

In the shoestore next door he asked for a certain make of English sandals of the size and style Staki had noticed on the outside of the box containing the Vatican diamonds. But he was directed to six different stores before he found the right pair of size twelve black Clarks men's sandals.

*　　*　　*

'Taylor to Forth.'

'Yes?'

'He's buying sandals.'

'Sandals? Masking tape, envelopes, tissue paper, bracelets and now sandals. Maybe he's getting married. What's Carbetti up to?'

'Sitting at an ice-cream bar opposite eating a High Jump.'

'What's a High Jump, for Chrissakes?'

'Five scoops of ice-cream, strawberry cordial, nuts, whipped cr –'

'Okay. He make contact with Moon?'

'Nope. He's tailing him, I'm convinced.'

'Maybe it just *looks* that way.'

'Well, I th—'

'Any sign of the black cat, whatzisname, Fish?'

'Sole? Not yet.'

'Huh?'

'Sole.'

'That's what I said.' Forth switched him off, glared at the speaker on the desk and buzzed the Squad O base in the Olympic Village. 'Yvon?'

'You just caught me.'

'Iranian kid left for the island yet?'

'He's in the chopper now and should land in a couple of minutes.'

'Any trouble with the horses?'

'Nothing.'

Forth killed the connection. He switched on a TV set next to his desk and twiddled the knobs until he had a full view of the dressage arena on St Helen's Island. The island was mid river in the St Lawrence, about eight kilometers by road from the Olympic Village, and a stone's throw by bridge from downtown Montreal. It lay next to Notre Dame Island where the canoeing events were being held. Both islands were used for the Expo 67 World Fair, and some of the disused pavilions were turned into temporary bases by Squad O.

As the Games were being held on some twenty-three different sites, Forth had designed a system whereby he could utilise the standard TV coverage of the Games for placing Squad O cameramen at strategic points. If any Squad O officer noticed anything out of the ordinary he'd transmit a message to the 'special' cameramen dotted all over the various sites, the action would be filmed and transmitted both to a helicopter above with two marksmen in it, to a control room, and direct to Forth's operations room with its line-up of video receivers. For additional mobility, Squad O cameramen joined the news cameraman on the auto-camera track buggy. This drove around on the inside of the track, taking close-ups of the race in progress. A helicopter at 305 metres relayed the video signals from the news cameras to a near-by mobile commentary unit. The Squad O cameraman filmed the rows of spectators closest to the track.

The co-ordination between the news and security cameraman was so fluid and natural looking that no outsider could guess there was any difference.

Forth used another innocent looking feature of the Games for speedy communication between the Squad O marksmen and ground forces. Electronic scoreboards. These utilized a system nicknamed 'Swiss Time' innovated for the 1976 Olympics by two Swiss watch manufacturers. They enabled spectators to see the timing and result of each event the instant it happened.

But the top of the scoreboards were used by Squad O for flashing signals to one another over the heads of thousands of spectators. This was done in such a way so as not to detract from the original purpose of the scoreboard. Signals were processed instantly by the computer in the operations room, and Forth was handed regular print-outs telling him exactly what was happening on the various sites.

If a man or group of men started to act suspiciously on any of the Olympic sites or at the Village, Forth's team would be alerted to watch the action on the video screen, and help co-ordinate ground and air forces via signals on the scoreboards where relevant. If anything happened at the equestrian site on St Helens' Island there was no way Forth or Squad O could be caught off guard. No way.

But surveillance outside the Olympic sites and Village still depended on prowling squad cars and old fashioned foot leather.

'Taylor to Forth.'

'Yes, Pete.'

'You're not going to believe this – Moon's on his hands and knees on a building site picking up stones.'

'C'mon, Pete.'

'I'm serious.'

'He doesn't need us, he needs a shrink.' Forth broke the connection immediately as another call flashed on his speaker. 'Forth.'

'Car 46, sir. Sole Dubois is backing his car up Jacques Cartier.'

'The whore with him?'

'Naw – she's shopping across the road.'

'Okay, 46, he's meeting Moon at twelve in a few minutes.'

'We're with him.'

* * *

Sole picked up Walter at the top of the stairs leading down to the metro station for McGill University. He was gaudily dressed in bright pink jeans, matching braces and a black T shirt. He pulled away from the pavement before Walter had closed the door. It was a trick they used to play on one another as boys to test their reflexes.

Walter didn't find it funny. 'You miserable bastard. Half the street saw that!'

Sole looked in the mirror and laughed at him. He noticed the squad car following behind. 'Assole, pretend you're looking at your shopping while I ditch our friends here. Don't look round!' He swung around the corner, headed for a hairpin bend, drove on for two blocks and shook his head. 'Tonight,' he began, 'after you make the switch, pick up a roving cab. I'm not risking hanging around in the shadows waiting for you. Don't come to the house – it makes Mama nervous. I'll meet you in Yoanniki's store across the road.'

Walter whistled. 'Thanks. Say if your plan fails?'

'It won't.'

'Can we go up to Mount Royal?'

'Why?'

'I want some fresh air. Somebody puke in your car this morning?'

'Jesus. It still smells back there? Spent an hour scrubbing it.'

The two lurched back violently in their seats as the taxi changed gear automatically for the climb.

'For Sunday,' said Sole, checking in his mirror to make sure they'd dropped the tail, 'I arranged like you suggested to switch this heap with a guy running a popcorn concession. He's a buddy of mine who used to drive a taxi so doesn't mind

84

for a day. Your five hundred bucks helped. Pull out that envelope between my seat and the door and you'll find a layout of the Olympic site.'

'Right.'

'See to the north east of the site there's the Maisonneuve sports centre? Okay. Joe will leave his van in the car park there and take you through the security gate. It takes a few minutes to walk from the gate to the back of the Velodrome.'

'Security checks?'

'Course. Everybody with concessions – popcorn, peanut, ice-cream, horse, shit, all carry special metal discs on their shirts. No disc, no way they can get in. Each guy has a special pass-word. It's the same in the Olympic Village. Baby, even the flies have discs on their balls.'

Walter chuckled and ruffled Sole's hair.

'Hey! Cut it out. The street'll think I'm driving the fairy queen!' He drove past some of the wealthiest homes in Mon-treal on his climb to the top of Mount Royal. They were grand, double-storey, leafy fronted homes, many of them built of large grey stone blocks.

'Remember when we used to deliver newspapers here?' said Walter turning in his seat to watch the houses go by.

'Mm hmm,' said Sole nonchalantly swinging the wheel for a corner.

'Next week you could buy a block.'

'Wouldn't waste my time.' He slowed down for a stop street. 'I've told Joe the best time to meet you on Sunday is somewhere between seven fifty and seven fifty-five, eh? If you take the metro to Viau you only have a short distance to walk to the car park.'

'Where will you be?'

'I'll come later on and wait in the van for you. While Joe collects my taxi from the other side of the site, I'll drive you and these cats you're meeting away someplace.'

'How can you trust this Joe character so easily?'

Sole knocked on the roof of his cab with his knuckles.

'Okay, long stuff. Now that we're at the top of Mount Royal will you *please* tell me how I switch these gems tonight?'

Instead of replying, Sole climbed out of the driver's seat. Walter followed.

The two stood and gazed over Montreal to the St Lawrence and the clean limbed bridges linking the shore with the islands beyond. The single view summed up all that Montreal was about. The quiet dignified elegance of the old French buildings with their peaked domes and green copper spires and pointed roofs fought for the skyline with the tall slabs of the commercial complexes, hotels and apartment blocks.

French Canada was fighting with America. And America was winning.

* * *

'Car 46 to Forth.'

'Mm?'

'They're walking around Mount Royal.'

'Can you hear what they're saying?'

'They're speaking Greek.'

'You mean to tell me there's nobody in Squad O that speaks Greek?'

'Andreas – but he's at the Village.'

Forth switched off without bothering to reply. He looked at the print-out lying on his desk from St Helen's Island. It was as clear as a baby's behind. He glanced at the latest telex report from Teheran. It confirmed that Iran's police minister was still missing.

'Why hasn't there been anything in the press?' Simma dumped a sheaf of telexes from the wire services on his desk.

'One party system in Iran, sweetheart. One man state. The Shah's. He says what news gets out and what doesn't. Okay, Taylor, what's that? This stuff is crap.' Forth gestured scornfully at a pile of files on Iranians in Quebec.

'Special security file on Jean-Claude Dubois known as "Sole".' Taylor put them down with a proud flourish. 'Taken at an anti-Iranian demo in Montreal three months ago,' he said spreading out a number of press photographs, 'biggest demo of lefty sympathizers in town protesting against the student executions. And look who's in the front line here – Dubois. See who's punching a cop there – Dubois. And who's that throwing a brick at the Iranian embassy window? Dubois –'

'Was he pulled in at the time?' Forth examined the blow-ups one by one.

'Na. Riot squad soon cooled everyone down,' Taylor smirked.

'How about the organizers of this?'

'Two flew up from New York and flew back the next day.

86

The others have kept a low profile in town since the demo.'

'Low profile, low profile. Jesus, Taylor in your book that means they're clean. In mine, it means they're keeping cool in the wings waiting to pounce! Have the squad check them out for Chrissakes.' Forth wiped the back of his solid neck with a Kleenex. 'Any beer on ice, Simma?'

'Sure.' She walked over to the fridge and hauled out two cardboard frames each linking six cans of beer. She pulled the seal off the frame and began handing the cans around the room.

Forth yanked the ring off his, drank half the beer in a gulp, slung a leg over his chair arm and began to leaf through Dubois' hefty file, reading occasional items out loud. 'Hmm, campaigned for both Indians and Half Breeds. Seen at Chicano demo in Los Angeles. Seen in Vancouver during Simon Fraser University student sit-ins. Jezuz, this trouble-maker moves around. Founder editor of *Moustique*. *Moustique*? Simma, what the hell's that? Sounds like after-shave.' He finished his beer and stood up to get another.

Simma rummaged in a pile of assorted magazines on Taylor's desk and pulled out the lastest issue of *Moustique*. She threw it expertly across the room and it landed at Forth's feet. He stooped to pick it up, beer can in hand, but noticed an item in Dubois' file. 'Christ – what the hell's this? Believed to be involved in the North American branch of the Middle East Revolutionary Front?'

'What surprises you, Saxon?' said Simma, not bothering to look up from her desk. 'You're the Middle East expert. I thought you knew about such things!'

'How many times do I have to tell you the revolution breeds groups like flies? Where the hell's that fella from the Shin Beth? I thought he was supposed to be here all the time.'

'We told you,' Simma shouted back, 'he's gone off to prove the Israeli gold medallist isn't a fairy.'

'Simma – get Washington to send us everything they know on the MERF. Top priority. Where the hell's Taylor? I want Dubois pulled in.'

'On what grounds?' Taylor turned from a group of men standing around a wall chart. 'Guy's done nothing!'

'I don't care.' He punched a switch on the speaker. 'Car 46?'

'Sir.'

'Where's Dubois?'

'Ummmm. We've lost him.'

'You've fucking what?'

'Lost him sir. He ran away from an MPD patrol car earlier and now we've lost him. We're waiting for him now at Jacques Cartier.'

'Yeah, you stupid parrot stuffed full o'crap, where you expect him to walk out in the open, smile sweetly, and say, "Hi guys – it's me, your buddy Sole!" Put out an APB on him, on Moon and Carbetti.'

'Sir.'

Taylor walked across to his desk as the speaker switched off. 'APB? Have you told the Prime Minister's office? Or the Iranian ambassador?'

'Why create unnecessary panic, Taylor? You don't solve this by telling everybody in town and have them bring out the army with Saracens and metal helmets. This isn't 1970. It's 1976. You use your *brains*. Create an outer atmosphere of calm, well being, peace, love light and keep everything cool. That way people get sloppy and careless.' He snapped his fingers by Taylor's eyes. 'That's when you break them.'

* * *

A white and blue 1964 Dodge laundry van cheerfully inscribed with the words 'La Paloma' rattled along route eleven.

'Do you always borrow the laundry van?' asked Walter nervously clinging on in the front seat.

'Sometimes. Makes me look more credible.'

'How much do they pay you for doing this?'

'Five bucks per delivery. But I paid the kid from McGill twice that to let me take over. He thought I was crazy.'

'Sole.'

'Mm hmm.'

'I'm sorry about last night. You should have told me about Mama's operation.'

'Aaah. If you'd been around you would have known.'

Walter looked away sadly.

'C'mon,' said Sole grinding the gears noisily, 'cut the sentiment. Me 'n Mama have put up with it for years. *Calice*. My taxi's like a Cadillac compared with this rattle trap! Hey. I put a pair of wide blue jeans and a dark shirt in the back. Jump over the seat and get changed. You'll be more comfortable than in those ball-slicing things you're wearing.'

Sole slowed down as Walter made his way carefully into the back seat of the van. The highway ahead, leading out of Montreal towards the Laurentian mountains, was deserted.

'Hungry? Couple of hours yet before we go to St Dominique's.'

'Sure,' came a muffled voice from behind.

Sole changed down, turned off the highway at a roadhouse and pulled up under a massive billboard. He swung his head around and smiled at Walter struggling into the jeans. 'Hot dogs here are the best in Quebec.'

'Fine. Boy, you ever tried changing back here?'

At the sight of the van a man came running out from a swingdoor that squeaked violently behind him. He rubbed his hands on a cloth and squinted at Sole. *'Bonjour, Bonjour. Qu'est-ce que vous voulez?'*

'Chiens chauds s'il vous plâit mon vieu – et café.'

The man's mouth fell open as two legs appeared over the seat next to Sole. *'Pour deux?'* he whispered anxiously leaning over to see if there was anyone else in the back of the van.

'Oui, deux. Merci mon vieu!' said Sole breezily.

'Chiens chauds,' Walter repeated as they watched the man disappear behind the swingdoor. 'I wonder when French-Canadians will stop transliterating Americanese? When I first went to Paris and said, *"mon truck est buster, je n'ai pas de wrench pour fixer"*, people thought I'd arrived from outer space. They said even the English spoke better French than I did!'

Sole eyed him up and down. 'More comfortable, eh? Imagine sitting four hours in the others. You'd come out of St Dominique's as *Wanda* Moon!'

'Then I wouldn't need to spend a coupla million bucks getting my mug changed, would I?'

'Coupla million? *Tabernacle*. I could start a revolution here on that!' Sole fitted his cap on his head in the driver's mirror.

Walter watched him affectionately. 'What will you do, you and Mama?'

'Stick around here, make life more comfortable – not too much otherwise the *flics* get suspicious – and wait till you call us.'

'That could be two or three years!'

Sole leaned on his wheel and avoided Walter's eyes. The

89

swingdoor burst open and the owner appeared carrying a tray. He hooked it on Sole's window and clapped his hands enthusiastically.

'*Merci mon vieu!*' Sole handed him a few notes without bothering to count them and carefully lifted two large hot dogs wrapped in paper napkins off the tray. He passed one to Walter, brought in the cups of coffee and placed them on the floor. Then he took out a cassette tape recorder. 'While you're eating I want you to listen to this. It's a taped conversation between the kid in the kitchen at St Dominique's and me. Listen, then try to imitate the kid's voice. He's a good kid. Nineteen or so. Parents live near to where your old man had his store. I think they sold him to the Church. I keep telling him to clear out.'

Sole pushed a button on the cassette and a snatch of conversation filled the laundry van. They ate their hot dogs and listened. He rewound it and replayed it until Walter had heard it half a dozen times. Walter practised imitating the kid's voice in an accent he'd spent years trying to get rid of. Sole played the tape a final time and Walter repeated the words, catching the kid's inflection exactly.

Sole sat back and smiled. 'That's just about right,' he snapped off the tape. 'Finish your coffee and later we'll test your recall. Although the kid – he's called Bobbie by the way – is off duty tonight nobody's going to be surprised to see him, or *think* they see him around midnight. He's a bit shorter than you are and much darker. But when the lights are off, who'll notice that? Let's check over the action.'

'I sit in the closet,' Walter began, sipping his coffee, 'and dial into Lancey's conversation, through the Hero. I'll know exactly where he and the others are from your layout. So, I'll know how to get to them, and how long it will take me, because you have timed the distances for me.'

'Check. How will you switch the gems?'

'I take your timing device, attach it to the fuse box in the kitchen closet and time the supply to switch off, giving me a few minutes to get from the closet to Lancey and the gems.'

'Check. Then what?'

'Soon as the lights go out I rush in pretending I'm Bobbie saying something like "*Sacre-bleu*, the lights have gone out, don't worry I'll fix them. I was on my way to the kitchen". Then I switch the diamonds with my box of stones and rush from the room before Lancey and the others have adjusted to the darkness. How do I know they'll stand still?'

'They won't.' Sole finished the last of his hot dog and wiped mustard off his fingers. 'And that's what you exploit. You've seen people in the dark – they grope around. But *your* eyes will be accustomed to the dark from sitting in the closet all those hours with just a flashlight when you need it. Right?'

'Right. What happens if they lock the door?'

'They can't. I checked that. There aren't any locks on the doors except the front door. Even the john doesn't have a lock.' Sole pulled his T shirt away from his chest and blew out. 'Getting warm, huh? Guess we'd better start putting your rocks in the envelopes. Boubolina's scales are in the kitbag in the back. What weight did you say the box had to be?'

'Two to three kilos.'

'Jesu, that's a lotta rocks.'

'We've got over an hour,' said Walter stretching to the back to get the shoebox, tissue paper, masking tape and envelopes, and the pile of stones he picked up from the building site.

'Another hot dog 'n coffee?'

'Sure.'

Sole toot-tooted on the horn and the roadhouse owner's face appeared at the hatch. Sole pointed at the tray and gestured that they wanted the same again. The face smiled and disappeared.

'Walter.'

'Hm?'

'How will you know exactly when to switch the gems?'

'Well, that tissue paper's bound to make a lot of noise. I guess Lancey will unwrap all the gems and then wrap them up again. I'll time him and that'll give me some idea of how long he'll take to rewrap them. Then when I think he's nearly there, I'll set the timing device. I'll –'

'Christ. Shh –'

They both turned as a Royal Canadian Mounted Police patrol car with the bilingual initials RCMP GRC slowed down behind them. Two Mounties in brown uniforms and wrap around sun glasses looked at the van curiously. Sole waved cheerfully, the policemen waved back and drove on.

'MPD car this afternoon and now these guys –' Walter watched the car accelerate down the highway.

'Yaaah,' said Sole scornfully. 'Everybody's nervous. If

91

MPD's out checking up on people like me it'll take a day before the GRC get the word. Shit, you should have seen the co-ordination during the kidnappings in 1970. GRC arranged a stakeout at a Montreal apartment. Some suspicious tenants contacted Montreal North PD and they sent a squad car around and the GRC guy had to show his credentials at the door. Boy. Some stakeout.' Sole shook his head in disgust. 'Hey, that reminds me,' he said, helping Walter fill the envelopes with stones, 'you'll find a gun and a coupla cartridges in cookie wrappers in the kitbag.'

'I won't need that,' Walter snapped.

'You think your pointed feet are enough, huh, fancy ballet dancer? *Calice* you're conceited!'

'Okay. Okay!' Walter sounded desperate.

'You'll find a silencer with the scales.'

'Quiet – here come the other hot dogs.'

The trays were exchanged and the owner scuttled back to the roadhouse.

'Aw *shit merde skata*,' shouted Sole banging the side of his head, 'Mama said she was making you pea soup for lunch. Better go call from the roadhouse and apologize. Say we got held up and you'll eat it tomorrow or something.'

*   *   *

Saxon Forth looked through the sheaf of print-outs from the dressage event on St Helen's Island and tried to dig a piece of meat from between his teeth with a pencil point. The event was nearly over but Forth still felt uneasy. He was happier when things happened than when they didn't.

He stretched and suddenly found the noise and clatter in the operations room unbearable. Normally he didn't notice the incessant clacking of the telex machines, the boys walking back and forth endlessly checking charts and print-outs, sending and receiving messages, decoding secret information, feeding it to the shredder, calling for reference material and punctuating everything with a steady stream of wisecracks.

Forth recognized the danger signals. When he noticed noise he was worried. Very worried.

He took the hint and walked to a little office next to the operations room. He rarely used it. The blinds were pulled down against the strong afternoon sun. The room was cool and quiet. Forth lay down on a studio couch and switched on the

92

portable TV set next to him, twiddling the knobs to see the Ladies One Mile event.

The faces approached him then the cameras cut quickly to a side view. '... looks as though number six Leafy Pond from Great Britain is determined to keep in the lead. Earlier this year she surprised everybody by winning the event at the Commonwealth Games, and – no – that's number forty nine Penny Kanda from Nigeria catching up on the inside and running at the most remarkable speed – amazing runner this girl and she's only eighteen and she looks as though – yes – she's neck and neck with Leafy Pond – if she k—'

'Saxon?' Simma leaned around the door.

Forth switched off the set. 'What?'

'Report in from Washington on the Middle East Revolutionary Front. And a telex in from Teheran. No sign of Ramshid. No word from any kidnappers. And the government's still keeping quiet.'

Forth swung his legs off the couch. 'Ask the bureau in Teheran for any private theories or speculations. Tell them the stuff they've sent over is about as helpful as a mouse's dick. Oh, and Simma –'

'Mm?' she stood at the door with a pencil poised over her notebook.

'Get Major Pink on the line in Washington. John Pink. The English "gentleman". Tell him to catch the next flight to Montreal. I want him here by dark.'

'*Pink?* Why?' She blinked rapidly behind her huge round spectacles.

Forth stood up. 'Tell him to bring everything he needs. He'll know what that means. Everything. For three men at least.'

Simma looked at him, turned and left the room.

Forth picked up the information sheet from Washington and stretched out again on the studio couch to read it.

EX WASHINGTON STOP MERF LATELY FORMED LINKING LIKEMINDED GROUPS IN LEBANON ISRAEL IRAN JORDAN OMAN SEEKING REVOLUTIONARY CHANGE IN SO CALLED REACTIONARY REGIMES STOP LEADERS IN TEHERAN JERUSALEM AND BEIRUT STOP POTENTIAL GROWTH CAUSING ANXIETY STOP INFILTRATION TOP PRIORITY STOP BELIEVE RECENT GUERRILLA ACTIVITIES CREDITED TO VARIOUS DIFFERENT GROUPS HAVE ROOTS IN MERF LEADERS STOP SECURITY CHIEFS FROM

ISRAEL IRAN LEBANON JORDAN OMAN CO-OPERATING VIA OUR
BUREAUX STOP MAJOR SOURCE MERF FUNDS FROM N AMERICA
AND BRITAIN STOP XXXCJH

'Simma? *Simma!*'

'I'm only around the corner, Saxon, for God's sake.'

'Telex Teheran and find out if Ramshid isn't on a security
mission someplace. He's probably meeting his godamn coun-
terparts from Israel, Oman and wherever the hell else on
somebody's private yacht.'

'Surely you would have heard if he was?' She stuck a pencil
into her frizzy hair.

'No, sweetheart. Not unless we ask!'

They both jumped at the sound of the speaker buzzing in
the operations room. Forth ran to answer it. 'Get this thing
working in both rooms by this evening. Yes?'

'Car 46, Sir. Fat Greek woman's going out with a shopping
basket.'

'Alone?'

'Yes.'

'Search it. Tell her it's routine. Be nice. Don't scare her.
Search other baskets or parcels on the square. Tell everyone
there's been a bomb scare.'

'Sir.'

CHAPTER SEVEN

Toni Carbetti walked listlessly up St Catherine street and looked in shop windows with the interest of a blind man. He loathed hanging around waiting for something to happen and wished Sunday would come and go. There was something much cleaner about being a hit man than a dumb bodyguard.

He paused at the *Rive Gauche* store on the corner of St Catherine and La Montagne and walked into a quiet arcade. He couldn't see any sign of the brasserie. A group of people emerged out of the floor and he waited until they casually walked by him into the street before moving across to a circular stairway that led down into the heart of *La Bergerie*.

Carbetti hesitated on the bottom stair and glanced around the brasserie before turning right to take a seat at the bar. He ordered a lager. Behind him the brasserie filled up rapidly as people lined its sheepskin covered seats along the walls. Slim elegantly dressed boys in tight fitting shirts and jeans served at the various tables. A clever designer had turned an ordinary basement into a cosy panelled interior with a relaxed and friendly atmosphere.

Carbetti was used to working alone. He didn't seem to notice that he wasn't part of the spirited chit-chat that went back and forth between the tables and the boys that served them.

He ordered a second lager and looked at his watch. It was seven twenty-five. The couple had said seven thirty. He listened idly as a group of people at the table behind him read through the menu badly mispronouncing the French names.

'Say, we're from Edmonton, Alberta. Could you help us with the menu please?'

Carbetti didn't move.

'Excuse me, we're from Ed—'

'Forget it, Daisy. He probably doesn't understand English. Waiter!'

Seven twenty-nine.

'M'sieu Ben-Or?'

Carbetti looked up. The barman held out a telephone.

Carbetti nodded once, took the receiver and pulled the wire free, half turning away from the inquisitive ears at the bar. He cupped his hand over the mouthpiece. 'Yes?'

'Carbetti?'

'Yes.'

'You'll find your instructions stuck under the second basin in the gents room.'

The line went dead.

Carbetti replaced the receiver, slid the phone back along the bar and quietly finished his beer. He ordered a third, dropped some notes next to the empty glass, slipped off the stool and walked towards the cloakroom door.

*   *   *

'Any sign of Carbetti?'

'No sir. He hasn't been back to his hotel yet either. We just checked.'

'Bananas.' Forth punched the switch on the speaker and fixed himself a glass of scotch and mineral water. A chef in Miami once told him it was the best way to treat nerves. 'Simma send out for some pizzas for the boys. Pizzas okay, fellas?'

'Sure. Why not? Okay. Jesus, again?'

'Taylor – I want you to collect Major Pink from the airport tonight and bring him straight here. See he gets through without any hassle. What the hell are you reading now?'

'My horoscope.'

'Yak.' Forth walked to the fridge and emptied half a tray of ice into his drink. Taylor watched him and while his back was turned gestured to Simma to step out into the corridor.

'Old man usually get like this?' he asked, nodding at the open door.

'Like what?' Simma turned her back to the operations room.

'Y'know – jumping about – mixing crazy drinks – eating telexes –'

'Oh. Don't you know about Saxon and Iran?'

'Saxon and Iran? What the hell does that mean?'

'He was part of the CIA team in Iran in the early fifties.'

Taylor scratched his head and looked at her. 'Hey, when the army was put in power and guys were paid to run through the streets shouting pro Shah slogans?'

She nodded deeply.

'Cheeesuss. But that was over twenty years ago!'

'So? Sax was one of eight agents that carried it out.'

'Classic style, huh? I wasn't even in high school then!'

'I know. But he's still part of the blueprint that gets edgy every time anything threatens America's long affair with the Shah.' Simma glanced nervously into the operations room but Forth was bellowing at the speaker.

'Like the blowing up of the American embassy last year?'

'You said it – I didn't.'

'Why's he so convinced *Carbetti* was involved?' Taylor asked unwinding the foil off a new packet of Camels.

Simma shrugged. 'He said at the time it had Carbetti's style and stamp – no thanks I don't smoke – nobody believed him at the time. Up till then Carbetti had always been hitman for *our* side.'

Taylor struck a match noisily and lit his cigarette. 'But yesterday he said Carbetti would jump whatever way fifty thousand bucks flew!'

'He didn't think that a year ago.'

'Cheeeesusss.' He inhaled a lungful of smoke.

'Saxon chasing Carbetti is like Saxon tracking down the man who's raped his daughter. Except the daughter here is Iran.'

'Why the hell didn't he do this a year ago?'

'Big daddy in Washington prevented it. But Saxon has an open field here,' she whispered making a sweeping gesture with her arms.

Taylor pursed his lips thoughtfully.

'It's not just Carbetti, Pete,' she added confidentially, 'Saxon wants to take credit for finding out who's behind him.'

'Yea,' replied Taylor cynically. 'Guess you'd better get his pizzas huh?' He turned and walked over to the elevator.

*   *   *

The La Paloma laundry van pulled up and parked noisily under a large tree two blocks away from St Dominique's. Walter and Sole sat in silence for a minute staring ahead at some kids playing ball in the street.

'Stick of gum?'

'Nuh.' Walter shook his head.

'Ready to go?'

'Guess so.'

'Beard itching?'

'Nuh.'

Sole smiled and punched him playfully on the cheek. 'C'mon.' He slung two laundry bags and a La Paloma jacket over his shoulder, and jumped out of the van. Walter followed more slowly, carefully lifting his kitbag over the seat. It contained the neatly packed shoebox full of stones in tiny envelopes wrapped in four tissue paper rolls, the Hero, the diagram of St Dominique's, Sole's gun, the timing device for the fuse box and a pocket flash light.

'So. I see you at Yoanniki's store, 1, maybe 2 a.m., depending?' said Sole cheerily, putting on the small laundry-man's jacket that barely stretched across his muscular shoulders. He removed a wide leather wrist band and stuffed it into his pocket. 'Must look the part eh? Nothing too hip.'

Walter didn't seem to hear.

'Walter?'

'Hm.'

'Talk like Bobbie, the kid in the kitchen?'

'*Le maudit Christ en tabernacle.*'

'*Merveilleux, merveilleux.* Let's go. Let me do all the talking when we get to the back door eh?'

They started to walk down the road. Sole paused after a while and pointed at a large imposing double fronted house, a piece of early French Canada built out of solid grey stone blocks and partially covered with ivy leaves. He led Walter into a beautifully kept rose garden that intoxicated the warm evening air.

The lone name 'St Dominique' was engraved on a highly polished brass plate hanging on a walnut front door.

They walked down the side of the house and Sole knocked twice on a stable door at the back. Within minutes the top half opened a fraction and then swung back to frame a stooped, pointed faced old man with spiky grey hair and a checked shirt. He smiled broadly and opened the bottom half of the door excitedly '*Bonsoir, los palomos!*' he said giggling to himself.

'*Bonsoir mon père – comment allez-vous ce soir?*' asked Sole kindly in his best altar boy voice.

The old priest nodded rapidly and explained he was busy

watching the Games on TV. Sole bent over and whispered to him to go back, promising faithfully to stack the clean laundry in the closet before locking himself out. The priest grinned, naughtily crinkling his eyes, and scuttled off leaving Walter and Sole alone in the kitchen.

Walter glanced about approvingly. The kitchen looked like something out of *Better Homes and Gardens*. 'Beautiful,' he murmured appreciatively at the black-and-white flagstone floor.

'*Sacre-bleu*. Get in the fucking closet!' Sole pushed him through a large pine door into a fitted interior measuring some seven feet in height by five feet in width. In spite of shelves at least three feet deep the two of them could turn around comfortably with the closet door shut. The top shelf held towels and table linen. The lower shelves were stacked high with dozens of varieties of canned food.

Sole began parting the cans to make a rough staircase for Walter to climb. He removed some of the towels and linen from the top shelf and placed them on the floor with the clean laundry. 'Here, climb up and I'll pile towels along the front of the shelf like a bank. Then if any wiseguy opens the closet door you can lie down behind them.'

'Oh thanks, with my knees in my mouth?'

'That's the idea! Here, let me give you a leg-up.'

'What'll they say about the towels on the floor?'

'They'll say *La Paloma*'s been kidding around.'

'*La Paloma? La Paloma?*'

Walter and Sole froze as the old priest shuffled back into the kitchen. Sole stepped out of the closet hastily and pulled the door closed behind him. '*Oui mon père?*'

The old man stretched out two cupped palms full of home-made cookies.

'*Merci mon père, vous étes très gentil, très gentil.*' Sole held out his hands and took them.

'*Où est ton ami?*' The old priest glanced around the kitchen for Walter. Sole quickly explained that he had to get back to the van because they left the keys in the lock.

'*Eh bien. Au revoir La Paloma. Jusqu'à demain*, until tomorrow!' He waved and turned to leave the kitchen. Sole waited until the echoing footsteps disappeared. He opened the closet door.

'*Jesus!*' Walter's ashen face appeared between two piles of towels.

'Here' – Sole handed him the cookies – 'you look real cute up there. Just like in a sauna. If you turn you'll see the fuse box by your head. You want me to connect the timer?'

'No – just go!'

'The box works just like the one at Boubolina's,' said Sole chattily. 'Timer'll cut the supply and turn it on again exactly as you set it. Hasn't failed me yet.'

'Okay, Sole, now for Christ's sake go!'

'Don't worry about running back in here after you switch the rocks to take the timer off. Once the lights go on again nobody's going to come in here to check the box. They'll think Bobbie's pulled the lever down.'

'You mean the timer stays here all *night*?'

'Sure. It's hidden by towels. I'll collect it tomorrow on my next laundry round. Say – you'll get thirsty up there. I'll find you a Coke.'

Walter lay back behind the towels and raised his legs upwards to rest on the grid of a ventilator. He sweated profusely. The direct rush of fresh air felt good. He heard Sole open the fridge.

'*Merde*. Not a Coke in sight. One, two, three, maybe half a dozen different sorts of wine –'

'Sole, *get out!*'

Sole pounced on the closet door. 'What was that? You should see the food in the fridge. Can I get you a little cold chicken? Some sliced salmon?'

'I want nothing. Just *go!*'

Sole turned back to the fridge. 'Hmm, guess I'll take a couple of bottles of rosè back to Mama. Beer okay for you Walter?' He kicked the fridge door shut with his foot, walked into the closet and swung a carton of four beers to the top shelf. Walter caught them and thumped his head against the wall.

'Hey – go easy up there!'

'You stupid bastard – can't you get your brown ass out of this kitchen?'

Sole laughed and held up his spare hand to pat Walter on the cheek. 'Just think – this time next week you'll be a millionaire Greek from the Bronx!'

'Thanks. *Jusqu'à demain*, huh?' he replied shortly.

'*Oui, jusqu'à demain –*' Sole smiled, hesitated and turned reluctantly to leave the kitchen.

* * *

Toni Carbetti read through the instructions he found carefully stuck under the hand basin as the caller described. He stood in the privacy of one of the toilets, relieved to be away from the laughter and noise of the brasserie. Noise irritated him.

He examined the envelope's contents a second time. One first-class air ticket to Zurich. A key to a locker at Zurich airport. A deposit slip counterfoil for fifty thousand dollars. A photograph of victim number two for Sunday.

He reread the letter. It told him that Walter Moon and the second victim had to be assassinated simultaneously. It gave him details of how to get to a room that had been leased for him in an apartment block opposite the Olympic site, and where to find the equipment he requested.

The letter was signed, simply, 'Zurich'.

Carbetti memorized the contents of the letter, the instructions and the photograph, so precisely that if he closed his eyes he could outline them in his mind. He tested his powers of recall three times, and then carefully tore the letter and photograph into tiny pieces. He flushed them down the toilet, waiting for a few minutes until the water cleared to make sure that every fragment had disappeared. He flushed the toilet again. He waited, then flushed it again before unlocking his door.

He walked to the sink, took out a comb and ran it through his long hair and droopy moustache. He needed a woman. He felt the same kind of spiciness in his groin that usually hit him immediately before or immediately after an assassination.

Not that he didn't always feel like a woman, but this was different. He had to find one he could take into a dark alley and do up against the wall. Lift her skirt, pull her panties away from her thigh and force himself in at the side. If she struggled he'd have to grip her buttocks so tightly that the wall behind her would tear the skin from his knuckles.

He had to find that woman.

Carbetti turned away from the mirror, opened the cloakroom door and walked into the noisy brasserie. A few young men looked up hopefully from the bar, but all Carbetti could see was the circular stairway. The barman tried to catch his eye. His third beer stood untouched on the counter. Carbetti didn't notice him.

A group of people crowded the base of the stairway. He pushed by them and ran up to street level, and through the short arcade. He paused where the *Rive Gauche* window curved, and wondered whether to turn left or right.

He was so obsessed with his thoughts he didn't notice a dark blue Ford pull out slowly into the stream of traffic. Two men in the back seat fitted on Hallowe'en masks and kept their heads down until the car drew level with the Italian.

The window rolled down as if by an invisible hand. Up popped Lurch and Grandma from the Addams Family. Two sub machine guns aimed just as Carbetti decided to turn right. A hail of bullets caught him in the chest and face. He smacked up against the store window. The bullets thudded down his body as he tried feebly to stop them with his hands. The vast pane of glass shattered behind him and he flipped over in a grotesque back somersault impaling himself on a jagged edge.

The Ford's wheels squealed away from the pavement. Passers-by looked around for the TV cameras. It took seconds for them to realize there were none.

The woman from Edmonton Alberta was the first to start screaming. She pointed in fascinated horror as Carbetti's intestines snaked out of an oozing hole in his stomach. Her husband hung over the broken window and clucked wistfully as Carbetti's brains slowly fouled a five hundred dollar hand-woven Saint-Laurent suit.

CHAPTER EIGHT

A black limousine pulled up smoothly outside St Dominique's.

The chauffeur, dressed in a pale aubergine uniform and peaked cap, jumped out and opened the back door. The Apostolic Delegate for Quebec appeared and waited for his friend the jeweller from New York to join him on the pavement.

Bernard 'Bucky' Lancey stepped out of the car and flexed his shoulders self-consciously. He was a tiny man who overcame it by wearing built up platform shoes. His trousers were cut expertly to flare out at just the right place around his ankles, to hide the wooden inches.

The Apostolic Delegate stood head and shoulders above him. He was a handsome man with a mop of curly white hair that contrasted well with his deep purple cassock. He smiled at his chauffeur and the limousine moved off quietly into the night air.

The door of St Dominique's opened. Brother Mark stood there in a long brown habit, and waited for the two men to walk casually through the rose garden. 'Your Eminence.' He stooped to kiss the Apostolic Delegate's huge square ruby ring.

'Brother Mark – welcome to Montreal. This is your first visit isn't it? Have you met Mr Bernard Lancey before? His friends call him Bucky.'

'No. How do you do, Mr Lancey.'

'Why hi there, just fine, how're you?'

The two men shook hands and Brother Mark stepped back to let them in.

'Aaah, wonderfully cool. A pleasure to leave the heat outside. Did you go to the Games today, Brother?' The Apostolic Delegate was a Montrealer of mixed Irish and French parentage. He had been a member of the Canadian ski team during his college days and was still a fanatical sports lover.

'No, but I hope to go tomorrow. Supper has been prepared for us in here, I think –'

The Franciscan pushed open two doors leading into the parlour. It was quiet and comfortable, dominated by a three-piece

103

suite covered in a thick oatmeal fabric. A handsome hand carved chest stood in one corner, a legacy from one of the first French families that settled the province.

A solid table built of British Columbian pine complemented one corner of the room. A buffet supper had been laid out on it, and covered over discreetly with a muslin cloth.

Oil paintings of the various Apostolic Delegates elected to serve Quebec through the generations decorated three walls. The fourth was lined with shelves of well-loved and frequently read books in French, English, Italian and German.

Lancey nodded approvingly and beamed at the two men. He walked over to a large bay window and gazed longingly at the rose garden. 'Well, they sure knew how to build houses in those days,' he said shaking his head. 'These stone walls should store up enough heat in the summer to keep you warm in winter eh?'

'I wish that were true, Bucky,' said the Apostolic Delegate, joining him at the window. 'Our heating bills wouldn't be so crippling. Where do you live in London, Brother Mark?'

'The Vatican allows me to live in one of its residences, very near to Regent's Park.'

'Regent's Park? Ah, yes,' replied the Apostolic Delegate with a toothy grin, 'very near to the American school? I remember walking through that very English park one day and seeing some kids playing baseball.'

The Franciscan nodded knowingly, tossed his long fair hair off his forehead and gestured at the table. 'Your Eminence, Mr Lancey – shall we eat first?'

'Good thinking.' The Apostolic Delegate rubbed his hands together vigorously, and then glanced expectantly around the room, like a schoolboy looking for a chocolate cake. 'Father hasn't forgotten that we don't all live on Coke and Holy Wine, has he?'

Lancey chuckled.

Brother Mark turned obediently to the door. 'I'll get something Your Eminence.'

'Excellent. There were two bottles of Pouilly Fuissé left last time I was here. See if they're still in the fridge, eh?' He winked broadly.

Lancey watched the Franciscan leave the room. 'Not very talkative, is he?'

The Apostolic Delegate shook his head. 'No. They did warn

me he was moody – but with an exceptional mind. I could do with him in Quebec. He's young. Looks modern. Healthy. I like that. Church depends on men like him.'

'He's also very English,' Lancey replied dryly.

Walter stiffened. Someone had walked into the kitchen. He knew it wasn't the old priest. The footsteps were too quick and lively. He heard the fridge door open and the clink of bottles. He heard sounds of someone opening several drawers. Then the footsteps moved away.

He glanced at his watch. It was eight forty-one and he'd been in the closet nearly an hour. At ten minute intervals he'd checked the various rooms in St Dominique's with the Hero but heard nothing except the TV, the old priest talking to himself, and the sound of somebody using the upstairs john.

The footsteps made him put down his can of beer and reach for the Hero. There were eight rooms in the house plus a kitchen and bathroom downstairs and another bathroom upstairs. Sole had listed all eleven readings neatly and accurately, with additional readings for the front porch, downstairs and upstairs corridors.

Walter dialled the first reading. 25.3098 A. Dining room next to kitchen. Nil. He dialled 60.2941 Z. Reception room next to dining room. Nil. He frowned, twiddled his earphones and dialled 39.541 P. Parlour. He waited, adjusted the sound and leaned back relieved against the wall. The voices sounded as beautiful as the trio from Mozart's *Cosi Fan Tutti.*

'Delicious salmon,' murmured Lancey between mouthfuls.

'Bobbie's a good cook,' agreed the Franciscan, passing him a plate of home-made brown bread. 'How long have you been a jeweller?'

'Thanks. All my life. Started in my father's keyhole in Brooklyn. As a kid I used to spend my afternoons pestering every watchmaker on the block. One of them hired me out of desperation when I left school. Jewellery business always does well in a depression,' he paused, helping himself to more salmon.

'Movies too,' added the Apostolic Delegate refilling all their glasses with wine. 'Jewellery because the rich panic buy to beat the diminishing dollar. Movies because everybody wants escapism.'

105

Walter groaned. Sports. Theatre. Wines. Philosophy. Everything but diamonds. He pulled the ring off a second beer can and tried to shift himself into a different position. The closet seemed so beautifully cool when he first walked in. Now it felt defiantly chilly. He took a couple of towels and placed them behind his back. He tried to lie down but had to pull his knees up against his chest.

Fearing the effect restlessness might have on his powers of concentration he re-examined the work he had done on the fuse box when Sole disappeared.

He had pulled the lever down at the side to switch off the electricity, confident that the old priest would fuss about the blank TV screen before he'd think about a blown fuse. That gave him a few precious seconds to undo the screws exposing the negative and positive terminals in the box. He then pushed the wires from the timer through the screw holes until they rested against the terminals. He taped over the holes to prevent the wires from falling out, and made a tentative adjustment to the timer to cut off the supply at eleven thirty.

Finally he pulled down the lever and switched on the supply.

Re-checking the fuse box reminded him to set his watch alarm to go off at eleven fifteen. He looked at the clock-like face of the timer and made doubly sure he'd set it correctly.

He sat back with a sigh of impatience and removed the earphones. He shook his head free of the parlour chit-chat and flexed his jaw muscles. He longed to stretch but sat bolt upright. He recognized a steady flip-flap-flip approaching the kitchen. It was the same footsteps he'd heard earlier. He listened again, aware of a soft swishing. He guessed it to be the sound of a monk's habit.

Walter crouched miserably on the shelf wondering if he'd ever feel a sensation in his legs again. He heard a cupboard door open and shut, some muffled banging noises, and a clatter. A coffee grinder whirred energetically for a few seconds, followed by a chink of cups. The stove was switched on. The footsteps echoed out of the kitchen.

Walter quickly turned on the flashlight and looked at his watch. It was nine forty-nine. He leaned back and listened to the sensuous bubbling of the coffee percolator. A delicious smell wafted its way through the cracks in the closet door. He wondered if there had ever been a time in his life when coffee smelled so tantalizingly good.

Yes, there was.

Cannes. July 1965.

He'd picked up clap from a Viennese fashion designer who'd left her husband and paid him five hundred dollars a night. He had to arrange twelve different spots in Cannes where he could make love to her to be seen by her husband's various colleagues who were in the resort on a conference.

She was so determined that it should be known she'd found herself an enviably young, handsome lover that she had photographs taken of his *peder* to send to her husband. But for Walter the frolic meant spending the rest of the summer working in a hotel kitchen. That's where he remembered the smell of coffee. Beautiful coffee. Trays of it being carried to impatient guests from eight in the morning to midday. If any of the staff were caught snatching a quick cup for themselves in those relays they were fired on the spot.

Coffee.

The footsteps flip-flap-flip-flapped back into the kitchen. The bubbling stopped. The fridge door opened and closed. Someone lifted a tray. The footsteps started again more slowly and gradually disappeared.

Walter replaced his earphones. He listened to the Apostolic Delegate offering liqueurs. And then he heard the coffee being poured.

The summer of 1966 had been easier.

An American on a yacht just wanted him to hang around the deck all day on view to his men friends and wear nothing but white jeans. At night he changed into a black suede G string to serve drinks and favours on board to the same group of friends. It was an easy way to earn twenty thousand dollars in three months.

The summer of 1967 was awful.

He spent a few weeks carrying trays to the private beaches of the plushiest hotel before being collared by a Hungarian millionairess with brown crinkled skin that hung from her arms and body like the jowls of a bloodhound. She liked to think of herself as the young prostitute, Walter as the middle aged gentleman, complete with ivory tipped walking stick and monocle. He'd have to pick her up in a bar, pretend to find a *stunden*, the Viennese hotel that lets out rooms discreetly for an hour, go through the act of asking the owner for the *schlüssel* to unlock the imagined room, and then ravish her. She'd paid him fifty thousand dollars for her fantasies.

He spent the winter cruising around the West Indies with two elderly Queens with an unquenchable taste for daisy-chains. He was paid to recruit young sailors to join them in their cabin. He'd make them all link up for inspection. Then the two elderly gentlemen would walk in, select themselves the choicest place in the chain, and set the line of men going with a series of yelps and whoops that sounded like a cross between an English Hunt and a rodeo.

Walter took the eighty thousand dollars he made during 1967 and bought himself a few years of university. Freedom from the men and women who purchased him like a pair of Gucci shoes each year. And enough capital to start the centres.

He doodled with one half of his mind and listened on via the earphones to the trio in the parlour. He closed his eyes. A vision of them drinking beer at a seventeenth-century English country pub flickered into view.

His brain cleared instantly as he heard the sound of something being dragged across the carpet.

'Where shall I put the card table, Mr Lancey?'

'Oh, anywhere near a power socket.'

'You'll need a strong light. Brother Mark, do you have one upstairs?'

'Certainly.'

As the Franciscan turned to leave the room, Lancey took a small felt object out of his pocket and opened it to remove his magnifier. He patted around for a piece of *chamois* leather, found it, and began polishing the precious magnifier vigorously. He blew on it and looked up at the Apostolic Delegate who watched with interest. 'Do you know much about diamonds, Your Eminence?'

'No, Bucky, course I don't. I'm a sportsman!'

'Oh yes,' Lancey laughed kindly, 'like you said.'

The Franciscan returned to the room with an orange angle-poise high intensity lamp. He plugged it into the wall next to one of the armchairs and stood it on the card table.

Lancey rubbed the tips of his fingers rapidly against his thumbs. 'Brother Mark, Your Eminence. As this is the first time for both of you, why not draw up a coupla chairs and watch me?'

'You wouldn't mind?'

'Course not!'

'Brother, perhaps you could give me a hand.'

The monk dragged some high-backed pine chairs from the table in the corner and arranged them around the card table.

Lancey sat down and continued rubbing his fingertips. 'Now, gentlemen, we need some diamonds, don't we?' he said busily.

The Apostolic Delegate hooted with laughter and turned to the row of paintings. 'Cardinal Guy Langlois 1905 where are you? Hmmm. 1902 Cardinal Jean Jacques ... 1903 Cardinal Robert Ford ... ah, here we are.' He slid his hand behind the face of a formidable looking Cardinal, quite bald under his skull cap.

The combinations to the six concealed safes in the room were known only by the Apostolic Delegate and two Cardinals of the Holy See in Rome. When Brother Mark arrived from London all he had to do was leave the box of diamonds in the safe behind a painting that was left slightly ajar for the purpose, and push it against the wall.

The Apostolic Delegate brought out the shoebox and held it carefully with both hands. 'A *shoe*box Brother?' he said, aware that his chaplain, who'd met the Franciscan, hadn't told him.

'Ah yes, Your Eminence. Very practical. If I'd brought them in a leather-bound case people would have wondered what it was. Far less conspicuous for a simple Franciscan to carry a humble shoebox!'

The Apostolic Delegate smiled at him warmly and placed the box in front of Lancey before sitting down at the card table. 'Bucky?' he asked.

'Uh huh?'

'Can we offer you more coffee?'

'No, thanks.'

Walter ran his tongue around the inside of his lips and reached for the third can of beer.

Lancey adjusted the anglepoise lamp, twisting it this way and that until it gave him a perfect slant of light. Then he polished his magnifier again and placed it around his head just above his right eye. He pulled down his cuffs, squared his shoulders and drew the shoebox gently towards him. He untied the string carefully and removed the lid. He read the labels on each roll of tissue paper and laid them in order. Before he opened the first, he took a pair of fine tweezers out of a side pocket and laid them neatly on the green baize top of the card table.

He winked at the two men sitting beside him. 'You realize,' he began, unwrapping the first tissue paper roll, 'that your investment advisers have moved at just the right time. Over the past eighteen months the diamond market has been trying to catch up with itself after a frenzy of buying during 1974. So you bought at a time when there was such a depreciation in the market – the polished market, that is – in the sale of the larger sizes that your buyer could select the very cream. And do a lot to boost the market too!'

Lancey folded back the tissue paper as he spoke and smoothed out several tiny envelopes. 'One diamond in each, gentlemen,' he explained, opening the envelopes and scattering the gems expertly before him on the table. 'You know why? Because diamonds are themselves the finest cutters known to man. To put two diamonds together in a packet would be disastrous.'

He placed the magnifier over his right eye and took a while to adjust it. 'You see what I mean by larger stones? His tweezers darted among the diamonds like an anteater's tongue. 'I can well understand your buyer taking several months to select these. Fewer and fewer of the larger varieties are coming out of the mines so you are doubly advantaged.'

The two men next to him watched every move with the eyes of children glued to their mother's mixing bowl.

'Hmmm,' murmured Lancey taking one stone and turning it round and round under the light with the tweezers. Gently he picked it up and examined it closely through the magnifier. 'This is a prize, gentlemen. I'd sell my mother for it. All these Wesseltons – our trade name for top grade stones that are just slightly off-white – are good, but this one! Mmmm.' The amateurs sitting beside him craned forward but saw no real difference between it and the others. 'Cheap at a million bucks, this one stone alone,' said Lancey. 'In a few years it could be double that!' He shook his head and replaced the gem reluctantly. 'Your Eminence, you're quite sure your bosses don't want to sell now?'

The Apostolic Delegate shook his head sadly. 'The stones

will be made to work hard, Bucky, you'll see. But not for a few years.'

Lancey pursed his lips. 'Normally,' he continued, 'a parcel of this value would give you between ten thousand to fifteen thousand diamonds. But because you've been able to select the larger stones you have, oh I'd say, under five thousand.' He opened the other rolls and scattered more gems. The anteater jumped and darted between them. Lancey grunted and squeaked in unison. It was a language that neither the courier nor the Apostolic Delegate dreamed existed.

Walter pulled the ring off the last can of beer and drank a long toast to himself. He finished off the cookies and felt quite heady with excitement. He glanced at his watch with the flashlight and hastily switched off the alarm due to sing out at eleven fifteen. It was eleven seven. He balanced the flashlight between his knees and adjusted the timer on the fuse box before settling down to another round of Lancey's wit.

'Gentlemen – these diamonds are called River Colour … and they're very, very hard to come by. Let me show you the ultimate in a colourless diamond. Exquisitely transparent. Frosty white. Gorgeous. Have a look for yourselves –' He pulled the magnifier off his head, passed it to the Apostolic Delegate, and waited until it was firmly in place before handing him the diamond carefully held between the fine points of the tweezers.

'Ah, this is a polished diamond?' asked the Apostolic Delegate concentrating fiercely on the stone but not really knowing what he was expected to say.

'Why sure!' Lancey chuckled, 'all of them are polished. Any jeweller – say like yours truly – could put that into a ring or a bracelet tomorrow. It's all ready to go.'

The Apostolic Delegate carefully passed the magnifier and stone across the table to the Franciscan. He took them gingerly, looked at the diamond, then turned it round and round, fascinated by the way it caught the light from the high intensity anglepoise lamp, twisting, teasing and playing with it in a hundred different ways.

'It has life,' he said after a while, 'I've never seen a stone I could say that about before. I always thought diamonds were dead somehow. But this one is aggressive, it seems to be

111

challenging me!' The Franciscan was in another world.

Lancey beamed delightedly. 'You have a rare eye when a stone vibrates for you. You either have it or you don't. It's God-given, if you'll forgive me. It can't be bought or acquired.'

Brother Mark flushed with pleasure and passed the stone back to him.

The Apostolic Delegate scratched his head. 'I don't know. It beats me, it really does. You could put a bunch of rhine-stones down there and I wouldn't know the difference –' He idly fingered some loose gems on the table, then looked up quickly. 'How about a Bourbon?'

'At this hour?' Lancey looked blankly around the room.

The Apostolic Delegate jumped nimbly to his feet and crossed over to the line of paintings on the wall. 'Now ... it's you, Cardinal Jean Jacques 1902, you crafty old hypocrite.' He slid his hand behind the robed figure and the Cardinal leaped forward. 'Do you know I believe he heard me? Now then, last time I was here there was a bottle of ole' sinners' fortified best.' His torso disappeared into the cavity behind the Cardinal. 'Why, a foowal bottle,' he cooed in a perfect South-ern drawl that echoed from the back of the safe. 'Course, Buck' Lancey, I could offer you any whisky or brandy – but this here Bourbon – mmmm hmmmm!' He swung the bottle out of the safe and pressed Jean Jacques back to the wall. 'Brother – you'll find some Bourbon glasses in that small closet over there.'

At the word 'closet' Walter nearly jumped off the shelf with fright. His legs felt so stiff that he decided somebody could wheel in a circular saw and pass it through his waistline and he wouldn't even feel it. He listened wistfully to the clink of glasses. It was going to be a long, long night.

* * *

Saxon Forth turned around savagely. 'What the hell do you mean *you* ordered those bird brained punks to drive around Montreal like a coupla hoods and spread Carbetti's guts about St Catherine?'

Mordechai Golan, head of the Shin Beth contingent that had been stationed in Montreal since Munich, looked at Forth and smiled.

The dozen or so men in the operations room turned from

their boards, charts, telex machines and computer video screens and looked across at Forth.

Forth couldn't have cared if half Montreal was listening. Golan had once served under him in Rome before he emigrated to Israel and changed his name from 'Mike Green' to 'Mordechai Golan'. He was one of several men from 'The Company' that moved into Israel's secret service in the late sixties.

'Have you gone crazy, Green? This isn't some grimy little Mediterranean port where you can do what you like. Who the fucking hell gave you orders to turn Montreal into a shooting gallery for those *shmucks* you run around with? Carbetti was my prime suspect, you mother fuckin' bastard – *mine*!' Forth crashed his fist on to the top of his desk and a wire basket jumped to the floor. The men in the room began to gather around.

Golan crossed his arms leisurely. 'You know what you are? Last month's leftovers.'

'And you're tomorrow's load of shit. Your oh-so-brilliant little tap dance has alerted the whole of MPD just when we wanted to keep cool and smoke out the guys behind Carbetti. Now every jackass in the force is out on the streets. What're ya trying to do? Turn an air raid siren on to scare the worms back into the woodwork? My puke has more brains in it than your skull has!'

Golan laughed loudly and reached inside his jacket for a pipe. He picked up Forth's Zippo and lit it slowly. 'We're not interested in your pet theories about Carbetti and Iran,' he said between puffs. 'You're cooking something out of the air.' He sucked in deeply. 'While you sit on your spreading ass jerking-off over telexes we discovered that Carbetti was planning to blow up six members of the Israeli team on Friday.'

'*Balls!*' Forth looked ready to burst.

Golan shrugged. 'Play it your own way then.'

'Where's your proof?' Forth snapped.

Golan tapped his temple.

'How the hell do you expect me to explain that to the Prime Minister tonight?'

'You don't need to, friend.' Golan scratched in his pipebowl with a pencil. 'We made it look like a syndicate job. You know as well as I do Carbetti's been used by the syndicate before now. You don't *need* our proof.'

113

'Who the hell gave you the freedom to use one of Montreal's busiest streets?'

'I take my orders from Jerusalem now – not Washington.' Golan puffed away contentedly.

'Who're you trying to kid, buddy-boy?' Forth looked around incredulously at the other men in the room. 'Je-ru-sa-lem *my assole*! It's me, Saxon Forth here, remember? Listen here, Green or Sinai or whatever the hell you call yours—'

'Golan.'

'If Carbetti was planning to mess up your team we would know about it. Jesus-son-of-Mary-and-Joseph-Christ! For the past four years Squad O has spent most of its time keeping tabs on every first, second, or third generation Arab in the city. Anybody whose mother's cousin's lover's brother-in-law happened to be Arab was watched. Not just Palestinian – but *any Arab*. That was Washington's order.'

'So?'

'– I've got a data bank over there full of totally useless information,' Forth gestured towards the back of the room. 'We've got complaints that you could paper this entire building with: from Lebanese bankers who resent the way their children's parties are monitored; from second generation Canadian born Palestinians who don't see why they should be required to give intimate details of their family's whereabouts; Jesus, even from a Moroccan doctor who refused to give the boys his list of patients. I haven't finished yet –'

Golan gazed at the ceiling.

'– When some Arab kids graduated from McGill last year and went up to the Laurentians to celebrate we had *five* boys from the Squad stick with them. When a third generation Iraqi kid was married to councillor Larouche's daughter last year we had our fellas at the reception. Jesus Christ, we even tailed Ralph Nader when he was here last March. So don't pussyfoot with me. There's no way Carbetti could have been involved with action against your team. No way.'

'After Munich we shoot first and talk later.' Golan shook his pipe at the floor.

'Listen, punk. You know as well as I know that what happened in Munich happens every day in the Middle East. *Your* raids into the south of Lebanon, right into the streets of Beirut if necessary; Palestinian raids into Israel; day after day. Only difference between that yo-yoing and Munich is the world's

TV cameras conveniently turn away when you guys drop booby trap toys and poisoned chocolate to the refugee kids in the camps – or napalm of course, depending on your mood.'

The men in the room froze. Golan didn't move a muscle.

Forth sat down and searched about his desk for a cigar. 'Sure, Carbetti and whoever's paying him are planning a little action,' he went on. 'I've known Carbetti long enough to know he never works alone. Never. He trains somebody on the spot to step in if necessary. So by killing him you don't kill the action. You warn his buddies. Teach them to be a little sharper on the day –'

Golan turned without saying a word.

'Okay fellas!' Forth pointed at each one in the room. 'We have tomorrow, Friday and Saturday to find out what's going on. I'll prove to you, Green,' he shouted at Golan's back, 'if it's the last godamn thing I do on earth, that Carbetti was on a different wavelength. Simma? I want to file a report to Washington. *Simma!*'

* * *

It was nearly midnight.

Walter wondered if he'd ever see the outside of St Dominique's. He had visions of himself sitting in the closet until dawn and being found, stupified, by the bewildered old priest. His mood ranged from fear to anger via self pity and from self pity to anger via fear.

The earphones hurt like hell. He slapped his cheeks quickly to brighten himself up.

'Now in this parcel we find what are called Capes Vague. You can see their distinctly yellowish tinge. Look closely gentlemen. Brother Mark, would you like the magnifier?' Lancey pulled it off his head and passed it across to the Franciscan.

Brother Mark was enjoying himself. He quickly acquired the expert way of examining a gem close up.

'You can see the difference, can't you?' said Lancey energetically. 'The others range from a pale to a strong yellow. Nice stones. Pretty stones. These here will make happy engagement rings.'

The Apostolic Delegate poured out another round of Bourbon. '*Engagement* rings?' he sounded quite disappointed. 'And

115

what will the others be used for?'

'Remember the first ones we looked at? The Wesseltons? They'll make nice bracelets for Elizabeth Taylor. But the River Colour – hmmmm mmmmm – the Jackie Onassis —'

Walter frowned. Lancey must be loosening his whistle with a shot of Bourbon, he decided. He waited. Not a squeak. He turned up the volume on the Hero. But he heard nothing except the sound of his own eyelashes blinking furiously. He pulled the earphones out quickly and shook them. He detached them from the Hero, reconnected them carefully and put them into his ears again. Nothing. He shook the Hero. Still nothing. He turned on his flashlight and shone it at the two dials in case one of them had been knocked out of place. It hadn't.

Very quickly he dialled another room in the house. But the Hero was silent. He sat for a full minute and willed it, willed it with every living fibre in his body, to work. He coo-cooed to it softly in the dark. He kissed it. He told it it was the most important being in his life and always would be. He begged it, pleaded with it.

But the Hero was dead.

Walter looked at it in disbelief and turned it over. He tried it again. Nothing. Then, gradually it began to dawn on him. The batteries had gone. He cursed Sole over the bodies of their respective dead parents, and vowed to kill him.

He looked miserably at the flashlight. There was no way that it could possibly have the same batteries as the Hero but he unscrewed the end to make sure, hastily screwing it back into place again to check the time. It was twelve twenty-eight and the timer was set to cut off the electricity supply at twelve thirty.

He felt nausea sweep over him and frantically pushed the timer forward to twelve fifty.

Although he had heard Lancey talking about various categories of diamond, and heard the frequent rustle of tissue paper, he had no way of telling if the diamonds were back in the shoebox or lying between the Bourbon glasses on the table. It had taken Sole and himself nearly an hour to put the stones from the building site into the envelopes and wrap them in tissue paper rolls. But that was no guide to the amount of time Lancey might take to pack the diamonds away in the parlour.

Walter knew his back was permanently crippled. After four

beers he needed to go to the john. Badly. The shelf was covered with cookie crumbs. The air from the ventilator had turned bitingly cold and he decided the circular saw might not be such a bad idea after all.

There was only one thing he could do. Chance it. Move his ass into the parlour and pick up whatever he saw, toss down a few of his own tissue rolls and decide on the spot if he should swap the shoeboxes.

He re-examined Sole's chart under the flashlight and checked that the parlour was a little under three minutes away from where he sat. Well, five minutes to give him enough time to get off the shelf and re-arrange the towels. He took the box of stones out of the laundry bag and ran his fingernail around the edge to break the seal of scotch tape.

Twelve thirty-five. Fifteen minutes to lights out. He set the second switch on the timer for one a.m., giving himself seven minutes to switch the gems, and three to run back to the kitchen, before the lights turned on again.

He began counting. He wrapped the beer cans in a towel and stuffed them into his kitbag. He moved the towels on the shelf to one side and jumped to the floor with the kitbag in one hand and the box of stones in the other. His legs buckled under him. His head crashed against the closet door and he sat star-gazing, fighting himself to get back on his feet again.

Then he heard a noise that made him reach for the gun in his kitbag. He strained to decipher it. Someone was unlocking the kitchen door.

He heard the top half opening, then the bottom half, and the sound of somebody whistling cheerily. A voice said 'merde'. He recognized it instantly. It was the kid who worked in the kitchen.

He didn't dare flash the light on his watch. He heard the fridge door open. Something rattled and the fridge door closed. A drawer opened. The voice said 'merde' a second time and the drawer closed noisily. Then Walter heard the slow steady footsteps of someone balancing objects precari-ously, moving towards the stable door.

The steps took a lifetime to leave the kitchen. Walter heard the bottom half of the door slam first, then the top half. He waited a minute. Then he opened the closet door and stepped into the dark kitchen.

Swiftly he moved over to the stable door and slid back the

117

lock. He left the kitbag with the Hero and the empty beer cans beside it, against the wall.

He put the box under one arm, carried two of the tissue paper rolls in one hand and the flashlight in the other. The kitchen door leading into the passageway stood open. His eyes were fully accustomed to the dark and he was relieved that the passage light was off.

The layout of the house was so firmly imprinted on his mind that he was almost surprised to find it exactly as Sole had drawn it. He recognized the parlour door as the second on the left, and a thin glow was just visible under it. He moved towards it quickly and waited for the lights to go out.

A burst of laughter broke the silence. Walter shuddered and looked around, panic stricken, all sense of timing lost. He heard the sound of footsteps shuffling along the floor above him. A door opened and closed. He waited. He heard a toilet flush, and then the lights went out.

He lost a second with shock. He turned the handle on the parlour door, stepped in quickly and heard a voice say in the east side French of his boyhood: '*Merde*. I came to get the supper dishes. *Merde* these lights.' He saw the outline of three men and prayed that the Bourbon would increase the time it would take for their eyes to grow accustomed to the dark.

'Is that you, Bobbie?' asked the Apostolic Delegate.

'What the hell happened to the lights?' said Lancey.

'It's okay, Bucky, it must be the fuses.'

The shapes moved uncertainly. Walter spotted the outlines of two rolls on the table. He exchanged them swiftly.

'The plates are over in the corner. Can't you wait till the lights go on?' snapped the Franciscan irritably.

'*Pardon?*' Walter replied, noticing that someone had his hands firmly around the box.

'Don't worry Brother. Bobbie, *attention, attention*,' said the Apostolic Delegate kindly. 'Leave the plates. Go and fix the fuse!'

Walter turned obediently. He closed the door behind him and bolted down the corridor. He was several feet away from the kitchen when the lights snapped on in the parlour.

The three men blinked at one another.

'That kid sure has fast feet!' said the Apostolic Delegate approvingly, 'he should go into athletics.' He took a deep breath. 'Where were we? Am I ever getting sleepy. How about

118

you two?'

Walter reached the kitchen, picked up the kitbag, opened the stable door and stepped out into the clear Montreal night.

The moon shone so vividly it made triangles dance before his eyes. He crouched down so as not to be seen from the bay window and ran swiftly to the road. He didn't stop running until he was four blocks away. He paused to catch his breath and hastily stuffed the two rolls of diamonds into the kitbag, together with his shoebox and its two rolls of pebbles.

He leaned against a fence for a second and then moved away slowly. He heard a steady squelching noise and glanced down at his shoes in horror. He'd wet himself and hadn't even noticed. One trouser leg was soaking. He looked up and down the road sheepishly and started to run, hoping the night air would dry him quickly.

CHAPTER NINE

After Sole had dropped Walter at St Dominique's he visited a friend to discuss the next issue of *Moustique* before driving home to Place Jacques Cartier. He decided to return the laundry van in the morning.

The square was full of people. The cheerful sound of voices, laughter and the clinking of glasses hit him as he turned off Notre Dame and drove down past a long line of hotel balconies.

The flower sellers at the top of the square were still folding up their stalls after a long day in the sun. Sole could hear the familiar swish-swish each time they threw successive buckets of water down Jacques Cartier. Young couples sitting on the benches in the middle of the square shrieked as the water trickled down over their feet.

The area was a well-known 'drop' for Montrealers. The sight of the police prowling around the perimeter in vehicles so wide they squealed and scraped against the cobbles in the middle of the square and the pavements on the outside, was too commonplace to be noticed any more. The locals knew the timing of the patrols by heart. But to the visitors, who flocked to Jacques Cartier for its unique mix of old French hotels, *pensions*, easy pavement chatter and pretty crêperie, the low wide police cars brought the only jarring reminder of 'America'.

Sole waited impatiently as one car took time to move its bulk around the bottom corner of the square. It turned right and Sole turned left to park a stone's throw away from the St Lawrence. He felt under the seat for Walter's clothes, stuffed them into his laundry bag, jumped out of the van and locked the door.

Boubolina's back gate was a few feet away. He let himself in and could her her singing loudly. He paused, smiled and tiptoed up the stairs. Then he burst into the kitchen.

She jumped violently. '*Christé* Sole, you crazy huh?' She smacked his cheeks playfully and kissed him warmly. 'Walter in the closet huh?'

He nodded shortly and took out the bottle of rosé with a flourish. 'From St Dominique's, Mama. With the compliments of the Apostolic Delegate.'

'*Themou*.' She dried her hands hastily on a tea towel. 'You didn't see him?'

'No. I stole it.' He bent over the stove and lifted a soup ladle to his lips. 'Mm, pea soup. Walter missed his. Too bad, eh?'

'Sole – you take this bottle from St Dominique's?' Her eyes widened.

He laughed and took a soup bowl from the drying rack. 'You had yours or you want me to give you some too?'

'*Oichi*, I didn't eat yet. I wait for you. Please, give me some too. Here, I'll warm some bread.'

Sole placed two steaming bowls on the table and hooked a chair out with his heel. He looked at the soup and smiled, remembering the day he brought the recipe to Boubolina from his *grandmaman*. It was distinctly French-Canadian, a clear soup, full of whole peas, and quite different from the thick green variety favoured by the European French.

Boubolina placed some warm bread next to him and drew up her chair. She looked at him fondly, stretched out a hand and tugged his T shirt. 'Dirty. Tomorrow I do a laundry.'

'Yilch. It's my turn.' He remembered the wine and stood up to uncork it. He picked up two glasses with one hand. 'Ice, Mama?'

'Sure.'

'I take you to the Games tomorrow?' He yanked the ice tray out of the fridge.

'Okay. You want to see the canoeing at Île Notre-Dame?'

'Why not? I'll fix up some press passes.' He dropped lumps of ice into the two glasses and poured wine over them slowly watching it trickle through the cracks. 'Hey Mama,' he said suddenly, 'you know all the foreign journalists are living on a boat on the St Lawrence? Today I heard some wiseguy took fifteen young French chicks across and auctioned them.'

Boubolina sighed. 'Twenty years ago I could made a fortune.'

Sole glanced at her quickly and didn't reply. 'My next *Moustique* is going to make that guy wish he never lived. He'll be the laughing stock of Montreal with his cringing pimpery. *Tabernacle*. I'll nail him. Some of those kids were under age.'

Boubolina dipped a piece of bread into her soup and looked at him. 'You're worried?'

'Walter'll be okay. The plan's a cinch. You coming across with me to Yoanniki's later to wait for him?'

She stared into her glass. 'Maybe. I'm tired tonight.'

Sole touched her face tenderly with his hand. 'After Sunday we take a holiday. Maybe to that nice hotel at Belle-Vue, Mont Tremblant? You can walk in the woods, sit by the lake.'

'Maybe.' She lifted the glass absent mindedly to her lips. 'Say if they find him in the closet?'

'They won't.'

'Sole?'

'Mmm.'

'Don't pretend you're not worried.'

'Yah! Tonight's no big hassle. It's next week that bothers me.'

'Next week?' She stood up to ladle more soup into their bowls.

'Sure. That's when my work begins and I start ass-hopping around the country.' He poured more wine for them both. 'After we finish eating, let's go through the accounts, see how much more we can pay on the house, fridge and stove without those finance company muthafuckas getting suspicious. *Skata.* You don't pay they screw you into the ground ... you pay more than you need and they send spies.' He tore a piece of bread apart and stirred it violently into his soup.

'Ass-hopping around *Canada*?' She looked at him sideways.

'*Certainement.* First we hit those Yankee companies like General Motors. They control us. They control *whole fucking towns.* Y'know Mama, kidnapping diplomats and cabinet ministers is kid's stuff. It's industrial bosses we go for now. Hurt GM here – real bad – and you put shit on GM plants all over the world.'

'*Oichi* Solaki, you think people will stop buying cars?'

He paused, then pushed his bowl aside. 'No, Mama, that's not really the point.'

She shrugged and pulled a low flat fruit basket towards him. '*Portokali?*'

He took an orange and began peeling it slowly. Boubolina stood up to make coffee and suddenly started shouting with laughter.

Sole looked at her in amazement. 'So what's the joke

Boubo?'

'Today ... today I was talking with Yoanniki in his store and ...' Tears started to roll down her cheeks, 'I forgot to tell you, he ...'

'What the hell is it? He say something funny?'

'He remind me ... you remember when I start to teach you and Walter Greek? You rem—' She broke off again and hung over the sink with the kettle hanging limply in her hand. 'You remember I made you shop at Yoanniki and I tell him not to serve you unless you speak Greek? Ask for food, talk money in Greek and everything?'

'*Endaksi, endaksi,* so what happened?'

'One day I ask Walter to get me three kilos black bread and he comes back and says Boubo they just laugh and laugh at me and Yoanniki's assistant won't give me bread and I asked many times? So I said Walter what did you say and he tell me like you say, three kilos of black *psoli.* He asked for three kilos black *psoli*!'

Sole choked on his orange.

'And Sole ... you remember his face when I tell him that *psomi* is bread? That he'd asked for three kilos black cock?'

They both doubled up with laughter.

Suddenly the night exploded outside.

'*Ouvrez.* Open up. Police.'

Sole stood up and rushed to the window. 'C'mon Mama, down the back – *c'mon.*' He seized her by the hand and pulled her to the door.

'*Yeti?* We done nothing! Let them in!'

'*Mama c'mon.*' He pushed her in front of him down the stairs and paused at the bottom.

But the police were still hammering at the front.

He opened the back door quietly. The road was deserted. The cops had been too anxious and hadn't reached there yet.

'Just walk like nothing's wrong to my van, and *don't argue.*' Nonchalantly Sole took the keys out of his back pocket and opened the doors for them. He started the engine and the old Dodge wheezed into action. He had parked facing a dead end, so turned the van carefully in the narrow road and started to edge it gently towards Le Royer. He paused at the bottom. People were shouting and running in the square but the sound of police car radios blared out above the noise.

'Bend over. Hide your head. I'll take it nice and easy until we're a block away from the square.' He turned left into Le Royer, right into Charles Dickens and then, as a police siren shattered the night air, he accelerated violently, flinging them against the back of their seats. *'Fuckers!'*

'Sole *Christemou*!' She covered her eyes. The old van hurtled wildly along the short routes of the St Lawrence quayside, darting up alleys, over pavements, in and out of side streets. It did complete circles, baffling the patrol car behind.

'Boy, this guy knows the roads. Car 46 to Forth.'

'Yuh?'

'Following suspect now, sir. He's in a stolen laundry van, an old white Dodge marked La Paloma and heading ... ah ... heading ... w-west along ... ah ... St Paul.'

'How the hell did you let him get away?'

'We didn't know it was him, sir. He went in the back way dressed as a laundry man and –'

'I want that boy brought in alive. D'ya hear?'

'Sir.'

Forth punched another switch in disgust. 'Forth to all cars south of Notre Dame and west of Jack Carter square. Suspect headed west along St Paul in a Dodge laundry van marked La Paloma. Intercept immediately.'

'Sole, maybe it's nothing!' Angrily she rolled down the window, hung out and cursed the car behind violently in Greek. *'Gamo to pragmatotita sou!'*

'Car 46 to Forth.'

'You got him?'

'No sir. There's a mad woman hanging out swearing at us. Must be the Greek whore.'

'Gamo tin panayia sou!'

'Mama, get back for fuck's sake. They'll arrest you for obscenity. *Mama*.' Sole swerved violently to avoid a pick-up truck.

Boubolina's head smacked up against the door rim. 'Oh *Themou*,' she whimpered.

Sole glanced in the mirror. The truck blocked his view of the patrol car. 'Hey look, Mama, look! That gives us a clear block. Roll up your fucking window and stay inside!'

He swung the car around, turned sharp right, sharp left on to Notre Dame and sharp left again for a major highway heading south out of Montreal.

'46 to Forth.'
'Where is he?'
'Route 10, sir.'

'Mama, check the fuel.'
'Nuh. Gallon, maybe less.'
'Shit!'
The patrol car began to grow in his rear mirror. 'Mama, hold on tight.' Road signs shot past.

'46 to Forth. He's turned down Pierre Dupuy headed for Pont de la Concorde.'
'Forth to O bases on St Helen's and Notre Dame islands. Suspect in old Dodge laundry van marked La Paloma headed your way across Concorde bridge. All bases stand by. Forth to Chopper Helen. Suspect headed your way in Dodge laundry van marked La Paloma. If he starts driving around those goddamn pavilions keep the boys on the ground informed.'

'Sole, maybe they got Walter.'
'Shaddup!'
Boubolina burst into tears and covered her face with her arms.
'Mama, listen. Soon the gas'll cut out. You gotta run with me.'
'I can't Sole, I *can't*.' She screamed at the outlines of the pavilions, most of them crumbling leftover shells from Expo 67. Those used for the annual 'Man and his World' cultural exhibition were lit up brightly against the night sky. Others loomed bleakly on the horizon like tombs of a mad circus of design.
Sole deliberately drove into one of the darker parts of Île Ste-Hélène and zig-zagged around the pavilions. He crashed through mansize weeds, bounced over blocks of cement and sent the van spinning into the back of a wall. Bricks crashed down on top of them. He reversed rapidly, spun around twice and bounced the car down a bank. He jammed his foot on the accelerator, thrashing up dirt with the wheels. The van zig-

125

zagged sickeningly for several hundred yards, steadied itself and dived over a bank. Sole wrenched the wheel and crashed inside the massive, rusting skeleton of the Italian pavilion.

For a split second he'd driven out of the sightline of the patrol cars. Sirens wailed around them.

'*Grigora*. Quickly. Come Mama, come.' He jumped out of the van, vaulted over the hood, pulled at her door and dragged her out.

'*I can't run,*' she said hysterically.

He struck her once. 'You think I'll leave you here for those pigs?' He took her by the hand and edged his way around the inside perimeter of the pavilion. The tall rusted iron structure creaked and groaned from the impact of the van thudding into its spine. They looked up through a thick forest of criss-cross iron bars swaying before the stars.

Car lights suddenly lit up the pavilion and a helicopter flayed the sky above.

'We'll climb up –' Sole pulled her out of the light beam and ran to a pile of wooden crates stacked in one corner.

Boubolina heard the sound of a hundred voices. Lights darted like huge flies around her. Her mind went blank. She knew nothing but the power of Sole leading her, pushing her behind the crates. helping her climb a broken metal structure with the words *Musica d'Italia* written on it.

'Shhh – they think they've lost us,' Sole whispered. 'I'll go first. You see that platform? I'll go then pull you up. *Grigora!*'

'DUBOIS COME OUT. WE'VE GOT YOU COVERED. COME OUT DUBOIS.'

The amplified voice echoed out first in English, then in French. It bounced off the concrete floor like a massive beach-ball.

'DUBOIS. THE PAVILION'S SURROUNDED BY POLICE.'

Sole froze and cupped his hand over Boubolina's mouth.

'DUBOIS. WE KNOW YOU'RE IN THERE. LET THE GREEK WOMAN GO UNLESS YOU WANT HER TO GET HURT.'

She struggled violently against his hand. He released her. 'Go, Mama. It's me they want.'

She shook her head.

'DUBOIS. WE'RE COMING IN TO GET YOU.'

126

Sole pointed upwards at the platform.

'WE'RE COUNTING TO FIVE. ONE –'

He jumped up nimbly, crouched on the platform and stretched out his arms to guide her.

'TWO.'

He hooked his feet on the edge of the platform and hung over as far as he could to lift her.

'THREE.'

Sole slid his arms under hers and locked his hands across her back as she climbed the bars towards him. He pulled, feeling his own strength double with the taut force caused by his feet pinned around the platform edge.

'FOUR.'

'Come Mama, one more step, you're nearly there. Jus—'

The structure gave way under her feet and crashed to the ground. Her fingernails tore into his flesh and she trod air frantically. Flashlights illuminated the corner and a shower of bullets spat around them. Sole gripped her struggling body, feeling the platform edge bite savagely into his ankles. His hands unlocked.

She looked up at him as he tried to clutch her blouse. She gasped as blood spurted from her mouth. 'Sole!' She fell heavily on to the twisted metal heaped up behind.

Sole somersaulted over the platform and landed on top of her.

'Sole, *Themou, Themou pethano*, my God I'm dying. Sole . . .'

'OKAY COME DOWN NOW DUBOIS.'

Sole heard nothing, saw nothing but the person he loved more than anything created, vomit up a stream of bile and clutch feebly at her throat. Blood pumped out of her nose and ears and her body began to jump violently. Sole held her tightly against his body and rested her head on his shoulder. He felt her life ebb away from under him.

'*Christé-mou . . . Chr . . . So . . .*'

He half turned. Thirty men from Squad O holstered their guns.

CHAPTER TEN

The black limousine purred silently through Montreal's empty streets and pulled up outside the Apostolic Delegate's residence.

'I'm so sorry you can't go with us to put these to bed,' said His Eminence patting the shoebox on his knee. 'One of the divine rights bestowed on me alone, I'm afraid, is access to the' – he crouched down naughtily – 'is the key to the secret of the stock exchange sewer!'

Lancey laughed. 'It's been a great evening. You can tell your boss in Rome or Heaven or wherever he sits that these little honies are making extra dollars by the second – just by *being*!'

Pierre the chauffeur jumped out and opened the back door.

The Apostolic Delegate placed his hand on Lancey's sleeve. 'I think Lisette will still be up if you wanted coffee – or something a little stronger?' He took a key from inside his belt. 'There's a small closet in my study if you get thirsty. But I should only be about thirty minutes.'

'Oh, I think I'll hit the sack. Been a real nice evening. Your Brother Mark has a job waiting for him any time he wants to throw away his brown habit. That boy's got a knack many jewellers would pay a million bucks to have!'

The Apostolic Delegate chuckled throatily. 'What time do you leave in the morning, Bucky?'

'Midday flight to New York.'

'Perfect. We'll breakfast together eh? Nine thirty-five too early for you?'

'No, that's fine. Just fine.' Lancey climbed out of the limousine. 'Good night, Your Eminence, and thank you again for the evening.'

'That's a real pleasure, and I enjoyed the jewellery lesson, although as I said I'm only a simple sportsman.' He turned to the chauffeur, 'Pierre, could you show Mr Lancey to the door?'

The Apostolic Delegate watched thoughtfully as his short friend walked up the wide path accompanied by his chauffeur.

It had been a long evening and he felt sleepy. He made a mental note to thank Bobbie at St Dominique's when he next saw the boy, for fixing the lights so quickly. He always thought the boy looked athletic. He would talk to him seriously about it. No shortage of scholarships for athletic boys wanting to enter the church, he mused. No shortage of scholarships for unathletic boys, either. The church had long ceased to afford the luxury of choice.

His chauffeur re-appeared at the gate.

'Thank you, Pierre.'

Pierre nodded politely and climbed into the driver's seat. He started up the limousine's engine and made a perfect U turn in the road. The stock exchange was a ten minute drive away in downtown Montreal.

'Pierre, I'd like you to come as far as the basement door with me. It's so dark down there at night. What time did you tell the security officer to expect us?'

'Between one-thirty and two, Your Eminence.'

'Ah, good.' He placed the shoebox next to him on the seat, and massaged the back of his neck.

'Are you having some trouble, Your Eminence?' Pierre asked politely, glancing at him in the rear mirror.

'Too much sitting around. Tsk. I didn't get out to see the freestyle wrestling preliminaries yesterday,' said the Apostolic Delegate wistfully.

'Oh – you missed a great fight. That huge fella from the Ukraine made hamburger out of Beefy Joe from Saskatchewan. Boy, Canada's great heavyweight hope huh?' Pierre shook his head in disgust.

The Cardinal chuckled. 'Stubble jumpers never make good wrestlers. I always said that. Y'know when I was a kid there was a fella in Quebec City who would have wiped his nose with some of the talent you see these days. He used to throw his opponents clear out of the ring if he thought they were cheating. Not just over the ropes but way over the spectators' heads. We paid an extra thirty cents for our seats. In *those* days!'

Pierre whistled loudly. 'Are you going to the volleyball finals? Should be some good matches. Canada against the Phillipines, and Japan against Yugoslavia.'

'Oh hey?' said the Apostolic Delegate enthusiastically. 'Where are they being held? Paul Sauvé Centre?

'No, that was just the preliminaries.' Pierre paused obediently at a set of street lights although there wasn't another
vehicle in sight. 'Today and Friday's finals are at the Forum
on St Catherine West.' The limousine changed gear automatically and smoothly as he accelerated up a short hill. He
raised his eyebrows in the mirror.

'Perhaps we could sneak away when Mr Lancey catches his
plane to New York eh Pierre?' the Apostolic Delegate said in
reply to the inquiring look.

Pierre smiled and drew up outside the stock exchange. It
was an impressively designed building with dark tinted windows, that stood out grandly against the Montreal skyline.

'Your Eminence, I have the key to the front door. We'll go
and talk to the guard on duty by the first set of elevators.' He
jumped out and the Apostolic Delegate joined him on the
pavement.

The two men walked towards the building and their shoes
echoed hollowly around the bare streets. Several blocks away a
car zoomed through the night. The stock exchange door slid
back silently, and they crossed the huge foyer.

'Hi there!' The security officer looked up and rubbed his
eyes as the two figures moved into focus. He saw the Apostolic
Delegate's cassock and jumped unsteadily to his feet. 'I'm
sorry Father, I must have dozed off. Gets lonely around here.
Shall I take you down?'

'No, it's all right officer. Pierre is going with me to the
door.'

They took a set of keys and turned towards the elevator.
The doors opened at the slightest touch of the button, and the
elevator whined gently as it descended.

When the doors opened in the lower basement the Apostolic
Delegate stepped out and switched on a light next to the
elevator. 'It's chilly down here,' he said to his chauffeur, 'but I
shouldn't be too long. Will you wait for me?'

'Of course, Your Eminence.' He leaned up against the wall
and took out a packet of cigarettes.

The Apostolic Delegate jangled the keys to break the mountain of silence and walked jauntily to the end of the corridor.
He tucked the shoebox under one arm and opened the last door
on his right, taking a moment to double-lock it behind him
before switching on the light.

To the innocent eye the cool chamber-like room looked like

part of a boiler room, or a typical basement subdivision designed to house part of an elaborate air conditioning and central heating plant. No building in North America was designed without a basement full of the most advanced technological designs.

The Vatican chamber was no exception.

Its various safes were fed by computer controlled heating and cooling ducts maintaining a steady all year round temperature throughout the vivid extremes of Montreal's climate. The tight warren of safes was impenetrable. Each one was locked by a special electronic device.

Burglar alarms attached to the outer door and to the locking devices couldn't be casually switched off by an ambitious thief because he wouldn't know where to find them or where to disconnect them. They were built into the design. Although the security officers held the master keys to the chambers, not one of them knew how to double-lock the doors behind them to switch off the alarm. If any of them chanced it, the device would light up the entire building and bring a police car within seconds. It would also seal the door, trapping the unfortunate man inside.

The Vatican had sent out a team of its own electronic engineers to design and fit the chamber with the most sophisticated safes in North America. They had to be. They held the destiny of the Catholic Church in Canada.

The Apostolic Delegate took a second bunch of keys from a fold in his cassock and walked across to a metal panel on one wall facing the door. He slipped the key into a minute hole. The panel slid back.

He placed the shoebox between his feet, felt inside the area protected by the panel, and pressed a button. A minute computer keyboard came out of the cavity. He hesitated and dived into a pocket near the hem of his cassock for a piece of paper where he scribbled the code to gain access to safe eight.

He read it twice, replaced the piece of paper, slipped the same key that opened the panel into the side of the keyboard and turned it until a tiny red light came on at the side.

He typed out an anagram based on the words 'Blessed are the Humble', then turned to watch a four-foot square metal panel slide back along the wall next to his elbow. He reached inside it and began tapping expertly on a line of electronic buttons. An inner panel slid back more slowly than the outer one, revealing a two foot square safe that was as deep again.

The interior lit up automatically. It was fitted out with rows of neat shelves, all of which were empty. The Apostolic Delegate bent down to lift up the shoebox and propped it against the edge of the safe. He removed the lid, running his finger around the edge to break the seal and took out one tissue roll at a time.

He unpicked the masking tape on each roll, and spread the tiny envelopes along the full length of the shelves.

It occurred to him that when TV thieves broke into bank safes, they often picked up handfuls of diamonds and bracelets all laid out on plush velvet. The antiseptic effect of the Vatican's electronically controlled safe was wise, he mused. It added some perspective to the dozens of tiny envelopes and their priceless contents.

He finished smoothing out the diamonds and retraced his steps, carefully and accurately.

It was nearly two-thirty.

He unlocked the door and stepped out into the corridor. By the time he reached his residence it would be after two forty-five. Or after seven forty-five in Rome. A little early to call Cardinal Zerelli perhaps. He'd fix himself a nightcap before dialling the Vatican to confirm that all the gems had been checked and verified, and safely locked away.

The twenty million dollar transfer was complete.

*   *   *

Saxon Forth squeaked backwards and forwards impatiently in his swivel chair. He felt around his desk for a cigar and glared at the angry, blood-spattered man sitting in front of him.

'Gene Cloud Du Boyce, if you weren't Black I'd beat the living shit out of you,' he said.

'Be my guest,' snapped Sole. 'Pronounce my name right first.'

'You must have seen enough TV movies to know that police start shooting if a suspect refuses to come out.'

'Not unless he's armed. I want my lawyer.'

'Lawyer? Oh, boy.' Forth chewed off his cigar butt and spat it on the floor.

'Your pigs shot an innocent woman. I'm a witness to that.'

Forth took out his Zippo and casually lit the cigar, never

allowing his eyes to leave Sole's face for a second.

'You were asked to come out. You were told to let the woman go. You were given a count to five.'

'They started shooting on four.'

'Nuts.'

'I'll tell my lawyer that.'

'With a record like yours, I'm surprised you can find one that's allowed to practice.'

'Big deal.'

'Where's Moon?'

'Who?'

'Don't pussy with me, Du Boyce. Where's Moon?'

'In sky.'

'Okay smartass. I got something for you.' Forth opened a drawer of the desk in his private office next to the operations room, and took out a cassette player. He scratched around for a tape, making a great show of examining four or five before slotting in the one he wanted. 'Let's see now, Ella Fitzgerald? Ray Charles? Oscar Peterson? No, maybe later. Here we go – Moon and Du Boyce.'

He twiddled the knobs. The tiny wheels within the cassette started to spin.

'Sole?'

'Uh-huh.'

Long silence.

'Feel like coming over for a night cap?'

'No.'

'We need to talk about tomorrow and Sunday.'

'Maybe.'

'For Christ's sake can't we spike what happened tonight until after Sunday?'

Another long silence.

'Sole?'

'You tell Boubolina yet you intend disappearing when it's all over?'

'How the hell can I?'

'*Maudit Christ en Tabernacle!*'

'Sole, if I don't speak to you you'll be driving a taxi for the rest of your life. It's for her sake as well as for ours.'

'Okay. Noon, usual place.'

'Can you bring something with you?'

'What?'

'Boubo's kitchen scales.'

Forth snapped off the cassette and blew out a thick cloud of smoke. Sole said nothing but his jaw muscles worked violently.

'Now, Du Boyce,' said Forth like a concerned bank manager. 'We can save an awful lot of time, you and I. So where would you like to begin? Why not tell me about these "kitchen scales" first? Then we can talk about Sunday, and for dessert we'll talk about Moon's disappearance. What was it you had to do to keep out of the taxi ranks for the rest of your life?'

Several minutes passed by. Sole crossed and uncrossed his legs twice.

Forth twisted his cigar around between his thumb and two forefingers. He sighed deeply and pressed the buzzer on the desk.

Simma knocked once and walked straight in. 'Yes?' She looked exhausted and fed up.

Forth glanced at Sole. 'Get Taylor to take Du Boyce to shower. He's beginning to stink. The only clothes that'll fit him in this building'll be in the cleaners' closet. Bring him back in an hour. Wake up Major Pink. He's in the apartment downstairs. He's slept long enough.'

Simma stood at the door looking from Forth to Sole, who sat staring straight ahead. 'Shouldn't I call his lawyer?'

'No, sweetheart. That's *after* you call his massoose.'

* * *

Walter walked all the way back from St Dominique's. He was too sensitive about his urine soaked trousers to risk taking a taxi. Four passed him by and slowed down hopefully but he waved them on. The walk felt good after the cramped hours in the closet.

It was a beautifully clear night. He felt drunk with excitement. He had two parcels of diamonds instead of four. So what? He had two parcels of diamonds. One of them had to contain the stone Lancey drooled over. The Jackie Onassis of stones.

He crossed Notre Dame in three elegant leaps, spun around on tiptoe and wondered if Nureyev ever did the same in a deserted street. He heard a lot of noise and shouting as he approached Jacques Cartier but took no notice. Raids were so familiar. He wondered idly what the 'stoolie' got for the information. Probably a week's supply of raw 'horse'.

Yoanniki's back door faced the street that ran parallel to the square. Walter didn't bother to walk the extra thirty paces around the corner to see what was happening in Jacques Cartier. He wanted to see Sole and Boubolina.

He started to bang cheerfully on the door. 'Hey you guys it's me, Walter!'

The door opened quickly and Walter rushed in. He swung Yoanniki around in his arms and ran into the back room. It was dark. 'Where's everybody? Didn't that son-of-a-bitch wait up for me? Yoanniki – why's everything so godamn dark –? How about some light around here?'

Yoanniki leaned against the door. Walter bent down to switch on a table lamp. The old man covered his face with his hands and sobbed.

Walter froze. It took several minutes for him to get the full story. The Greek community was tightly knit in Montreal and Officer Andreas Constantin from MPD had taken time to drive to Yoanniki's store to tell him what happened.

'You didn't tell Andreas you expected me?' asked Walter glancing around nervously.

'*Oichi*. Andreas serves *his* people first. But no. I didn't. Is that all you can say after –' He covered his face with his arms again and cried unashamedly.

Walter's mind raced like a fairground switchback out of control. He began to shiver violently.

The old man crossed the room and took Walter's face in his hands. 'You hear the police cars? They go through Boubo's house – curtains, floorboards, everything. Come, Walter. Sit.'

Walter dropped the kitbag on the floor and sat down slowly on a sofa in the corner. It was years since he'd cried. 'Where is she?' he asked.

'Police morgue. Somewhere. I'll find out who did it. *Kolombarás*,' he hissed vehemently. '*Bumfucker!*'

'They hit Sole?' Walter didn't look up.

'No. He wasn't hurt. But they're holding him.'

'Why, *why* for Christ's sake?'

Yoanniki shrugged and sighed. 'Andreas said he didn't know why and I believe him.' He stood up and walked over to a large closet, took out a bottle of brandy and two glasses and poured generous shots for them both. '*Waltakimou*,' he said handing him a drink, 'we searched everywhere for you tonight. Jean's brasserie around the corner. In the crêperie here and in

135

three of your favourite bars downtown. We didn't want you to hear the news from anybody else.'

Walter squeezed his arm. The two men spoke Greek and not the mixed-up Greekfranglais of Boubolina's kitchen.

'Has Andreas seen her?' he asked, downing the brandy.

The old man nodded and began to cry again, 'All her face –'

'I don't want to know.'

They sat in silence, sharing one another's thoughts, each drawing comfort from the unspoken knowledge of what the loss meant to the other.

Yoanniki stood up to pour them second brandies. 'Maybe they're connecting you with Sole and his politics? They've searched here already. I'll make a bed for you in my attic.'

Walter shook his head. His first reaction made him blame Sole. He feared word had got out about the gems switch. Probably thanks to Sole and his endlessly indiscreet outbursts. Walter suddenly felt bitterly angry. It helped to blot out Boubolina's death. There was only one thing he could do. Hasten the disappearance of Walter Moon.

Yoanniki watched his face anxiously. 'I'll make us coffee,' he said taking Walter's glass from him.

Walter nodded briefly. His mind worked feverishly on a solution to take him to Sunday. 'Yoanniki – do you have an old coat?'

Yoanniki paused by the door, 'All my coats are old.'

'I mean *really* old.'

'*Ena lepta.* Just a minute, I'll have a look.' He disappeared into the kitchen. After a while he came back carrying a tray with a pot of coffee and two small cups, which he placed on a stool by Walter's feet. Then he turned to his closet.

Walter had known Yoanniki's closet for over twenty years. It was the standing joke of the Greek community. There was nothing it couldn't produce. You lost something? Look in Yoanni's closet. You need wooden buttons? Try Yoanni's closet. You want a new husband? Ask Yoanni's closet.

It had never failed anyone yet. The old man backed out into the room from its doors, carrying a thin grey tatty coat wrapped in a pile of yellowing Greek newspapers. '*Endaksi* Walter? From the Greek civil war,' he explained proudly. 'Okay?'

'*Thavma.* Wonderful. I'll take good care of it. Now, can you find me a needle and some cotton?'

'Something so simple?' Yoanniki disappeared a second time into the closet and came out with a sewing basket.

Walter poured coffee for them both before pulling the kitbag towards him and taking out the shoebox, the tissue paper rolls and the towel wrapped empty beer cans. He took the coffee pot and cups off the tray and raised it to his knees. 'Do you have a piece of dark cloth?' he asked.

Yoanniki sipped his coffee and nodded. Within seconds he held out a stretch of black felt. He watched, fascinated, as Walter smoothed it out carefully on the tray, lifted up two tissue rolls, undid them by peeling back strips of masking tape, and scattered several tiny envelopes on to the cloth.

Walter paused to drink his coffee, then opened the envelopes one by one and shook out precious gems around the tray.

The old man blinked and stretched out his hand. He took the shade off the table lamp, raised a diamond to his eye against the naked bulb, and replaced it on the tray. He looked at Walter, looked back at the gems, looked at Walter again and said nothing. He poured out more coffee for them both, drank his, and asked simply: 'Was Boubolina involved?'

'No.'

Yoanniki nodded once and looked away.

Walter took several minutes to shake out the first load of envelopes. The tray began to look like a mass of twinkling glow-worms. He took it off his knees and placed it carefully on the floor, before picking up the old grey coat to test the material for strength. It had an interesting smell, but the cloth was thick and taut. He patted it, bent over to scratch around in the sewing basket for a pair of scissors, and slowly began unpicking the hems.

Yoanniki watched and frowned as Walter started inserting the diamonds at regular intervals into the small holes he had picked in the hems. His fingers worked nimbly and quickly like those of a master tailor. The old man tumbled the diamonds thoughtfully, picked up a sleeve of the coat, shrugged, and started unpicking its hem. He dampened the end of a piece of cotton and threaded a needle, sewing up the holes as fast as Walter filled them.

Within a while the two men were working rhythmically and speedily. There were a couple of thousand diamonds to conceal. They took turns to break off and make coffee.

137

After three hours Walter counted up the remaining diamonds on the tray. One hundred and twelve. He yawned, stretched out and ruffled the old man's hair. 'Can I fix us some food?' he suggested.

'No, Waltaki. I'll do it. What more do you need?'

'You have trousers to match this?'

The old man clicked his tongue. 'Not the same – but I'll find something.' He left the room and returned ten minutes later carrying a pair of soiled grey flannels over one arm, and a basket full of bread, yoghurt, honey, olives and fruit over the other. '*Nearly* the same,' he said handing Walter the flannels, 'but eat first, *endaksi*?'

Walter put down his sewing obediently. He picked up a carton of yoghurt and spooned in some honey. The mixture felt cool and deliciously sweet. They broke off bits of bread and dipped them in the yoghurt. Walter took an apple out of the basket and sank his teeth into it hungrily. He hadn't eaten for hours. Yoanniki took time to peel an orange. When they had finished eating, he poured out brandy for them both.

Walter swilled his around and around in the glass watching the effect of the colour on the diamonds. It made him feel sick. Hastily he put down the glass and picked up the flannels, familiar from his boyhood in the fifties. He felt them over and tested the hems.

'Try the waistband,' said Yoanniki rubbing his eyes wearily.

Walter looked at him anxiously. The old man's face was drawn with tiredness and weeping. 'Yoanniki,' he whispered kindly, 'I'm nearly there. Tell me where I can find nail clippers, a razor and some dirt.'

'Dirt?'

'Well, perhaps some soil from your plants?'

'Soil?'

'Sure.'

'*Yeti?*'

'To make me look like a tramp.'

The old man frowned. He took a sip of brandy and left the room. Walter heard him banging around, and he re-appeared with a bowl of warm water, a cut-throat razor that he began sharpening deftly on a worn leather-strop, a mirror, and some shaving cream. 'Soil, hah?' he asked opening up a handkerchief. 'From the avocado plant. You better thank him or he'll die on me.'

138

'Thanks avocado, I sure appreciate that!'

'Don't overdo it. You want me to finish your sewing while you shave?'

Walter passed him the flannels, stood up, then suddenly sat down again, remembering the state of his trousers. 'Could I shower?' he asked sheepishly.

'Shower, then rub in dirt?' Yoanniki put his hands on his hips and looked at Walter in amazement. 'Okay, quick, though. It's light outside.'

Hastily Walter passed him the last of the sewing, picked up the shaving kit and ran upstairs.

While he was gone the old man sewed the remaining diamonds into the waistband. The stones meant nothing to him. He didn't want to know where they came from, or why. It wasn't his business. Walter's safety was.

Walter stripped and showered vigorously. He gave the razor a few more swipes on the strop and set to work on his face to make his beard look more like a few days of untidy stubble. He wrapped a towel around his waist and trotted back downstairs.

Yoanniki held out the completed flannels. Walter let the towel drop to the floor and pulled them on.

'No underpants?'

'No. It doesn't matter.' The trousers bagged around him, making his hips look four times their normal size.

The old man started to laugh. 'Waltikimou at fifteen,' he said fondly and handed him his own belt. The tears started to spill down his cheeks and he quickly brushed them away. 'You need a shirt?' he asked, turning to the closet.

'No. I'll wear this one.' Walter's voice cracked like an adolescent's.

'It looks too good. Try this?' He held out a yellow, heavily sweat-stained vest.

'Perfect.' He pulled it over his head and bent over the handkerchief full of soil from the avocado plant. He rubbed it into his damp hair and beard, around his freshly scrubbed neck, ears, throat, hands, wrists and finally concentrated on his fingernails and cuticles.

'Put dirt on your ankles. They look too clean,' said Yoanniki pointing down at them.

Walter crouched down and rubbed his feet with soil before putting on his sneakers. He looked up, 'Is my hair dirty enough?'

139

'Nnnnn, *etsi-ketsi*. Put *more* soil on it.'

'Okay,' Walter rubbed in a handful. 'Now?'

'*Kala*, good. Very good.' He looked at Walter sadly. 'Where will you go *pethimou*?'

Walter shrugged. 'Railway line. Building site. I don't know,' he said honestly.

'Do you have any money?' asked the old man.

Walter felt in the kitbag. He drew out five dollars. His travellers cheques and passport were locked up in his hotel room and that was where they would stay. Staki had fixed up a direct Montreal to Los Angeles flight for him, and he didn't need a passport for that.

Walter Moon had simply disappeared.

Yoanniki picked up a corner of his carpet and tapped at a loose floorboard underneath. He drew out a sheaf of notes. 'Please –' he said handing a pile to Walter, 'pay me back when you can.'

Walter shook his head, took the old man's hands and kissed him.

'Okay, but you *must* take some food huh?' He showed Walter a packet and then quickly put it into the kitbag.

Walter fought back his tears. He gathered up the shirt and trousers Sole had given him, the shoebox half full of pebbles and the towel full of beer cans.

'Leave them,' Yoanniki said looking anxiously at the light filtering through the curtains.

Walter dropped them in a pile, pulled on the Greek army coat and shouldered the kitbag. He clasped the old man in his arms and turned to the door.

Yoanniki covered his eyes as he let Walter out into the early morning light of Montreal's Thursday. The door closed quickly. Walter found himself alone on the street. He paused, felt a nauseating rush through his body, and was violently sick in the gutter.

CHAPTER ELEVEN

Saxon Forth hung over a hand basin and splashed his face energetically. He had precisely four hours sleep but it was as much as he needed, he told himself. Cold water, strong black coffee and a plateload of waffles covered with butter and warm syrup would do the trick.

He washed his face again, vaguely aware of voices filtering through the ventilator grill above his head.

'Pssst, you guys. Come and look at this.'

'For Christ's sake, Taylor!'

'Look! Williams, look! She's only got one tit! All these years Montreal's been jerking off on one tit!'

'Where?'

'See!'

'*Jesus* Taylor, that doesn't mean she was born that way. She's had a masectomy.'

'Oh. Wonder how she managed it with only one?'

'Cut it out.'

'Seriously you guys – let's find out what half Canada raved about.'

'Taylor, pull up that fucking sheet.'

'Why? Aren't you guys curious? Hey, here we got something Canadians used to drive *thousands* of miles to see. Wonder what she's like down below. We could probably run a wheelbarrow up her ...'

Forth shook his head and splashed water in his ears. He listened again. Angrily he picked up a towel and stormed next door.

Taylor hastily pulled a sheet over a shape on a slab in the middle of the room. Williams and Constantin from Squad O both looked at Forth and shook their heads. Taylor tried desperately to zip up his fly but Forth grabbed him by the collar and flung him to the far end of the makeshift morgue. He crumpled up against the tiled wall.

'Saxon, leave him. He was only kidding,' said Williams.

'Only kidding huh? Okay. Taylor show us what you were about to do. C'mon, don't tell me you're shy all of a sudden.'

141

Forth moved towards him.

Taylor climbed unsteadily to his feet. Forth kicked his legs brutally from under him. 'Come along,' he snapped, 'the boys and I are waiting.'

Taylor tried a second time to get up and Forth slammed a clenched fist into his stomach. He doubled over in agony, gasping for air.

Forth turned from him casually and buttoned his shirt. He squinted up at the fluorescent tube that gave the only light to the windowless morgue, and nodded towards the covered shape. 'I thought she was supposed to be in the MPD morgue.'

'They refuse to have her,' said Williams. 'They say if they take her they'll be forced to investigate. They don't want to know.'

'So try the RCMP.'

'They're refusing for the same reasons,' added Constantin bluntly.

'*Goddamn*, where's all that friendly co-operation I was promised? Get up Taylor, for fuck's sake, and put that one inch hard-on away. It's embarrassing. We can't keep her here. *Jezuz* what a mess. Taylor, see she's put on the flying meat wagon to Washington. I haven't got time to waste pussying around some bureaucrat with a crown on his cap here. See she's outa here within an hour.'

Taylor groped feebly at the wall to try and haul himself up.

'We'll take care of it.' Williams turned to the door.

'No. Taylor, get the right forms from Simma. Clear everything first with Robert at air security. Make immediate contact with Washington. And for Chrissakes wash your face –' Forth looked at him pityingly.

Constantin frowned. 'But the Greek community plan to bury her.'

'So let them unplan. Move, Taylor.' Forth turned and left the morgue.

Back in the bathroom he rewashed his hands and face and ran a comb through his hair. He knew damn well Major John Pink was waiting for him. He liked to keep people waiting. It sharpened their reflexes.

He left the bathroom and put his head around the operations room door. The mid morning shift was taking over from the dawn shift. Empty bottles and crumpled papers littered the

142

floor. Forth shuddered. He hated mess.

Disgruntled, he walked into his small office, buzzed the kitchen downstairs and ordered some breakfast. Then he buzzed a different number. 'Is Williams down there?'

'Yes sir, he just walked in.'

'Yes?'

'Williams?' Forth pulled a face at the speaker.

'Yes.'

'Du Boyce still refusing to shower?'

'Taylor saw to it,' Williams replied shortly.

'Uh huh? Is Taylor getting that broad moved?'

'He is.'

'Okay. Where's Du Boyce now?'

'Next door.'

'Give him something to eat.'

Williams drew in his breath. 'We're trying to,' he said in exasperation.

'So stop trying. Let him go hungry. Is Major Pink anywhere near you?'

'Two doors away.'

'Send him up. Ask him if he wants waffles and coffee with me in here.'

Forth switched him off impatiently and picked at a pimple on his neck.

Major John Pink sat alone in a box-like room below. It stank of sweat and stale cigarette smoke. He hadn't slept well after his short flight from Washington and brief meeting with Forth. He loathed strange beds. His head twitched every now and then, and he twisted a lock of hair nervously against his ear lobe.

His face was gaunt but there was something slightly fleshy about the jowls. He kept rubbing the corners of his mouth with his fingertips, like an elderly dowager. The dark blue suit, light pinstripe shirt with stiff collar, and tightly knotted polka dot tie were quite out of place in Montreal's midday heat. But it would take more than that for Major Pink, recently retired early from the Coldstream Guards, to roll up his sleeves.

'Retired early' was a euphemism.

Pink became an embarrassment to his regiment when his involvement in the 'hooded man' technique of breaking fourteen Irishmen in a British Army experiment in Northern

143

Ireland between August and October 1971 was made public knowledge. Pink wasn't the only officer involved. But it had been noted that his involvement went beyond the call of duty. The Compton report whitewashed much of the distasteful affair. But it had been agreed, for the sake of army prestige, to dismiss certain senior officers to avoid a public outcry.

The CIA had offered Pink a post as soon as he was singled out for dismissal. The British DI6 didn't comment.

'Major Pink?' Adams a young FBI officer seconded to Montreal for the Games, looked casually around the door. 'Mr Forth wants to see you.'

'Ah!' Pink jumped to his feet and followed the officer along the corridor.

'He's having breakfast, Major, and wondered if you'd like some waffles and coffee with him?'

'Oh, good heavens, it's nearly lunchtime. Coffee will do.'

The officer, a fresh faced young Black New Yorker glanced at him briefly and shrugged. He led the way up a single flight of stairs and knocked on Forth's door.

Forth opened it and stretched his face in a watermelon-like smile. His shirt sleeves hung limply below his elbows and his paunch had forced its way past three buttons. 'Morning, Major, did you sleep well? Thanks Adams.'

The officer winked and walked away.

'Take a seat Major.' Forth took in his appearance in a single glance. 'I'm sorry about that false alarm last night. The boys had a little trouble getting our subject to shower.'

'As you said,' Pink replied irritably. He reached inside his jacket for a worn silver cigarette case, opened it with a slight thumb tap and offered it to Forth.

'Thanks, no, I'm a cigar man. Let me give you a light.' Forth stretched out his Zippo, turned down the flame before lighting the Major's cigarette, and turned it up before re-lighting his cigar.

The two men studied one another.

Forth turned to the speaker and buzzed downstairs. 'Williams? Put Du Boyce in the little room next door.'

'Now?' a voice crackled into the office.

'Yes.' Forth switched him off. He stood up and pulled a cord on a venetian blind to reveal a pane of glass set into one wall. 'We've got a two-way mirror here. The subject will appear in a few minutes. Curious guy. Half Negro. Half

144

French-Canadian. With double the chips from both sides.'

'As you said last night,' Pink reminded him.

'Yuh, well –' he jumped up quickly at the sound of scuffling in the passage outside. The back of Williams' head flashed past the two-way mirror. A door banged loudly and was double-locked. Angry footsteps echoed towards the stairs.

Forth and Pink looked through the mirror. Sole stood alone in the room. He wore the same blood spattered clothes: jeans, braces, T shirt. Forth turned and punched at the speaker. 'Adams? What's the matter with you guys downstairs? Couldn't even *you* get your Brother changed into fresh clothes?'

A long drawn out sigh came over the speaker. 'You try,' said a voice sarcastically.

Forth snapped him off and turned back to the mirror. 'One of those guys that'll take a long, long time to crack Major.'

Pink was eyeing Sole's crotch. At that precise moment Sole unzipped himself quickly and pissed up against the mirror. 'You think I don't know you *bastard*s are watching me through that?' he bellowed to himself in the sound-proof room.

Forth and Pink stepped back hastily as the mirror clouded over for several seconds.

Forth yanked down the blind and cleared his throat. The two men returned to their seats. The lighting up ritual was repeated, and then breakfast arrived bringing with it a brief chance for small talk.

Forth soaked his waffles in syrup before pouring coffee for them both. 'Y'know Major,' he said slicing through the multi-storey block of waffles, 'my colleagues think I'm soft because I disagree with the electric shock method. I'll admit it to you, I can't stand to see a man suffer.' He opened his mouth wide and began to chew noisily.

The Major helped himself to cream and sugar. He stirred his coffee and watched a line of syrup trickle down Forth's chin.

Forth sliced another large mouthful. 'Which is why I sent for you,' he took a gulp of coffee, 'with your way the suffering goes on in the man's mind. I can't see it so I can't relate to it.' He ran a piece of waffle around his plate to soak up the syrup. 'I'm a simple man at heart.' He smiled briefly. The sight of Pink's soft gold family crest ring on his little finger irritated him almost as much as the way Pink held his cigarette long-

145

ways between the index and second fingers.

'Have you had any experience of the hooded man method, Mr Forth?' asked the major politely.

Forth shook his head and pushed his plate aside. 'You probably know that a coupla blocks away, McGill University carried out experiments in the fifties after Korea. They tested various sensory deprivation techniques. Volunteer students wore translucent goggles and could only see a blur of light.' He poured out second cups of coffee for them both. 'They were played buzzing sounds,' he added. 'Nearly drove them crazy.' He chuckled.

'That was sponsored by the Canadian Defence Research Board, wasn't it?' Pink poised the cream jug in mid air and looked at Forth inquiringly.

'Sure.' Forth caught the expression. 'I was reluctant to call in the CDRB,' he explained. 'We don't want to involve the Canadians – the Olympic hosts – in anything embarrassing or politically touchy. This centre here is international. We answer to no one. Our task is to protect those hundreds of thousands of spectators and athletes –'

'You don't need to explain,' said Pink curtly.

'Well I just thought I oughta put you fully in the picture – you coming in cold to this scene and so on –'

Pink lit another cigarette. 'I appreciate your concern.'

Forth played with his dead cigar. 'I'd like to have most of the day to try my own way first,' he said nodding towards the blind, 'tonight I'd like you to take over.'

Pink tapped his cigarette against an ashtray.

'I'm aware of my limits,' Forth admitted bluntly, 'and I wouldn't let a little Saxon Forth pride prevent me from protecting Jesus knows how many thousand innocent people.'

'I follow your reasoning. I too am dedicated to law and order. I did service in Malaya and Aden. Before my retirement I was in Commander "Pip" Johnstone's team in Ulster. Fine man. Believed in scientific interrogation methods on one side, and community involvement for the army on the other. Brilliant strategist. Worked excellently for army morale.'

Forth nodded uncertainly. 'I, ah, is there any preparation you'd advise for Du Boyce?'

'Yes indeed. The whole purpose of SD is to break down the psychological defences,' said Pink gesturing with his hands, 'to unravel the outer shell of a man's confidence and sensory/intellectual control. In short, dismember him mentally. Deny him food, and the loo –'

'Loo?' Forth looked puzzled.

'Toilet.'

'Oh.'

'Deny him both. By tonight we'll see him in a more settled frame of mind than the one we saw him in just now.' Pink put the cigarette to his lips.

* * *

Walter heard a clock tower clanging out the angelus.

He stretched along the full length of the park bench. His bones ached. Montreal's parks and building sites spelt 'home' to hundreds of vagrants and drop-outs in the summer months, in the same way that the subterranean city and various metro platforms spelt 'home' in winter.

Walter glanced around. He had no idea there were so many bums. He hadn't noticed them before.

A couple in one corner of the park put down their meths bottles. They stood up shakily at the sound of the angelus to cross themselves, before sinking in a heap on the grass. A park attendant with a long spiked pole speared rubbish in a neat circle around them.

Walter watched, fascinated.

The bells continued to ring out across the city. He sat bolt upright. They reminded him of something. His mind cleared instantly. If the authorities had Sole then Sole couldn't remove the timer from the fuse box at St Dominique's.

Walter swung his legs off the park bench, picked up the kitbag and started to run. The meths drinkers in the corner shouted something at him but he didn't hear them. He left the park and hesitated, looking from left to right to get his bearings.

Montreal's streets were hopelessly crowded. The city hadn't been built to accommodate hundreds of thousands of extra people, and it was like walking through a noisy fairground downtown. Foreign pedestrians took no notice whatsoever of the 'little green man' crossings and the police had long since given up trying to fine them. Normally it was easier to get away with robbing a bank than with jay walking, so it gave Montrealers a special thrill to shove their way across the roads in the midst of a visiting group of Germans or Japanese.

147

Walter fought his way through the crowds, keeping his head well down in case anybody recognized him. He was forced to wait outside a vast bank complex built entirely of glass as a coachload of visitors spilled out on to the pavement. A long line of them rushed into the bank to change travellers' cheques. He watched the cashiers deftly counting out notes, pressing their fingers every now and again on moisturised sponges.

He moved on when the empty coach pulled away. A smell of food wafted out of an expensive French restaurant. It made his stomach heave. The early morning onslaught on his insides made him feel he didn't want to see food again. The smell of his father's store got him the same way. While kids on the block would rush in to sniff freely at the pungent cheeses and salamis, he'd slope away around the corner to breathe in stinking gas fumes from the passing cars.

The sun beat down and he could feel the heat of the pavement through his thin sneakers. The grey trousers and coat felt stiff and impersonal from lack of use. The material was rough against his sensitive skin and he stopped every few minutes to scratch himself.

*　　*　　*

Officer Andreas Constantin stood at the two-way mirror and looked down at Sole sitting in a corner of the room next door.

Forth glanced at the Greek officer's heavy blue five o'clock shadow, put a cigar between his lips and dampened the end. 'You're soft, Constantin,' he said.

Constantin shook his head. 'I know this guy. You don't. He's a political nobody who's lived off a whore for years. He's a nuisance, that's all.'

'*Yuk*,' replied Forth in disgust. 'You think this guy Moon's also a misguided politico? Not the first time a whore-house has been used for subversive activities.'

'But the fellas found nothing there. Some political posters, pamphlets and dozens of press cuttings. Since when is that illegal?' Constantin faced him squarely.

'What the hell did you expect to find? Arms caches? Blueprints of Sunday's action? Handbooks on how to build bombs? What kind of fools do you think we're dealing with?'

Constantin shrugged and turned back to the window. 'I still say you're wrong.'

'How about those photographs of the Olympic site you found?'

'For Christ's sake, every newspaperman in town has those – they're standard handouts!' shouted Constantin.

'Okay, officer – then perhaps you can tell me why Moon's disappeared? Why he hasn't shown up at the house?'

'He has other friends in Montreal.'

'Ah yes, these "friends",' said Forth sneeringly, tempting the end of his cigar with the Zippo flame, 'I want you to liven up the talkers in the Greek community. Spread the word around there's a thousand bucks for whoever brings in Moon.'

'A *thousand*?' Constantin looked at him in amazement.

'Yea. Move it, officer.'

*   *   *

Walter sat down under a spreading tree in a Hampstead crescent a few blocks away from St Dominique's. He placed his coat gently across his knees and wiped the sweat off his face. The houses seemed deserted. He looked around at them and their neatly kept gardens. They seemed to symbolize the difference between the distance and privacy only the very rich could afford, and the glaringly exposed lives of the poor.

A large silver Mercedes-Benz started to back out of a driveway into the crescent. Walter leaped hastily to his feet. He turned and walked towards St Dominique's. The car pulled away and a tiny long haired dog jumped around frantically in the back window.

Walter watched it disappear down the avenue. He felt his muscles tighten with fear as he approached St Dominique's. It was as though somebody else's legs carried him up the path to the open kitchen door.

He heard somebody whistling. He shuffled up to the door, shielding his face from the sun. '*M'sieu, d'eau s'il vous plaît, j'ai soif.*'

Bobbie stopped whistling in surprise and looked out at the cringing figure. '*Certainement mon vieu* – come in – don't be afraid, I'm alone here today,' he said in French.

Walter moved reluctantly into the kitchen. He hovered, embarrassed, in the middle of the floor.

The boy pulled out a stool and gestured to him to sit down. The kitchen smelt of baking. Some cakes had been placed on wire racks to cool. The boy smiled and turned to the sink to pour some water into a cup.

Walter stood up quickly and gave him a swift rabbit punch

149

with the side of his hand. The boy slumped over the sink. Walter caught him in his arms and dragged him over to a corner of the kitchen. He lowered him slowly to the floor and propped him up against the wall.

Hastily he ran over to the closet, opened it and stepped inside, taking care to close the door behind him. He moved the cans of food aside, in the same way that Sole had done the night before. He climbed to the top shelf. The towels were exactly as he had left them. Feverishly he reached over and pushed up the handle on the fuse box, tore off the pieces of tape, pulled out the timer's wires and patted around the shelf for the screws. He twisted them into the holes covering the terminals, with his thumbnail, and pulled down the lever.

He straightened out the towels, put the timer into his kitbag and jumped off the shelf, pausing only a few seconds to tidy the food cans.

Slowly he emerged out of the closet. The boy was beginning to stir in the corner. Walter moved quickly across the kitchen floor and out of the stable door.

He turned the corner of the house at a run, to see the Franciscan and a priest in a shiny black suit opening the gate at the bottom of the garden. Walter glanced around panic stricken to see if he could vault over the hedge into the next house. But the two priests had spotted him. Cold logic stopped him from running headlong past them. He affected a stiff limp and hobbled down the path.

Within seconds the two men drew level with him. Walter nodded and crossed himself. The two priests nodded back and carried on walking towards the front door.

CHAPTER TWELVE

Staki wished the ringing would stop. It didn't.

She hung over the side of the bed in Walter's London apartment and groped about for the telephone. She picked up the receiver and tried to find the light.

'Hello?'

'Staki?' The girl's voice sounded vaguely familiar.

'Who the hell's that, it must be midnight,' Staki said tonelessly.

'It's Belinda and it's only eight seventeen. Hey, did I wake you?'

'Uh huh. Belinda who?'

'*Belinda*, dumb-dumb. I just flew in from Montreal with you. Remember? We served lunch together?'

Staki found the light. 'Oh, wow.' The room swung into focus. 'Gosh, I'm sorry, I cut out completely. Hey, what's up? Somebody died and I have to fly back in an hour?'

'Nah,' Belinda chuckled. 'Just wondered if you heard about the strike? I'm calling all the girls who're down to fly back to Canada tomorrow.'

'Strike?' Staki picked up a tin of Coke she'd left by the bed.

'Jeannie and I organized it. Weren't you around when we discussed it three weeks ago?'

'Honey, I was on the Pacific run.' The Coke tasted warm and flat.

'Oh – oh. So you don't know?'

'Know what?' Staki asked impatiently.

'Staki, is somebody in bed with you?'

'*No* for Christ's sake. I would have told you.'

'Sure, sure, well you just sounded a little out of touch,' Belinda said anxiously. 'You see a few months back there was an incident at a San Francisco hotel swimming pool when the manager caught Sue Carter – you've flown with Sue haven't you? – and John Stiles together.'

'Stiles?'

151

'Y'know, Flight Captain Stiles?'

'Oh him.' Staki searched for a Kleenex.

'Jesus, sister, where you been the last two months? I thought the whole airline knew,' Belinda sounded exasperated. 'There's been an inquiry at head office and it's leaked out that Sue and John weren't just skinny dipping. She was doing a blow-job on him under water. But get this. He's been suspended for three months, but Sue's been *fired*. How d'ya like that?'

Staki lay back and rolled her eyes at the ceiling. 'Liberated Air Canada huh?'

'So we're calling a strike tomorrow,' Belinda added busily, 'and we'll *stay* on strike until Sue is reinstated. I'm giving the story to the papers this afternoon. Can you think of a better time to strike?'

'*Christ*. You mean ground the airline at the end of the Olympics?' Staki sat up horrified. How the hell would she fly out of Montreal on Sunday?

'Sure. We make our point that way. The girls I've called all agree.'

'Oh my God Belinda, but I'd arranged to meet somebody in Montreal tomorrow. There's no way I can contact him. Can't you postpone it till Saturday?'

'You mean some date is more important than Sue's rights?' said Belinda with disdain.

'It's not just a date, it's –'

'That's rough kid,' Belinda snapped, 'but we can't back down. If we want to make the point we have to move now. If we take everybody's personal life into account we'd *never* strike.'

Staki groaned helplessly and slammed down the receiver. She needed the Air Canada cover desperately. It was the only way she could get through customs. Air hostesses enjoyed no such luxuries on other airlines. Only their own. She tried not to think about it, but concentrated on getting herself across the Atlantic. Audibly she cursed whichever government it was that gave Air Canada and British Airways the exclusive run between Britain and Canada. It left her no choice. She hung over the bed, and hauled out the A–D directory.

She dialled a Mayfair number, and asked for reservations. A crisp female voice came on the line.

152

'This is Staki Lin of Air Canada,' she drawled hoping she sounded like the president's daughter. 'Can you book me on a flight to Montreal tomorrow?'

'I'm sorry madam but all flights to Canada are fully booked,' the voice said efficiently.

'Aw, c'mon honey. If I said my father was dying you'd find me a seat,' Staki pleaded.

'I beg your pardon, madam,' snapped the affronted voice, 'we don't indulge in preferential treatment for our passengers!'

'Like hell you don't!' replied Staki angrily.

There was a tight lipped British silence at the other end.

'Okay,' said Staki with forced resignation, 'could you put me down on the waiting list?'

'What is your number, please?'

'Zero one, double two nine, seven two seven zero. Staki Lin.' Staki could tell instinctively that the details weren't being recorded. She hung up sourly. Stupid English pussy. Probably hadn't opened her knees for years.

She jumped out of bed and walked over to the fridge, helped herself to a Carlsberg and drank it straight from the bottle. She had duplicate keys to all Walter's apartments and used them freely.

An unopened tin of cashew nuts stood on top of the fridge. She took it back to bed with her and the Carlsberg. Drinking and chewing helped. She was tempted to call Montreal. But, knowing full well that all international calls to and from the city of the Big Games were carefully monitored for the slightest hint of a guerrilla attack, decided against it.

She drained the last of the lager and returned to the fridge for more. She refused to let herself worry about how she'd get the diamonds out of Montreal. She had to find a way of flying herself across the Atlantic first. She groaned at the thought of plane hopping.

A sudden clap of thunder enveloped the apartment block. Rain thrashed down on the skylights and echoed around the room. Staki shuddered and uncorked the Carlsberg. Since when did London have such violent summer storms? It reminded her of Vancouver.

She looked up and watched the rain beat at the window panes. If the pace kept up she might never fly out of London. Angrily she turned over and picked up the phone from the carpet. She'd have every son-of-a-bitch travel agent in town jumping for her.

*   *   *

The late afternoon flight from Montreal to Toronto arrived at a little after six thirty.

A man who travelled under the name of Thomas A. Harbaker of Miami moved jauntily across the burning tarmac wearing a blue check shirt and white trousers, with matching white buck shoes.

He walked into the cool interior of the airport building and glanced about expectantly. He spotted the beige uniform and cap of the driver from the hotel and waved cheerily. 'Hi there!' he said.

'Mr Harbaker? If you give me your baggage ticket sir, I'll –'

'This is all I got!' said Harbaker swinging a neat black attache case.

The driver, a pleasantly fat-faced young Portuguese immigrant, smiled and gestured towards the exit. A fawn limousine waited to whisk them away to the hotel, a few minutes drive from the airport.

'Did you have a good flight?' asked the driver with a newly acquired twang coating his Mediterranean accent.

'Perfect. Glad to get away from Montreal for the night,' Harbaker replied.

'Just one night sir?' He opened the door politely.

'Sure thing!'

The limousine pulled away from the loading pavement and its wheels hummed towards the road leading out of the airport. Harbaker leaned back in his seat and forced himself to relax for the first time that week.

As soon as the limousine pulled up outside the Bristol Place, he checked in quickly.

He stood and looked about the impressively designed foyer. It was dominated by a large Vasarely in ceramic relief, a fountain and expansive bare brick walls. The man called Harbaker took the wide open stairway to the first floor and walked into the bar.

He hesitated before choosing a seat. A nicely proportioned girl in brief khaki shorts, shirt, leopard skin boots and matching belt, moved across to him with a list of drinks. 'Hello,' she

154

said pleasantly, 'do you care for one of our Olympic specials?'

'What'n the hell are those?' he asked eyeing her up and down appreciatively.

'Well now,' she began, 'you could have a Gold Medal – that's cognac mixed with champagne on a bed of crushed ice. Or, something a little more refreshing perhaps, a Silver Medal? That's Vodka, fresh grapefruit juice and frothed white of egg –'

'Jesus honey, whataya think up for Bronze?' he asked smiling at her.

She giggled. 'Rye, peach bitters, peach slices. On the rocks!'

He shook his head. 'Y'know I just don't know. What would you have?'

She winked at him. 'My favourite's Olympiad 21 – raspberry cordial, white wine, shaved ice and whole raspberries. Beautiful. Don't tell anyone but I think we pinched that idea from Montreal!' she whispered.

He chuckled and let his eyes linger over the taut line of her breasts. 'I'll have that then, and oh honey?'

'Yes?'

'Could you bring me a telephone?'

'Sure!' She scribbled down his order and walked towards the bar.

The lounge was half empty. Low slung mock Zebra skin, thirties-style sofas were arranged in comfortable groups around the room, offering everybody a generous plateglass view of the airport. Tall plants in tubs and drum tables completed the setting.

The hotel was built mainly for businessmen in transit. Clusters of them sat around the lounge pouring over folded out progress charts, or blueprints the size of bedsheets.

The girl in khaki shorts returned with a tall, lavishly garnished Olympiad 21 in one hand, and a telephone dragging a long wire, in the other. Harbaker gave her a ten dollar bill and waved away the change.

'Hope you enjoy it, sir!' she smiled warmly.

'I'm sure I will!' He picked up the glass and stabbed at a circle of sugar frosted raspberries with a long red cocktail stick. It had Montreal's Olympic logo on one side, and the hotel's crest on the other. He stirred the drink vigorously and sipped it through two wide straws. It tasted deliciously sweet.

155

He picked up the telephone.

'Can I help you?' a voice asked brightly.

'I wanna call Zurich. How long will it take?'

'One moment, sir.'

Harbaker's eyes darted about the room. A girl in a tight fitting, long pale yellow dress moved elegantly across the floor. She took a window seat and ordered a drink.

'It'll take an hour, sir.'

'Oh. As long as that?'

'We'll do our best, sir.'

Harbaker cupped his hand over the mouthpiece and gave the operator the necessary details. He said he would take the call in his room. As he spoke he kept his eyes on the girl. She caught his glance and half turned as if entranced with the airport view. She crossed her legs and the soft material of her dress fell apart easily, revealing a shapely thigh. Harbaker removed the straws from his glass and drank deeply, feeling the syrupy mix roll around his tongue. The girl continued to stare ahead.

Harbaker turned to the bar and waved at the girl in khaki.

'Another drink, sir?' she asked enthusiastically.

'No thanks honey. I'm on my way to my room. I think my sister was at college with the young lady by the window. Could you give her this note?' Hastily he scribbled down his room number on the back of a card. He drained the rest of his drink and left the bar before the girl in khaki was half way across the room.

He took two flights of stairs in a matter of seconds and walked down a long corridor to his room. The quiet hum of an air conditioner met him as he walked through the door. Somebody had been sensitive enough to pull down the blinds, leaving the room cool and soothing.

He opened the fridge by the bed and took out a bottle of chilled Baby Duck. His few days in Canada had given him a taste for its wines.

He took out two glasses and poured one. There was a knock on the door. 'Come in,' he said, and poured another.

The girl in the pale yellow dress moved into the room like a shadow and closed the door gently behind her.

Harbaker smiled and handed her the glass.

She took it. 'Two hundred dollars down payment,' she said in a strong Torontonian accent.

'Don't undersell yourself, honey,' he said sharply. He would have argued her down in price but simply didn't have the time and didn't particularly want to waste their energies. He was annoyed at the contrast between her willowy good looks and the rasping voice. He felt in his back pocket for a wallet, opened it and peeled off a number of notes.

She took them, counted them carefully and slid them into a pencil slim purse.

Without saying a word she turned, unzipped the back of her dress in a single movement and let it fall to the floor. Harbaker faced a smoothly tanned back and the minutest pair of panties. She turned again quickly and her shoulder length chestnut hair swept across her face in a perfectly rehearsed swing. Her eyes were challenging and insolent.

Harbaker watched and sipped his wine as she moved towards him. Her nipples were neat and slightly pointed, exactly as he'd imagined them. Nothing switched him off faster than huge, dark ringed nipples. She wore a gold chain around her throat and a matching chain around her waistline, that hung provocatively below her navel. She was clearly accustomed to sunbathing in the nude. Her entire body was an even, silkily-smooth café au lait.

Harbaker put down his glass and casually poured more wine for them both. Then slowly, he undid his belt. She pushed his hands away, unzipped him expertly and reached into his trousers. He felt himself arch in her grip. He pulled her towards him and began to knead her firm buttocks.

She began doing quick circular movements with her hips. He slid his right hand down and forced his fingers between her thighs. She opened and closed her legs quickly, trapping his fingers in a sensuously moist cave that moved tantalizingly with a life of its own.

Suddenly she drew back. She nodded at the phone.

As he moved to answer it his trousers dropped to the floor. He stepped out of them and unbuttoned his shirt. 'Yes?' he said crossly into the mouthpiece.

'Mr Harbaker?'

'Yes.'

'We have your call to Zurich –'

'Just hold it a minute,' he snapped. He dropped the receiver on the pillow, stretched out and pulled the girl down beside him on the bed. He mounted her and pushed his way deep into

157

her. He picked up the receiver. 'Okay,' he said.

'You're through to Zurich.' The line crackled.

'Hello?' said a foreign voice in the distance.

'Borg?' asked Harbaker, dropping his acquired Miami accent.

The girl looked up in surprise. He turned her head to one side, arched his back, pinned her between his legs and twisted his body, making sure she didn't move with him. He pumped her violently, knowing that the position was excessively painful for her.

'Hello, *hello*?' said the voice impatiently in his ear.

'Borg? It's me,' said Harbaker in an English public school voice. 'You heard Toni got knocked out of the race?'

'I can't hear,' said Borg refusing to shout, 'there seems to be something wrong with the line.'

Harbaker twisted the girl a bit more. Her body gripped him with a savage hostility. He withdrew slightly and then rammed at her.

'Can you hear me now?' he barked at the mouthpiece. '*Did you get my message about Toni?*'

'I know about him. But you can continue the arrangement for Sunday. Why do you bother to ring me?'

'Last night went perfectly,' Harbaker added.

'Thank you,' Borg butted in, 'just make sure you're not careless like Toni.'

The line went dead.

Harbaker replaced the receiver. The girl began to struggle under him but he twisted her around even further. He moved his hips so vehemently she screamed like a twelve year old virgin. He started to flood into her and withdrew sharply, ejecting a stream of semen into her face.

She curled herself up, rolled off the bed and crawled towards the open door of his bathroom.

He reached out for the glass of wine. There was less than an hour to kill before he checked out in a hurry and caught the return flight to Montreal.

*   *   *

Saxon Forth lit up his twentieth cigar of the day and blew a cloud of smoke into Sole's eyes. 'Aren't you getting hungry?' he said, 'I can get the fellas to fix you a nice thick steak, rare, french fries, baked potato with sour cream and chives, coupla cold beers –'

Sole clenched his jaw muscles and folded his arms.

Forth sucked on his cigar. 'Okay. Let's run over the main points again. Spice up your memory a little. What was Toni Carbetti sent here to do and by whom?'

Sole said nothing.

'Carbetti *alias* Shimon Ben-Or, was watching your friend Walter Moon, making sure he didn't slip up or anything. But he kept out of the picture when you appeared. You expect us to think that's coincidence?'

Sole shrugged. 'I said a hundred times I don't know any Carbetti or Ben-Shimon –'

'Ben-Or.'

'I don't know him either.'

'How many members of the Middle East Revolutionary Front are involved in this?'

'Involved in what?'

'C'mon, Du Boyce. We got one of them at the back crying like a baby.'

'So show him to me.'

'In time. I want to see if your story matches his.'

Sole sighed and glanced at the ceiling.

'What did you and Moon discuss on Mount Royal?'

'Girls.'

'So why talk in Greek about girls?'

'It's poetic.'

Forth laughed. 'And it's poetic to steal laundry vans?'

'I didn't. Like I said, why don't you check with La Paloma?'

'We did. They don't know you.'

'So you spoke to the wrong La Paloma.'

'We used the number you gave us and asked for Levebre. He's never heard of you.'

Sole shook his head. 'Jesus, you're transparent.'

'Where's Moon?'

'Find him.'

'What's happening on Sunday?'

'Check your wall chart.'

'You're a pain in the ass. And dumb.'

'Coincidence. That's just what I was thinking about you.' Sole uncrossed his arms and crossed his legs.

'Need the john?' smirked Forth.

'How could I? You haven't fed me all day.'

Forth stood up impatiently and paced around the room. He glanced at his watch. 7.30 p.m. He weighed up the odds against Dubois. First, the connection with Carbetti via Moon. Second, the phone conversation with Moon mentioning some 'action'. Third, his attempted escape in a laundry van. Fourth, his refusal to give himself up. Fifth, his godamn stubbornness.

He buzzed the speaker. 'Taylor? Did you get that Melas woman flown to Washington?' He paused and glanced at Sole.

'Sure,' came Taylor's voice.

'No problems with the police at this end?'

'They weren't involved,' Taylor replied. 'We used Air America.'

Sole looked up quickly. Forth snapped off the speaker. It was no secret that the CIA owned Air America. Sole nodded and smiled. 'Very neat. That'll look great in the *Washington Post*. I guess you know it's illegal to move a body without the family's permission – even by *you* guys?'

'Family?' said Forth scratching his head. 'I didn't know you were married to her? You didn't tell me.'

Sole looked at him in disgust.

'I'll get her back for you,' added Forth. 'I can do just that by picking up this phone and calling Washington. You want to arrange a funeral for her? Next week you could hold it at the Olympic stadium. You'll need it for all the men who've had her.' He paused, hoping for some reaction. There wasn't one. 'But first,' he continued, 'I want some facts. Names. Addresses of your comrades.'

Sole laughed at him.

Forth stretched for the speaker. 'Williams? Ask Major Pink to come upstairs, and see the air conditioner is turned off next door.'

*   *   *

Walter woke up brutally.

Two faces hung over him.

He tried to focus his eyes, but a double set of features danced and swam above him against a backdrop of swaying trees. He closed his eyes.

Somebody pulled him roughly to his feet. 'C'mon Mac, stand up.'

Two policemen, one French-Canadian, one English, frisked

him quickly. They failed to notice the kitbag tucked under the slats of the bench.

Walter glanced across the park. A line of armadillo-like paddy wagons were parked at the curb, with their double rear doors standing wide open. Several other vagrants were being frisked and led away.

'Okay, pal. Go join your friends. Parks are being cleared for the mayor's receptions.' Walter felt a sharp jab in his back and lurched forward on to the grass.

They yanked him to his feet. 'Jeeeee-zuz, this one stinks,' said a policeman's voice at his elbow. 'Last time he had a bath was in his mother's after-birth. C'mon pal, *move*!'

Walter scampered obediently and was shoved into the back of a waiting paddy wagon.

The meths drinking couple he saw earlier in the day lolled inside with four other men. They were purple faced and exchanged a stream of cheerful abuse through the grill with the policemen in the front seat. The atmosphere had a touch of *bonhomie* and familiarity about it for everyone but Walter. He was the newcomer, eyed suspiciously by the other bums, who thought he was a welfare office spy, and by the policemen, who liked to think they knew everybody on the block.

The wagon squealed away from the kerb and shot down the block. The couple began to sing loudly and played the child's game of patta-cake-patta-cake on their knees.

'Shaddup Lilly, for Godssakes. I can't hear the car radio,' said one of the policemen through the grill.

'Shaddup Lilly for Godssakes,' imitated Lilly in a deep voice. 'Hey. You giving us a meal?'

Walter recognized an Italian accent mixed with her Montreal French. The man with her didn't utter a word but clutched her and swayed around the wagon. The stench of meths combined with the smell of clothes and bodies matted with layers of dirt and sweat was overpowering in the airless van.

Walter turned away and glanced through the back window. A long line of flashing lights stretched behind as far as he could see. The wagons didn't need a siren. The laughter and shouting heralded the convoy all the way across town.

'Hey, Mac.' One of the policemen put his face to the grill and nodded at Walter. 'Got your welfare card?'

Meths-drinking Lilly leaned over and punched him. 'He's

talking to you,' she drooled.

Walter blinked. *'Bitte?'*

'Jesus. *Where's your welfare card?'*

Walter nodded rapidly. 'Frederich Hagengroll. Frederich Hagengroll. Frederich Hagengroll. Frederich Hag—'

'He's nuts!' Lilly shrieked with delight.

Walter rolled his eyes and broke into an aria from Beethoven's *Fidelio.*

'Fucking kraut,' sneered one of the men at the back.

'Nein. Nein. Wien, Wien,' Walter protested.

'Can't you make him shaddup?' Lilly screamed.

'Belt up, Lilly,' said one of the men with her, 'he sings better than you do!'

She turned on Walter and began pounding his arm. Then she stopped and looked up at him curiously through watery eyes glazed over with years on meths. Her features were pouched and bloated. Strands of wispy hair struggled to free themselves from a soiled cap pulled down over her ears. Yet it was still possible to see she had once been beautiful.

'I am an Italian countess,' she said suddenly in English, and drooped her eyelids.

'I know,' whispered Walter in Italian.

'You see, you motherfuckers, he knows, he knows what I am, not like you rats from the sewers!' She began swinging her arms around wildly landing punches on the unfortunate bodies surrounding her. An arm shot out and thumped her face. She sank down into a whimpering bundle.

The paddy wagon pulled up smartly outside a low-slung slab of a prison on the outskirts of town.

'Okay you guys – you know where to go. Move!' said one of the policemen as the double doors opened from the outside.

The convoy of vans stopped one after the other. Out spilled a collection of throw-aways, the broken and discarded debris of an affluent society. From professional meths drinkers to men down on their luck. From elderly prostitutes to junkies suffering from advanced withdrawal symptoms. From kids on the run to crimson faced ex-servicemen. They were White, Black, Indian, Half-Breed, with a criss-cross of variations in between. They spoke as many languages.

Montreal's mayor planned a series of receptions to celebrate the end of the Games. His office had asked both the police and the refuse collectors to clear the pollution off the streets.

The long line of people swayed, tripped, groped and shoved their way into the prison's desolate grey and green tiled entrance. It was empty except for a lone brown desk at one end. Walter shuffled along, keeping as close to the Italian woman as he could. An assortment of identity cards and welfare cards were produced out of collars and socks, knickers and underwear.

Walter cringed by the desk amidst a confusion of bodies producing papers to prove their humanity. He hoped nobody would notice he had nothing on him. He prayed nobody would bother to check his name. Frederich Hagengroll. He wondered how the hell he'd thought it up. No-one stopped him to find out.

They all moved on down a corridor. Walter heard sounds of a number of doors clanging open. Prison officers in light blue shirts and dark blue trousers lined the way. They barked out cell numbers in between exchanging greetings. 'Hiya Pierre – how'rya doing Gino? Where'ya been Lilly? *Bonsoir mon capitaine, bonsoir!*'

A paunchy woman prison officer with a docked haircut gripped Lilly firmly by the arm. Lilly blew Walter a kiss. Sadly, he watched her go, and felt himself being moved by the crowd into a cell. The noise momentarily blocked out. He looked around at his five cellmates.

A bare bulb swung above. Six bunks faced him. Six identical sets of sheets and blankets. Five were taken. He stared bewildered at the empty one. The door clanged open behind him and a trolley was wheeled in. It bore a huge metal coffee-urn, white cups stacked dangerously high, and several plateloads of bread and cheese. Several pairs of hands dived for the trolley and for once nobody was counting. Walter took three large lumps of bread and a handful of cheese. He waited patiently until some coffee was poured, and took it to an empty corner by the door.

The trolley reversed and the door banged shut. Walter clucked to himself in his father's tongue, hoping nobody would try and talk to him. Only two of the men, the meths drinkers he'd seen in the park, seemed to know one another.

'Squadron Leader Beaky Bannering, sir, Royal Air Force.' A man with a nicotine stained handlebar moustache, a shabby brown herringbone sports jacket and baggy trousers stood to attention in the middle of the room.

163

'Oh *merde le maudit anglais*. Shit, that bloody Englishman,' said one of the meths drinkers.

'Seddown, *mange la merde*, shaddup,' chorused the others.

The man sank down to the floor and stared straight ahead.

Walter studied him. He pulled the Greek army coat with its seams full of millions of dollars worth of diamonds protectively around himself. His head was spinning with fear. He fought to rationalize the situation. The authorities had Sole and had to be after him. If Sole broke down and told them about the diamonds, the last place they'd look for him was prison. Fine. But what if a prison officer suddenly got curious? Or somebody decided to take fingerprints?

And how in Christ's name was he going to get the diamonds to Hammond at the Olympic site on Sunday? He thought about Staki. She was the only one who could get him and the money safely out of Montreal. But what if she couldn't find him?

He thought about Boubolina and looked around the cell in a wild moment of grief.

A man with Slavic features sat on the top bunk and idly scratched the wall with his fingernails. The two men under him talked intimately in French about a girl they'd shared. The fourth man rolled about his bunk in an alcoholic stupor.

Walter stared at the man on the floor with him. 'Bring your coffee here,' he heard himself say.

'Good Lord,' the man said, picking up his cup, 'I thought you were "gerry".'

'No,' Walter's eyes filled with tears. 'I'm Freddie,' he said. 'How, how long will they keep us here?'

The man looked at him in amazement. 'Pull yourself together and don't ask damn fool questions. Till the end of the bloody war of course.'

CHAPTER THIRTEEN

Saxon Forth and Major John Pink stood at the two-way mirror and watched as Williams pulled a hooded Sole to his feet.

Williams wore headphones, to block out the high-pitched hum in the room.

Pink spoke to him via a microphone on Forth's desk. 'Get him to stand with his feet wide apart at least two feet from the wall. You've been making it too easy for him. And his arms should be wider apart than that.' Pink paused. 'That's it. Make sure only his fingertips are touching the wall.' He switched off the microphone.

Forth watched as Williams carried out the instructions meticulously. He glanced at his watch. It was midday and Sole had been under the hood for several hours.

Pink glanced at him and rubbed the corners of his mouth. 'In Ulster we had the advantage of moving our subjects from place to place in a helicopter which helped accelerate the process of disorientation.'

'Well, that's impossible here,' said Forth bluntly.

'I realize that, as long as you realize the process will take longer. He's an extraordinarily resilient young man. You notice he's taken time to quieten down. Normally the hood brings about such disorientation and vertigo that the subject stops struggling very quickly.'

'So you've said.'

Pink turned to the microphone. 'Williams, come out now. It's time to switch the air conditioner on again.'

Williams looked at them, wiped the sweat off his brow and left the room.

The air conditioner was turned off at hourly intervals. The temperature was over ninety degrees. The air conditioner brought it down to thirty degrees in a matter of minutes.

Williams joined them at the mirror. They watched and waited. Sole fell to the floor.

Forth moved quickly. 'Okay, question time again. Headphones please Williams.'

Williams passed them to him. 'Give the air conditioner a chance,' he advised. 'I'm going down to shower.'

Forth shrugged. He walked out of his office and pulled on the headphones before joining Sole next door. He wished he'd taken Williams' advice. The room stank like Monday's dawn in a dive bar. He glanced uneasily at the blank mirror. He preferred being on the opposite side.

Sole crouched in a corner. Forth yanked him to his feet and removed the hood. Sole staggered backwards slamming his head against the wall. Forth dragged him towards the middle of the room. Sole buckled at the knees.

Forth let him fall to the floor. 'Who's behind you? Who're you working with in Montreal? Who did your instructions come from in Iran?'

Sole closed his eyes.

Forth pulled him up by his T shirt. 'What's happening on Sunday?'

Sole hung limply in his grip.

Forth shook him. 'Where's Moon? What did you discuss with him about Sunday? Why did you have to talk about Sunday?'

Sole's lips didn't move.

'What was Carbetti doing here? Who were his contacts in the city? Why was he watching Moon? What was Moon sent to do?'

Sole shook his head slowly.

Forth let him drop. 'Who sent Carbetti?'

Sole stared at the floor.

'*Who sent Carbetti?* How did he know Moon? Where is Moon? Who's hiding him? A girlfriend? Boyfriend?'

Sole tried to get to his feet.

Forth hauled him up. 'Who're Moon's friends? Names. Addresses. Who sent him? Who sent Carbetti?'

Sole suddenly shivered as the air conditioner pumped an icy blast into the fœtid room.

Forth shoved him into a corner. 'Where's Moon?' He struck him across the face. 'Where's Moon?' He struck him again. Sole's nose started to bleed.

'I wouldn't advise that,' said a voice in Forth's ears. He jumped in surprise and turned angrily to the mirror. He raised two fingers at the invisible Pink.

He looked down at Sole, pursed his lips and left the room.

166

He locked the door behind him and pulled off the headphones.

Back in his own office, he patted around the desk for a cigar and lit it slowly. 'Perhaps I should have tried something tougher,' he said dryly.

Pink removed his hands from his pockets and turned from the mirror. 'This method is fool proof,' he replied quietly. 'Usually it takes less than six or eight hours. Wait. In a while you'll have him crying at your feet.'

Forth grunted and chewed on the cigar.

'When it's all over you won't have him running to his liberal friends,' added Pink smugly. 'That's why the SD method is so effective. It doesn't sound horrifying at all. Not a bruise in sight! Imagine your reaction if somebody told you he'd been made to stand against a wall with a hood over his head – you'd think that was pretty soft stuff, wouldn't you?'

'Maybe,' Forth said sourly. He found the major embarrassing, and sank down in his chair to contemplate the last remark.

Williams walked in, freshly showered, wearing a turquoise beach shirt. He picked up the headphones from Forth's desk.

'Get that cologne,' Forth said sarcastically.

Williams took no notice. He looked through the mirror, and turned to leave the room.

'Wait,' snapped Forth. He bent over the speaker and buzzed downstairs. 'Is Adams around?'

'Adams speaking,' said the voice flatly.

'Come up and try your friend next door.' Forth switched him off. He looked at Williams. 'Okay. Get the hood back on.'

Williams left the office.

Forth relit his cigar.

Pink watched Williams rehood Sole and pull him up to the wall. He reached for the microphone. 'Don't let him edge his feet together when you're not looking. His hands should be farther apart.'

Adams hung his head around the door.

'Let the major tell you when it's time to go in,' Forth said nodding towards the mirror. He stood up. 'I'll be in the operations room. Bring him in here, Adams, offer him a cigar, coffee, beer, anything.'

Adams nodded and took out a cigarette.

Forth glanced at Pink. 'I'll ask my secretary to fix you some lunch.'

He left the two of them and walked into the operations room.

It seemed fuller and noisier than usual. He stretched out in his swivel chair, forcing his eyes to move idly around the flickering charts on the walls, to remind everybody he was still involved.

'What the hell's this?' He pulled at a newspaper taped around a bottle of Canadian Club. It was the latest copy of *Moustique*.

'Gift from the boys,' said Simma moving towards him with a roll of print-outs.

Forth flattened out the paper. 'Jesus. Why wasn't I shown this before?'

'You were.' She chuckled. 'It's going around the Olympic Village.'

'It's *what*? You mean the fellas there allow it?'

'Sure, why not? It's like encouraging the *Daily Worker*. Keeps you up to date with what the opposition thinks.'

He grunted and opened a drawer for a paper cup. He screwed the cap off the Canadian Club and poured himself a shot. He raised it to his lips, frowned and replaced it on the desk. 'Hey – why'd the boys give me this?' he asked watching Simma lay out the day's papers.

'Check out the cartoon inside,' she said, 'see the big guy trying to recruit a Chinese team? Recognize the cigar?'

Forth glared at her and flung the paper into his wastebin. He downed the contents of the cup and switched on the video screen next to him.

It flickered dismally. He adjusted it and turned down the sound. 'Simma –'

She was half way across the room and looked back over her shoulder. 'Yes, lovie?' she said, wiggling her hips.

Forth blushed. 'Damn you, come back. I want the number of marksmen doubled on the site on Sunday – see they're all told in the next half hour. Get those reservists off their butts. I want them here at midnight – we'll talk in the conference room downstairs. And Simma –'

'Mmm hmmm?'

'Major John Algernon Ponsonby Pink is feeling a little peckish next door,' said Forth see-sawing his shoulders and pursing his lips. 'See he eats downstairs. I'm going to crash in

168

the apartment for a couple of hours.'

*   *   *

'Cigarette?' Officer Adams handed Sole his pack.

'No thanks.'

'Coffee?'

'No.'

'Hey, man, you're not gonna let these honkeys get the better of you. How about a Coke?'

Sole ran his tongue around the inside of his lips. 'Okay,' he said shortly.

Adams jumped up and opened a small fridge standing in the corner. He took out two cans with one hand and pulled the rings off both. He put one down in front of Sole, and sat down opposite him across Forth's desk.

Sole looked at the can blankly. Gingerly he touched the dried blood around his nose.

Adams jumped up a second time, went to the fridge and hauled out the ice tray. He squeezed out a couple of lumps and tied them in a handkerchief. He handed it to Sole.

'Thanks.' Sole put it to his face and leaned back.

Adams watched him and took a swig of Coke. He waited until Sole rubbed his face all over with the ice. 'Better?' he asked.

Sole said nothing, but reached for his Coke.

Adams stood up and shook a cigarette out of a pack. 'Is there anybody you'd like me to call?'

Sole shook his head.

'Lawyer?'

Sole looked at him.

'Listen, man. I'm not one of Forth's lackeys. I could have you out of here in an hour.'

Sole continued to look at him.

Adams lit his cigarette. 'Those whiteys are trying to drive you nuts. For good. You wanna give them that satisfaction? You want them to break you here?' He tapped his temple. 'That English guy's been flown up from Washington for this job. He was kicked out of the British army for putting some paddies away for good. You want to wind up on a funny-farm like them?'

Sole closed his eyes and placed the dripping handkerchief to his nose again.

Adams inhaled deeply. 'Why protect Moon, huh? What's he done for you?'

Sole half opened his eyes and stretched out for the Coke. He poured half of it down his throat.

'Listen man, who's getting the most out of this? You or Moon? What's so big deal about Moon you gotta lose your mind over him?'

Sole finished his Coke and said nothing.

'What's so important about Sunday? Listen, man, if there's some political action planned, do you think your buddies are gonna stick around and wait for you?' Adams stood up and took another Coke out of the fridge. He opened it and placed it in front of Sole.

Sole picked it up.

'Okay. Let's talk about alternatives,' persisted Adams. 'You cover up for Moon. Sunday blows up. *Pow!*' He slammed a fist into his open palm. 'That means you take the rap, because we got you here. That's choice one. Choice two – you tell us about Sunday and where to find Moon. Or, just tell us about Sunday. I can understand you not wanting to talk about Moon, even if those honkeys outside can't.' He squashed out his cigarette.

Sole sighed.

'If you decide on choice two, I'll arrange a cover for you until the Games are over. Ticket to Mexico? Hawaii? You can take a nice chick. Penthouse suite in a first class hotel. Coupla thousand dollars expenses.' Adams sat back and looked at him. 'Jesus, man, we'll fix you up a new ID if that's what you want!'

Sole started to laugh.

Adams looked puzzled. 'What's so funny about a new ID?' he asked.

Sole shook his head and laughed until the tears flowed down his cheeks.

Williams burst into the room. 'Okay Dubois, move your ass next door.'

*   *   *

Walter stretched out on his cell bunk and waited for his turn to shower. He persuaded himself to think of prison as the safest place for him to be. But for how long? The afternoon trolley clanged its way down the corridor. The door smacked

170

open againt the wall. Walter rolled off the bunk.

A man in blue overalls pushed a trolley into the centre of the cell.

'How long do we have to stay here?' Walter asked in French, reaching out for a cup.

The man removed a cigarette from his lips. An inch of ash dropped on to the trolley. 'I don't know. Saturday. Sunday.' He shrugged. 'You guys know?' he said to the three other men in the cell.

'No. Who cares?' said two of them. The third didn't seem to hear.

Cups were passed around the cell, and the trolley backed out.

Walter lay back and stared miserably at the bunk above. He *had* to find a way out.

*   *   *

The speaker on Forth's empty desk in the operations room shrilled loudly.

'Car 46 to Forth.'

The patrol car voice paused.

'Car 46 to Forth?'

Taylor ran across the room and punched the switch. 'Taylor here. Forth's getting his beauty sleep.'

'Suspect Moon's been spotted, Pete. Brasserie Guy off Notre Dame.'

'Okay, I'll tell Forth.'

Patrol car 46 pulled up outside the workman's brasserie. Two officers got out, unclipped their gun holsters and walked in.

Every man inside stopped talking immediately. They left a collection of beers, sandwiches, hamburgers and hot rolls untouched to watch the two officers. The feeling of hostility was intense. Some customers began to tap their feet on the bare wooden floor. Montrealers were sick of the way the police behaved in Olympics year. It had turned the city's stomach.

The proprietor glanced at them and carried on wiping glasses. *'Oui,'* he said tonelessly.

The officers didn't reply. They stopped by a young man with dyed blond hair. sitting alone at a table in the corner. They pulled him to his feet.

'Hey, what the hell?' the man protested.

171

'C'mon Moon,' said one of the officers. 'Move it.'

'My name's not Moon! What the hell's this about?'

'Dyed blond hair doesn't suit you, Moon,' said the other officer.

'Jesus Christ!' shouted the man. He looked around the brasserie angrily. 'You talk about New York cops!'

Several pairs of eyes watched sullenly as the two officers dragged the struggling man outside.

They shoved him up against the car and frisked him quickly.

'What's happened to your fancy Montreal French, Moon?' said one of them.

'Yea. We were told you were brought up here.'

'You guys are clean outa your minds. My name's Ted Grange. Edward George Grange and I'm from New York. Who's this Moon cat?'

One of the officers removed his wallet. There was an American ID card inside and several hundred dollars. They handcuffed him and pushed him into the back seat.

'Where are you staying?' said the officer in the front seat pulling out his hand mike.

'My name's *Grange* you bastards. Check me out with my landlady. Madame Daoust, twenty-six Berri top floor. I've been there since Monday.' Grange's eyes rolled nervously.

The officer in front pressed the button on his hand mike. 'Car 46 to any car vicinity Berri.'

The speaker crackled. 'Yes, 46. Car 18 headed down Sherbrooke now.'

'Check twenty-six Berri, Madame Daoust, top floor. See if Edward George Grange lives there.'

'Right away.'

The speaker died.

The officer punched the button again. 'Car 46 to Taylor.'

'Yes 46?' Came Taylor's voice over the speaker.

'Bringing in suspect now.'

'Bring him to office fifteen.'

Taylor's voice died.

The speaker crackled. 'Car 18 to 46.'

'Yes 18?'

'Grange's story checked. He arrived on Monday. He's been watching the Games ever since. According to Madame Daoust.'

'Thanks 18.'

'Ten four.'

The blond man shouted from the back seat. 'You see? Now drop me at the end of the block.'

'That doesn't mean a thing. Any punk can check into two places.' The officer in front braked and eased the car over to the kerb.

'Look, I know you guys are jumpy,' protested Grange.

'C'mon. Out!' said the officer next to him as the car pulled up.

The two men hustled him out of the car, and through a side door. They walked him briskly to an elevator, and straight up to the tenth floor. The elevator doors parted and they turned him towards office fifteen.

One of the officers knocked loudly and walked in. Forth looked up from his desk.

'Moon, sir, we found him in Brasserie Guy.'

'He better be or I'll kill Taylor for waking me. Okay, bring him in.'

Grange struggled violently as they dragged him through the door. 'My name's *Grange* for fuck's sake,' he said hysterically. 'You saw my ID card. Why the hell can't you call my mother in New York?'

Forth eyed him up and down. 'Okay fellas,' he said to the officers, 'thanks. Sit down Mr Grange, Moon or whatever.'

The two officers left and closed the door.

'Got any ID?' Forth said, unlocking his cuffs.

'Sure I have. Look!' Grange produced his wallet.

Forth glanced at it. 'Your pal's behind those blinds,' he said, jerking a thumb at the wall.

Grange looked panic stricken. 'Which pal? Who?'

'Sole.'

'What the hell are you on about? I don't know anybody called Sole!'

Forth stood up and opened the door. He shouted down the corridor, 'Taylor, come here.'

Taylor emerged from the john.

Forth slipped out of the office and closed the door behind him. 'Friend of yours in there, Taylor.'

'Who?'

'Go and look.'

Taylor opened the door and glanced around it. He with-

173

drew, closed the door and looked quizzically at Forth. 'So?'

'You don't recognize him?'

'No. Should I?'

'How about putting an auburn beard on him?'

'Cheeesusss. You think *that* fairy is Moon? You're nuts! Okay, so maybe he dresses like Moon and is about the same height. But Moon's face is totally different.'

'Certain?'

'I followed him half of Wednesday, didn't I?'

'Okay, Taylor. Thanks.'

Taylor glared at him and slouched back into the john.

Forth pushed open his office door and grinned broadly at Grange. 'Guess we owe you an apology, friend. We were looking for a lost ballet dancer. His momma can't find him anywhere.' Forth stood back.

Grange looked at him, looked at the pack of cigars on the desk, helped himself to a handful, looked up at Forth again, and walked casually out of the room to the elevator.

* * *

Julius Hammond arrived on Friday's final flight from Chicago to Montreal.

He took a taxi from the airport direct to the Queen Elizabeth hotel, downtown.

He checked in at the front desk and asked for the dinner menu to be sent to his room. He was expecting a guest. He walked past a long line of boutiques that gave the hotel the appearance of a mini town. But Hammond, the seasoned traveller, wasn't interested. He'd had a heavy day in Chicago. There was only one thing he wanted to do before his next appointment. Soak in a bath.

A man in a tailcoat and white gloves showed him to his suite on the twelfth floor. He hovered around, opening doors, demonstrating a panel of switches by the bed that operated the colour TV, radio, twenty-four hour room service, and anything else Mr Hammond wished, until Mr Hammond eventually took the hint and tipped him a five dollar bill.

As soon as the door closed Hammond unbuttoned his blazer and loosened the knot of a dazzlingly striped necktie. He checked his cuffs. Although he hadn't changed his shirt since the morning, it was still crisply white.

He walked over to the green marble bathroom and turned on

two chunky gold taps. A bottle of yellow bath salts stood by the basin. He emptied half of it over the side, watching a jet of water whip the grains into sweet-smelling bubbles.

He returned to the bedroom, crossed the carpet and walked into the lounge. It was tastefully furnished with loose covered chintzy sofas and arm chairs, a leather topped desk, a deep pile carpet, and a discreet drinks cabinet. He opened it, took out a bottle of Chivas Regal, and poured himself a generous tot, squirting just a dash of soda in to liven it up.

By the time he returned to the bathroom, glass in hand, bubbles were frothing enticingly over the top of the bath. Hammond turned off the taps and tested the water. It felt perfect. He removed his clothes and hung them neatly on a coat hanger behind the door, dropping his shirt and underpants into a pile on the floor.

As he climbed into the bath feeling himself disappear luxuriously into the bubbles, he wondered for the umpteenth time why North Americans always raved about a shower. So uncouth.

He rubbed himself rapidly with a loofah provided with the compliments of the hotel. Then he lay back and contemplated the next two days.

He felt slightly annoyed that Moon had insisted on doing the diamond sale on Sunday, and even more annoyed that there was no way he could contact the man. Odd fellow, Moon. Fancy arranging a diamond sale for the Olympics Finale. Man obviously had some kind of kink about selling diamonds when half the world leaped about hysterically. Must be some hidden climax fetish.

Hammond shrugged and sipped his drink. He watched his toes playing idly with the bubbles. He felt himself drift off into a soft yellow cloud.

The bathroom phone purred gently in his ear.

He sat up, and reached for the receiver. 'Yes?' he snapped.

'Mr Hammond? There's a gentleman downstairs to see you.'

'Damn. The man's early. Could you show him into the bar, order him a drink from me, and say I'll be detained ten minutes?'

'Certainly, Mr Hammond.'

Hammond sighed and sipped more Chivas Regal. He loathed being rushed. He refused to allow anyone to see him

175

pad apologetically across the carpet with a stream of water trailing from under a towel. All too schoolboyish for words.

He finished his drink leisurely, let the water out and dried himself in a voluminous white towel before springing back into the bedroom.

His black leather suitcase lay open on the luggage rack. He selected a soft rich plum-and-cream striped shirt, cream flannels and shoes to match.

There was a polite knock on the door.

He did up his last button, looked at himself in the mirror, combed his greying hair, and nodded approvingly.

He moved to the door, opened it wide and beamed. 'Bucky Lancey, how nice it is to see you again. *Do* come in.'

CHAPTER FOURTEEN

The conference room was blue with cigarette smoke.

Two hundred pairs of marksmen's eyes watched as Saxon Forth climbed up on a platform at one end. He carried a model of the Olympic site under one arm, and a screen under the other.

It was past midnight.

'Sorry to keep you fellas waiting,' said Forth, placing the model on a table and hooking the screen up on its stand. He snapped his fingers at Taylor standing at the back of the room with a projector and a tray of slides.

'Half of you have been over this with me before,' said Forth, as Taylor adjusted the light beam from the projector to fit the screen. 'But it'll do you good to hear it again. Get some inspiration from the questions of the other guys.' He held up the model and turned it on its side. The men at the back scraped their chairs and crowded forward for a better view.

'Compact designs with excellent sightlines, fellas. You all know the stadia and this may seem like kidsplay. But remember, *you're* used to seeing them crammed with people and athletes, and that can be very distorting.'

The men nodded in agreement. Half of them had done target practice in the empty stadia before the Games began. The other half only knew the stadia at the height of the activities.

They watched as Forth tapped the bowl-like main stadium. He ran his hand down the arched dominating mast behind the stadium, that fanned out naturally at the base to cover a stingray shaped swimming pool. The Velodrome cycling track lay adjacent to the stadium and mast, like a triangular desert tent pinned down at the peak, and at three points along its base line.

'I want you all on the site later today. There'll be athletics and football at the main stadium, and judo at the Velodrome. That means we have to think of seventy thousand spectators in the main stadium, a few thousand guys using the practice rooms in these sixteen storeys of rooms on the inside of the mast looking down over the main stadium, and another seven and a half thousand spectators at the Velodrome. Add to that another thousand athletes and footballers and judoists, and all the guys running the services.'

Forth paused to light a cigar. 'That's a lot of bodies to protect,' he added, puffing out a cloud of smoke. 'My real worry is Sunday, not today. Then, only the main stadium will be involved. The equestrian events take up most of the day followed by the closing ceremonies.' He squinted through the smoke. 'I want you guys to be so high by Sunday that you'll jump if somebody so much as raises his arm.'

He turned the model around, enabling them to see the stadia from all angles. Then he turned to the screen.

'We'll look at the main stadium first. Kick those slides into action, Taylor. Could the guy nearest the door switch off the light?'

The room went dark. A cross-section of the main stadium edged its way into position on the screen.

'It looks like a bowl,' Forth began, 'measuring three hundred metres by two fifty and with sightlines among the best in North America. The distance from the back seats on the top balcony to the other side of the field is only one seventy-one metres.'

Taylor ran through a series of slides showing spectators' and athletes' entrances and exits. Close-up cross sections of the stadium's multi-tiered underbelly followed, showing shops, restaurants, offices, changing rooms, bars, boutiques and areas for pedestrian traffic.

'Mast please, Taylor,' said Forth.

Four different views slid into position. The first showed the front of the mast facing the stadium bowl, constructed to give sixteen storeys of gyms and practice rooms a magnificent view of the athletics ring below. The second slide showed the twin storey restaurant at the top of the mast. The third showed the stadium canopy being lowered on steel ropes from the top of the mast. The fourth slide showed the parabolic spine of the mast with its twin panoramic elevators plying up and down the arched structure.

Forth's ruler darted around the slides, pointing out positions, offering advice, showing suitable cover-points. 'You all work in shifts so everybody has a chance to see the action – either from the cheapest and best seats in one of the gyms'

178

windows in the mast – or from the stadium. So no poor sucker is stuck down in the kitchens or the parking lot for longer than a coupla hours at a time.'

A row of men at the back began to shift about restlessly.

'Just one more set fellas. Velodrome please, Taylor,' said Forth clearing his throat noisily. 'As you all know this is used for cycling and judo. Track inside measures two eighty-five point seven metres by seven point fifty metres. It's on three levels,' he added as a cross-section came into view, 'underneath you get the usual shamozzle, changing rooms, johns, bars, gyms and so on.'

The screen cleared as the last slide was removed. The men started to scrape back their chairs.

'Hold it –' Forth shouted. 'Two slides at the very end – yea –' An architect's diagram flashed on the screen. 'This is just to remind you about *pedestrian* traffic flow, and *athletes* traffic flow,' Forth explained. 'See how the structures have been designed to prevent them from coinciding – except in the communal areas, like shops, drugstores and so on. Okay boys. Lights please somebody!'

Two hundred and one pairs of eyes blinked against the light.

'Any questions?' asked Forth rolling up the screen.

A lone hand went up. 'Why are you doubling the marksmen at the main stadium, and not at the Olympic Village?' asked a Russian speaking officer from the Canadian army.

Forth faced him, hands on hips. 'We know something's planned for Sunday, at the main site,' he said shortly. 'You'll find your shift-and-site sheets on your way out fellas, all worked out by the computer. Any more questions? No? Okay. I want the first shift in position at zero eight hundred – that'll give you a few hours sleep. We'll meet again after midnight tonight for a final briefing on Sunday's action.'

* * *

London's freak storm continued to lash out wildly.

Staki was delayed at Heathrow for nearly eight hours. She was merely one of thousands of disgruntled travellers forced by the storm and Air Canada's crippling strike to take the best route-mix available.

Eventually she took her turn on one of the few flights out of Heathrow between cloudbursts, to get to Paris. From Paris she just made the connecting flight to New York, and sat around Kennedy for several hours waiting to get a seat on a direct flight to Montreal.

By the time she touched down on Canadian tarmac she felt raw with despair. For the first time in her own flying career she felt a twinge of sympathy for the rude, globe-trotting passenger she often had to cope with in the air.

It was noon on Saturday by the time she checked through customs. She headed straight for the Air Canada desk and showed them her card.

'Oh hi,' said one of the ground staff grinning toothily behind a red peaked cap, 'come to find out about the strike?'

Staki nodded glumly. 'I have to fly out of Montreal on Sunday night,' she explained feebly.

The girl laughed. 'You and several hundred thousand others,' she said gesturing at a blank video screen behind the desk. 'Were you *down* to fly out on Sunday?'

'Sure – I'm on the Europe-run again.'

The girl looked at her sympathetically. 'You just arrived from Europe?'

Staki raised her eyebrows. 'I heard about the strike in London.'

'Listen,' said the girl leaning over the desk to make sure nobody overheard them. 'The airline's not going to give in. No way. British Airways and Air France between them may fly Air Canada passengers out of here on Sunday. Right now that's unofficial. You want me to try and get you on a flight? Or try one of the regular flights to Europe?'

Staki smiled and shook her head. 'Thanks anyway. I'll call later.' She turned to leave the airport.

The girl looked after her and shrugged. 'One minute the kid has to get out of Montreal. The next minute she says no thanks,' she said to a colleague. 'I don't get it.'

Staki took a taxi straight to her hotel. She felt miserable and annoyed. There was no way she was going to risk leaving Montreal with the money, on another airline. Airport security was too tight. That meant taking a train out of the province and staying put in Toronto or Vancouver until the strike was over.

She checked in to the hotel sullenly and asked for some iced coffee to be sent up to her room.

A message to call her family awaited her. She felt overcome

with guilt and immediately resented it. How the hell could she get through to Vancouver from Heathrow?

She saw herself to her room and flopped out on the bed. But she knew damn well she wouldn't shower or do anything before calling her family. She picked up the phone.

There was a tap on the door. A petite girl in a mauve-and-white striped uniform bustled into the room with a tray of iced coffee. *'Bonjour Madame,'* she said cheerfully and placed the tray by Staki's feet.

'Bonjour,' Staki replied and wondered how much the girl earned. There was no real difference in their work. So why did people treat them differently? Staki crooked the receiver by her ear and scratched around in her handbag. She gave the girl a fistful of dollars. The girl flushed with confusion and left the room.

'We have your call to Vancouver, Ms Lin. Go ahead please.'

Staki adjusted the receiver, stretched over and picked up the glass of iced coffee. As was the custom with her family, she spoke to her grandmother first. Then to her parents. Then only to her sisters.

There was trouble at home. Damn. When wasn't there trouble at home? She replaced the receiver after a solid hour and lay back to finish her coffee. She wondered if her family would ever know that she agreed to a role in the gems' switch solely for them. Not for herself.

The thought made her feel rebellious. Stifled. Resentful. Guilty.

Only once before had she felt it so intensely.

Chinatown, Vancouver. August, 1975.

She had stood at her window, relieved to be away from the formality of the family meal and the staring unblinking eyes of her grandmother. The old lady spoke once to her all evening. *Bù guān ny de shì.* A polite way of saying, mind your own bloody business. Period. Disapproval oozed from the old lady's unsmiling lips.

It wasn't surprising.

Walter was staying the night. Separate bedrooms didn't make any difference to Laŏ Lin.

Staki thought about her family. Her grandmother hadn't budged out of Chinatown and didn't want to. Her parents straddled an uneasy middle road between their fear and re-

181

spect for her, and the 'old ways', and a nagging need to acknowledge North America. And her sisters? They cluttered the house with pop records and college sweaters, Vancouver slang and banana bread.

She couldn't take the extremes.

Staki cried softly as she stood at her window soothed by the quiet breeze. She knew that further up, Hastings Street would still be active, with late night movie houses just emptying. The remote sound of cars starting up, of horns sounding at the traffic lights, and the squeal of hot rubber on the road, hung dull and heavy in the hot late summer night air.

Lower down Hastings Street the beer parlours were still sucking in the regulars, filling them up ready to spew them out again into the street. And from there to Victory Square, where, if they were lucky, they'd find a bench for the night providing the meths drinkers or the cops hadn't got there first.

Amidst the Half Breeds hovering in alcoholic escape between the White world and the Indian, the druggies and the winos, the meths drinkers and broken down whores, came the lines of maimed and shell shocked war vets, to lurch around the Cenotaph commemorating the brave and dead of two world wars.

Victory Square.

Shit.

Staki hung out of the window bitterly and echoed her thoughts to the night air.

The door behind her opened abruptly. She turned as Walter swung optimistically into her room, long silk kimono flapping.

'Hi butterfly,' he said, 'boy, am I glad to see you alone!' He flung himself down on her bed.

She didn't move.

'Hey? Come here!' he said in a loud whisper.

'Shaddup. Do you want my grandmother in here?' she snapped.

Walter sat up, bewildered. 'Staki,' he said more softly, 'what's wrong?'

Staki moved towards the bed. She did up the top button on her loose fitting satin pyjamas.

Walter frowned. He held out his arms to her hesitantly. She looked down at him with contempt ... He wore the same expression as the sweaty-palmed boys who used to shout abuses at her when she refused to neck in her parent's front room.

182

Walter gripped her arms and pulled her towards him. He tried to kiss her but she turned her head away. He ran his hands over her breasts, feeling her nipples tighten under the satin. He started to undo her buttons.

'No,' she whispered. 'Not in my father's house.'

He looked at her angrily.

She pushed him back on the bed. His kimono fell open. He looked down at himself, humiliated, and tried to cover himself up.

She took his hands and leaned on them. She bent over him quickly and took him violently in her mouth, sucking him half way to orgasm. Then she withdrew.

'*Jesus*, Staki,' he said vehemently.

She turned without a word and left him alone in the room.

Thinking about the incident nearly a year later embarrassed her. She'd used Walter as an outlet from her suffocating home. It hadn't worked. He'd never forgiven her. He'd never even *tried* to understand.

She was exasperated. And sad. The thought of Sunday heightened the extremes that seemed determined to maim her inside.

Damn. Maybe this was just what the rest of the world called 'jet-lag'.

She got up to shower.

* * *

Walter's thoughts were softer about Staki, at that moment.

He sat in the corner of the prison courtyard feeling stupidly happy. God alone knew why. His destiny lay in somebody else's hands. He thought dreamily of Los Angeles. Staki. Himself. His new self that was. And a few million bucks to spare. He'd have to arrange to re-meet her somewhere in his second generation, Greek-from-the-Bronx, frame.

He lay back blissfully in his stinking coat and stretched luxuriously.

The courtyard looked like a fairground. Two guards played football with 'Squadron Leader' Bannering. Lilly's purple faced companion sat talking to a young man hitch-hiking his way rough to Alaska, and two characters who claimed they'd lived on welfare for over a decade.

A group of meths drinking companions bribed a prison

183

officer to bring in a supply. A face under a crumpled brown hat tried to puff at a thread of tobacco. An old violin maker who'd given up long ago sat discussing French-Canadian history with two Indians from the north of Quebec.

And then Walter saw him. A sweating, trembling mass gazing in terror at the faces around him. Walter had never seen advanced D.t.'s before. Two prison officers appeared from a door, walked over to the man, and dragged him inside.

Walter watched the man's shoes bounce and bump across the courtyard, and up some steps.

He looked away, and rubbed the diamonds in his hems for comfort.

*　*　*

The door of Saxon Forth's office opened violently and crashed againt the wall.

Mordechai Golan, head of the Shin Beth contingent in the city, dragged Forth up by his collar and smashed him in the mouth. Forth staggered back, more surprised than hurt.

Golan kicked the door shut and reached out for him.

'*For Christ's sake!*' shouted Forth nursing a bruised cheek bone, and swinging out an arm to prevent Golan from touching him.

'You motherfucker,' said Golan. 'Did you think we wouldn't find out, you double crossing swine?'

'Aw, sit down Green, you look like a pig's bladder,' said Forth dismissively with a sweep of the hand. He drew out his own chair and searched about for a Kleenex.

Golan remained standing. 'Iran's police minister Ramshid's been here all the fucking time, incognito, to watch his kid jump. So what the hell are you playing at with your telexes from Teheran saying he's been kidnapped? What kind of bullshit have you been pumping us?'

Forth sighed deeply and scratched the back of his head.

'– And that *Carbetti* creep,' Golan yelled, 'damn you, *and* your fuckingly cosy informer network. How long did you think it would take us to trace back that false crap you fed through to Tel Aviv via Beirut that Carbetti had our team lined up for the clouds?' Golan grabbed Forth angrily by the shirt.

Forth swatted his hand away like an annoying fly. 'C'mon Green, grow up.'

'Grow up? Damn your miserable assole. You get *me* to do

184

your stinking work for you by ridding the streets of Carbetti. Just like calling in a rat catcher!'

'I know how your mind works,' Forth replied searching the desk for his cigars, 'and take your hands off me, this is a clean shirt.'

Golan stood back abruptly. 'Now that we did you a favour, it's your turn to tell me what footsy-footsy's going on with Ramshid.'

Forth touched his cheek bone gingerly and tested his jaw. 'We guaranteed to protect him. Nobody knows he's here except his bodyguards and his kid. Trouble was,' Forth chuckled and shook his head, 'my staff are too efficient. They discovered Ramshid's kid in a fruit joint same time as Carbetti –'

'– So you think Carbetti was tailing the kid hoping he'd lead him to Ramshid? Bullshit!'

Forth lit a cigar and said nothing.

'*Jesus!*' Golan protested loudly, 'you got the whole operations room turned over because of this Ramshid affair. His kid's locked up with a Squad O guy. Even his horse is locked up!'

'Security precautions. You should know that,' Forth replied dryly.

Golan twisted away angrily. He caught sight of Sole behind the two-way mirror. 'What the hell's going on in there with that Black fella under hoods?' He looked at Forth. 'You get *us* to do Carbetti, and some creep of an English major to do this!'

In the next room, Sole fell heavily to his knees. Pink and Williams hauled him to his feet, removed the hood and slapped his cheeks. His face and hair ran with sweat. His eyes lolled back in his skull. Williams drew up a chair and made him sit down. Pink held his face and patted it with a towel. They handed him something to drink.

Golan watched silently for a minute. 'Boy,' he said shaking his head in disgust. '*We* don't take this long to get information. Why don't you get a couple of Blacks from the squad to work him over? We often use Moroccan or Iraqi Jews to work over an Arab suspect who's proving difficult.'

Forth stood up and yanked down the blind over the mirror. 'Get out, Green,' he said shortly.

'I warn you,' added Golan, 'if whatever you're cooking in

your stinking brain endangers our team, I'll have your ex-wife and kids mowed down by a hit and run driver –'

Forth pulled a face. 'Don't talk crap. And don't bother telling the fellas in the operations room about the telexes from Iran, because they won't believe you. Go ahead. Try.' He stood up and opened the door.

Golan didn't move.

Forth walked into the corridor, 'Okay, I'll do it for you.' He opened the operations room door. 'Hey fellas!' he bellowed loud enough for half Montreal to hear. 'Golan thinks I sent those telexes to myself. You know? Those messages from Teheran saying Ramshid's been kidnapped?'

There was a burst of laughter followed by a series of hoots and cat calls.

Forth returned to his office.

Golan had gone.

He shrugged, salvaged his smouldering cigar from the ashtray, and released the blind. He frowned anxiously and picked up the microphone. 'Well?' he asked.

Williams glanced back and shook his head.

'Shit. Ask Pink to join me here.' Forth watched as the message was communicated. He switched off the mike. Pink raised his thumb to the mirror and disappeared. A moment later he tapped politely on the door and walked in.

'Dubois has been in there nearly forty-eight hours,' Forth said anxiously. 'That leaves us tonight and tomorrow morning.' He continued looking through the mirror.

'Oh, he's hallucinating nicely,' Pink replied like a surgeon talking about a post-operative patient. 'It shouldn't take much longer. We've heard all about his grandmother and grandfather and their house with the mud floor by the railway line. It explained a lot.' Pink removed his cigarette case and joined Forth at the mirror. He flicked a stray lock of hair away from his ear lobe.

'Explained *what*?' asked Forth suspiciously, watching Williams walk Sole up and down the room next door.

'Why he's taking so long, of course,' Pink paused to light his cigarette. He threw his head back to inhale. 'He comes from the slums, that's why. He's tough. Mentally and physically. He's still fighting us. If he came from the middle classes we would have broken him thirty-six hours ago.' He sighed and shook his head. 'If he came from the upper classes we would

186

have had him *forty*-six hours ago.'

Forth looked at him in amazement. 'You mean you work out how long it takes to crack somebody by their –'

'Class background?' interrupted Pink. 'Indeed, yes.'

Forth turned away. He had no time for that kind of bull. 'So how the hell do you intend to do *him*?' he said jerking his head at the mirror.

Pink's face twitched. 'He's nearly there now.' He switched on the microphone. 'Williams, come out now. Turn the air conditioner on. Leave him in there alone. We'll start again – in two hours.'

CHAPTER FIFTEEN

Bill O'Dowd waited anxiously at the gate of number 14 Regent's Canal Path for the Harrods cold storage van to appear.

He knew how dangerous it was to leave electricity on in a flooded house. And he knew the house had to be tidy for Tuesday.

O'Dowd had taken care of Vatican properties in London for years. He was handsomely paid to organize carpenters, electricians, plumbers, builders and decorators. He was also paid to stay out of the way, to give the appearance of some invisible power behind the clockwork running order of the properties.

It was nearly noon, but the houses on either side of the Path still looked heavy with sleep. The rains had taken their revenge. Fragments of prize gardens and precious blooms floated miserably down the swollen canal.

Although Sunday started dry, the people were beyond caring.

The van started to back giddily down the narrow Path, snapping off twigs and trailing yards of cultivated ivy.

'Bloody shrubbery!' the driver cursed.

'Hold it Tom,' shouted O'Dowd stepping hastily into the middle of the Path to guide the van down. This wasn't the first emergency service the two men had handled together.

The driver edged to a halt and jumped out shaking his head. 'Morning Bill,' he said brightly, 'shouldn't you be at mass?'

'I'll give you mass. Come and look at this basement.' He crinkled his nose and opened the gate. The garden smelt dank from the heavy rains. Both men took care to keep on the paved way leading down to the basement door that stood half open in a pool of muddy water.

'Come in bare foot,' O'Dowd advised in a strong Cork accent, 'otherwise you can kiss your boots good-bye!'

'What a way to spend a bleeding Sunday,' Tom complained rolling up his trousers and wading knee deep into the water.

O'Dowd shoved back the door and pointed to the corner of the basement. 'I think you delivered this freezer nearly a year ago didn't you?'

'Probably,' said Tom grimly.

They waded towards it. O'Dowd pulled out the plug, noticing with some relief that it was still an inch higher than the water level. He wrapped the electric cord around his arm and laid it on top of the freezer. 'I'll take this end,' he said, bending down and plunging his hands in the stinking water to get under the cabinet.

The Harrods man bent down opposite him. 'Christ Almighty, I can't lift that!' He stood up painfully and rubbed the small of his back.

'Come on, let's try again. It can't be *that* heavy,' O'Dowd replied.

They tried again. But the freezer weighed a ton.

'Must be full of food. Let's fill the van with that first and then carry it out.' Tom banged on the lid. 'We'd need eight blokes to heave this out. Where you going to get eight blokes on a Sunday?'

O'Dowd nodded and tried the lid. It was locked. He tried it again. It wouldn't open.

'And you don't have a key?' sang Tom, resting his elbow on the lid.

O'Dowd shook his head.

'Jesus Christ, mate. Don't they trust you? How many years you been doing this job? Ten? Fifteen? Tom shook his head in disgust and glanced helplessly around the basement for a possible key board. There wasn't one. 'Right,' he said, rubbing his hands together. 'Any idea where we can find a paperclip or thick needle?'

O'Dowd shrugged. 'Wait – would my pipe cleaner do?' He took a metal spike out of an inner pocket.

The Harrods man looked at it and sniffed, 'Wouldn't do for a post office safe.' He bent over the lock, spiked it twice with the cleaner, twisted it right and left, twiddled it, and very gently moved it from side to side.

The lock slid back.

O'Dowd laughed approvingly and crouched down to lift the lid with the base of his hands. It wouldn't budge.

Tom ran his finger around the inside of the rim. 'Shit – stuck down with ice,' he said in disgust.

'Well, that shouldn't be too difficult,' O'Dowd replied, trying hard to be lighthearted. He moved towards the door and unhooked a spade off the wall.

Tom took it, inserted it under the lid, banged the end heartily and jammed it hard. Then he placed his weight on the handle and swung on it.

O'Dowd took over and began chipping away angrily at the solid ice, edging his way around the lid gradually. 'Hilary was knighted for doing this on Everest,' he said dryly, leaning on the handle every few inches.

Tom took over and eased the lid a bit more.

O'Dowd began picking away at some stubborn lumps of ice with the wooden end of a plunger.

Between them it took nearly fifteen minutes to hack the ice clear. When it was done they stood back against the wall and panted noisily.

'This is going to cost your purple frocked bosses a couple of hundred quid, and it'll cost you a few pints mate!' grumbled Tom, wiping his mouth.

O'Dowd laughed, 'I'll hold you to that,' he said, throwing back the lid. He reached inside and immediately staggered back against the wall. 'Holy Mother!' His cheeks bulged.

Tom looked at him in horror. He bent over the freezer. His guts somersaulted. He turned away, then fascination forced him to look back at the frozen man. 'Who is it?' He glanced around for O'Dowd.

Somebody was being hideously sick outside.

*   *   *

The magnificently designed Olympic stadia looked cool and stately in the early Sunday morning air. The ribbed roofing effect on the main stadium and Velodrome, and the slatted side of the dominant mast provided a pleasing visual empathy, and relief from the solid post-stressed concrete blocks of all three structures.

The couple paused in front of the main gate, soothed by the view. Suddenly two coachloads of spectators swung eagerly around the corner, determined to be the first in the queue.

The couple turned hastily to cross the road. They walked towards an untidy line of low income apartment blocks.

Montreal had tried to convince the people that the soaring millions required to stage the Olympics was raised through self-financing gimmicks, but somehow the message died here, a stone's throw away from the stadia. Debris from the previous day's crowds littered the gutters and the exposed ground between the apartment blocks. The early breezes scuffed up the chalk lines of the children's own athletics' rings drawn crudely on the paving stones.

The couple entered block three.

Babies yelled lustily, mothers screamed at their kids. The smell of scalded coffee hung around the building like a mangy stray. The couple climbed two flights of stairs and knocked at the first door on the left.

It opened a few inches. A child in a grey vest looked up at them. '*Maman* . . .'

A woman appeared with two more children in her arms and another very much on the way. She couldn't have been more than twenty-two, but her face was heavily lined. Lank strands of black hair stuck to her forehead. '*Oui,*' she eyed the couple suspiciously. The children struggled to get down.

Briefly they explained they were friends of M Shimon Ben-Or who had rented a room in her apartment. He'd had to return to the Middle East. He asked them to collect his things.

'*Eh bien,*' she said flatly. She stood back to let them in.

Her three children eyed them from head to foot. They trailed behind as she led the couple through a room with a double mattress on the floor, two cots, some chairs and a pile of clothes. A man stood at an expensive looking stove in a kitchen leading out of the room. He nodded at them and turned down the heat under a saucepan frothing with milk.

He was fully dressed and seemed exhausted as though he'd just come home from a late night shift at a near-by factory.

The woman patted her apron. '*Merde. La clé.*' She left them by the door. Within seconds she returned dragging a box spilling over with bits of kid's toys, books without covers, two broken saucepans, a collection of bills and socks, several decaying apple cores, torn up Olympic picture books, an unused sanitary towel that she hastily pocketed, and eventually, a bunch of keys.

She shook the keys, tried three of them. The door opened with the fourth. She turned and left the couple to it. The room was once hers and her husband's. That was before they were forced to rent it out to help keep up the payments on a three piece bedroom suite they'd bought to put in it.

The couple closed the door and locked it. They felt under the double bed. One of them forced open the cupboard door, splintering the wood instantly around a flimsy lock. Together they felt inside and pulled out a plastic carrier bag. It contained three .38 revolvers, three silencers and magazines; six of them.

'I thought Borg said there'd be explosives,' said the man looking angrily around the room.

His female companion shrugged.

He pulled back the covers from the bed and bounced the mattress. He removed a knife from his pocket and slashed at it, exposing the inner springs, but finding nothing else. They emptied out the contents of a chest of drawers, one by one, pulled up the floor lino, and tapped around the edge of the walls, but found no concealed hiding place.

They sat down on the floor, anxious and annoyed.

'Bloody mess, and it stinks of Carbetti's perfume,' said the man cynically kicking a pile of string vests.

His companion started to tidy up the floor. 'I'd better give the family something for it,' she said folding up a pair of long-johns.

'You're mad. They've been paid for the room already.'

'I don't care,' she turned on him bitterly. 'I'll ask her to make us some food – we better stay here today.'

'Stay *here*?' said the man glaring at her. 'But Moon's not meeting Hammond until eight tonight!'

'So what? We need time to think.'

'*You* do, but I'm not sitting around this stinking hole all day.'

'Okay, so give up on me. But the explosives *must* be here somewhere,' she said emphatically, looking around the room for a possible hiding place.

The man eyed her curiously. 'What's so special about explosives? I'll just have to shoot Moon and Hammond in the popcorn van.'

'I thought Borg told you you had to make it difficult for the police to identify them.'

'Shhhh – those wretched children might be eavesdropping.'

'They can't speak English.'

'Borg can shove his orders,' said the man bluntly. 'Anyway, shooting's easier. While Moon and Hammond are in the back of the van doing their coy trading, I'll force the driver to take us to a quiet spot. Moon and Hammond won't see me, only the back of the driver's head. After that it's a straight hold-up.'

'You make it sound so simple,' she said feeling around the edge of the window frame.

'It is. By the way, Borg's meeting us in London. To take collection of Moon's diamonds and Hammond's dollars.' He watched her closely.

She turned from the window. 'How do you know that?'

'Because I flew to Toronto yesterday to phone him.'

'Christ. That was a chance!' She began to tap the wall under the window.

'Not really.' He affected an east Florida accent. 'Ma name's Thomas Harbaker from Miama.'

'Original. Who did you pick that up from?' she dropped to the floor and knocked her knuckles along the skirting board.

The man stood up impatiently. 'Why don't you ask that woman outside to make us some coffee? You're beginning to irritate me.'

* * *

Sole heard beautiful music and people singing in the crêperie courtyard.

He knelt on his bed to look through the window. Boys and girls were dancing around in a lively circle. Tables and chairs had been pushed back along the cobbles to clear the centre of the courtyard.

> *'Derrier' chez-nous 'y' avait un champ de pois*
> PAMBELIBELO PAN PAN LA BOBINO
> *J'en cueuillis deux, j'en mangis trois –'*

Sole laughed and threw open the window.

A girl with a head full of curls dropped her partners' hands and waved to him. 'Come and dance with us Sole. Do you know *Pambelibelo*?'

'Sure! My granma sang it to me. It's about a girl who gets sick from eating too many peas.' He swung his legs out of the window and jumped nimbly to the cobbles. 'Everybody visits her except her boyfriend. Right?'

The girl nodded happily and kissed him. She clapped her hands at the circle of people watching them. 'Come on all of you – sing with us!' She raised her head and sang out joyfully to the sky to start the chorus.

> PAMBELI PAMBELO
> PAN PAN LA BOBINETTE

PAMBELIBELO PAN PAN LA BOBINETTE
PAMBELIBELO PAN PAN LA BOBINO
PAMBELIBELO PAN PAN LA BOBINO

'*J'en cueuillis deux, j'en mangis trois*', sang the girl alone.
PAMBELIBELO PAN PAN LA BOBINO, chorused the others.

> '*J'en fus malad' au lit trois mois*
> *Tous mes parents venaient m'y voir*'
> PAMBELIBELO PAN PAN LA BOBINO

'*Celui que j'aime ne vint pas . . .*'
Sole swirled and danced faster and faster. Philippe the proprietor emerged, smiling, a fresh white apron reached down to
his toes. Two shutters smacked open against the wall above.
Boubolina appeared. She saw Sole and laughed and joined in
the chorus, her voice soaring above the others.

Sole fell to the ground. The singing stopped. The people
turned on him angrily. He fought back wildly and clutched on
to a pair of sneakers.

Forth hauled him up and pulled off his hood. 'Who's working with you and where are they?' he demanded.

The face folded in and out of itself like a Yogi's stomach.
'*What are your friends planning to do?*' said the mouth.

'*Pam-beli-belo pan pan –*' sang Sole.

'Who was Carbetti instructed to kill?' said the eyes in the
head.

'*Pan pan la la la bobinette . . .*' sang Sole.

Forth kicked his legs from under him. Sole crashed heavily
to the floor.

'Who do they plan to kill?' shouted Forth.

'*Pam-beli-belo pan pan –*' The singing grew softer and
softer. Boubolina called out. Sole tried to get up.

Forth kicked him in the face. 'Where's Moon? What's he
been told to do?'

Sole fell back against the wall. '*Paammmmmmbe-beli-be-lo-
be-li pa-an . . .*'

Forth sweated profusely. He turned to cool his forehead on
the wall. He scratched noisily in his armpits, withdrew his
hand and flexed his fingers.

Sole crawled about the floor, singing gently like somebody
doing Ophelia in drag.

Forth closed his eyes.

Williams spoke to him through the headphones, 'The major's just got up. Do you want him in there?'

Forth blinked at the mirror and shook his head. He wiped his face on his shirt sleeve and gestured that he was coming out.

He returned to his office. He took some rye from the top drawer of his desk and drank it straight from the bottle. 'Williams,' he said hoarsely, 'come with me.'

Williams looked at Pink who stood by the mirror, fresh from a few hours sleep.

Forth ignored him and left the office. Williams followed obediently.

Next door they tried to revive Sole. Williams dropped to his knees and began to massage his shoulders and back expertly. He helped him into a sitting position. Forth threw a bucket of water over him.

Sole began to struggle violently.

Forth held him by the back of his head and forced him to make eye contact. 'Duboyce. Who the hell are you protecting? A fat Greek whore? She's dead. *Dead* do you hear? And Moon? He's laughing at you. Because you'll be blamed for what he does today. He told us all about you. He told us where to find you. You didn't know that did you? Moon told us. Yes. Your good friend Moon. Don't you want to find him? We'll find him for you!'

Sole's eyes swivelled around. He opened his lips '*bob-bob-bob-bob-bob-bob-bob-bob* –'

'Jesus fucking *Christ*!' Forth let him drop to the floor.

Williams helped Sole to his feet and tried to put on the hood.

'Forget it,' said Forth sourly. 'We've got to stop this. Take him downstairs and put him under a cold shower. Get Adams to sweeten him up, give him coffee, food, whatever. How long's the heat been on in here?'

'Four hours,' Williams replied, supporting Sole with his arms.

'Blast some cool air in. Bring him back when I tell you.' Forth turned to go, leaving the door wide open. Two Squad O men passing by looked in curiously and shook their heads.

Forth walked into his office and stretched out for the bottle of rye.

Pink glanced at him nervously. He rubbed the corners of his

mouth. 'In Belf—'

'In Belfast in Belfast!' shouted Forth slamming the bottle down aggressively. 'Why don't you shove Belfast up your miserable assole? If it's as big as your mouth you shouldn't have any problems.'

Pink looked horrified. 'I really don't thi—'

'I don't give a three cent blow-job *what* you think. If we don't crack that Black bastard there's going to be one almighty row. Your head will roll with mine. I'll see to it.' Forth raised the bottle to his lips.

Pink stared unhappily through the mirror at the empty room. 'I can't understand it,' he began, shaking his head. 'We've been at him in shifts since Thursday *night*!'

'And it's now nearly sixteen hundred hours Sunday. That leaves us precisely *three and a half* godamn hours to the closing ceremony!' Forth looked at him with contempt.

Pink shifted uneasily from one foot to the other. Then he squared his shoulders. 'I did advise you not to start hitting him about. It doesn't help. It would have been more helpful if you had arranged to keep moving him around by car and helicopter. That *really* dismembers the senses.' Pink removed a cigarette and tapped it smartly on his silver case. He put it between his lips and lit it, drawing smoke down to the depths of his lungs.

Forth wanted to kill Pink.

It was easier to kill a man than drive him insane. The one was final. Clean. The other meant a lifetime of coping with a conscience that carried the weight of another man's broken mind on it.

Forth turned his back on the major and switched on the TV set next to him to help clear his thinking. The picture focused itself. It was the finals of the Grand Prix jumping event. A horse thudded up to the camera. There was a pause, a gasp from the crowd, and the animal cleared the wall. A second camera took over from the side view for the water jump. The horse surged forward, collected itself, surged again and flew through the air. The crowd roared its approval.

The young Yugoslavian army officer had jumped a clear round.

'Hallelujah,' said Forth.

A member of the British team came trotting busily into the ring. His horse's tail swished from side to side. The rider

196

checked his mount, grinned at the crowds, dug his heel's into the animal's sides and hurtled towards the first jump, knocking it flying.

The crowd burst out laughing.

Forth watched the camera pan around the faces. He agreed with it. Enough horseflesh was enough. He turned down the sound.

He stared thoughtfully at the special video screen standing next to the standard TV, linked to Squad O cameramen all over the site. He leaned over and fiddled with the speaker on his desk to make contact with the camera control room, at the same time as switching on the video.

'Control room,' a voice crackled chestily.

Forth looked at the video screen in amazement, and back at the standard TV.

'*Control*,' repeated the voice impatiently.

'Forth here. What the hell's going on? Get the boys to turn their cameras off those godamn horses. What're they trying to do for Chrissakes? Compete with Canadian Broadcasting?'

'Oh,' said the voice dejectedly, 'sorry.'

'Pan around the interior of the stadium. News cameras did it a second ago. Get your fellas to do it more slowly. I want to know what seventy thousand faces look like.'

'Yes, sir.'

Forth leaned forward and clarified the picture. He waited until the cameramen picked up the message from control and began to sweep around the stadium, giving him nice easy shots of the various tiers. Forth then glanced down the site chart to check the positioning of the marksmen, cameramen and assorted Squad O officers.

He ringed one name with a pencil, and switched himself through to the earphones of Officer Yvon Benoit. 'Yvon?'

'Yes, sir?'

'Iranian kid okay?'

'Sure. He's jumped twice. Each time we've had the programme varied. The way he moves he's safer in that ring than outside of it.'

'Hmm. How's he done?'

'He won a gold medal in the last event, and he jumps for the last time in the next event. Nice kid. I'll be sorry to say goodbye –'

There was a long pause.

'Yvon?'

'I'm still here,' said the voice.

'Hear me out. Take the kid to his father –' Forth double checked his list. 'He's on row DE, four rows down from the back on stand 7. He's not with the Iranian delegation for security reasons. He's got five gorillas with him. Pass a note down saying "Saxon thought you'd like to see your son's gold medal" and then let Dwajan wait for him at the security room at the top of stand 7. Give him five minutes with the kid.'

A puzzled silence came over the speaker.

'His *father*?' asked Yvon in amazement.

'Yea. The kid knows he's here. Move your ass.'

Forth switched him off and buzzed the camera control room.

'Control,' said the chesty voice.

'Forth again. Get the camera nearest to DE stand 7 to hold it there. Four rows down from the back.'

'Check.'

Forth switched him off and adjusted his video screen.

He sat forward with interest and reached across the desk for his cigars. Yvon Benoit picked his way down the stand, showed his ID to a tightly packed group of six men, and pointed upwards. Three of the men rose as one body and followed him up the stand, out of the camera's view.

Forth pursed his lips and lit his cigar thoughtfully. He flicked the speaker to connect him to the apartment downstairs.

'Adams,' said a voice quickly.

'You finished showering Dubois?' asked Forth.

'Sure, he seems in slightly better shape.'

'He still singing?'

'No.'

'Great. Bring him back to me here. Could you and Williams get that stinking room cleaned up next door? Make it smell nice. Williams'll give you his fancy cologne. Squirt some around eh? Put a decent chair and table in there and a coffee perc. Get a TV and a video screen and sit Dubois in front of them. Fix him a nice steak and french fries – whatever he wants.'

A deep sigh hissed through the speaker.

Forth turned on it angrily, '*You get that Adams?*'

'I guess so, bu—'

Forth switched him off mid voice. He glanced up at Pink who was staring at the video screen.

'Surprised, major?' he asked slowly.

'No, Forth. But I'm curious to know what you *really* want out of Dubois.'

CHAPTER SIXTEEN

Walter was released from prison at 5 p.m. He'd forgotten what the outside world felt like.

He stepped out of the paddy wagon into a lightheaded sickly, daisy-fresh, ring-of-confidence, spun from the adman's dream TV commercial.

He wore nothing but several million dollars' worth of diamonds sewn into soiled trousers and a shabby coat, reeking with memories of the Greek civil war.

An officer gave him a token ten dollars and a brisk pat on the back. Lilly and her friends rushed off to the drug stores open on Sundays to catch up on meths supplies. The others used their ten dollars to return to favourite park benches and buy a couple of snacks.

Walter started on the long walk down Sherbrooke Avenue that linked downtown Montreal with the Olympic site. His limbs and joints ached. He'd grown accustomed to his own smell. But what would the impeccable Julius Hammond say? 'I know you said disguise, but this really goes a little too far, Moon. Good Lord, man, you don't expect *me* to pick the diamonds out of your coat like picking at a headful of lice do you? Disgraceful!'

Walter chuckled lustily. He wouldn't miss this for anything. Then he caught sight of himself in a shop window and sobered up instantly.

His face was streaked with weariness. Large bags hung under his eyes. The hair and beard he'd spent hundreds of dollars grooming over the years, looked stiff with dirt. He shuddered and walked on.

He paused once opposite the road leading to Place Jacques Cartier and looked down it longingly, before breaking into an agitated trot. From the height of the sun he judged it to be after 6 p.m. At a run he could make the site four or five kilometres away, in time.

But he'd underestimated the effect prison had on his normally peak condition.

He slowed down and sat on the pavement, closed his eyes and forced Yoga to take over.

*   *   *

'Mr Hammond?'

'Yes?'

'Front desk here, sir. Mr Lancey has arrived. Shall I send him up to your room or will you be down soon?'

'No, would you send him up, please?'

'Certainly, sir.'

Julius Hammond fastened his mother-of-pearl cuff links, before opening his door. It would be a matter of seconds before the high speed lift brought Lancey to his floor.

He heard the familiar whine and stepped into the corridor. The elevator doors parted and out came Lancey, stretching up to add another half-inch to his five feet height.

'Hello Bucky,' said Hammond warmly, 'exactly six sixteen. You're only a minute late!'

'Where I was brought up if you were a second late you went hungry!' said Lancey.

Hammond laughed politely and stood back to let the jeweller in. 'Drink?' he asked.

'Why not?' Lancey followed him into the lounge and nodded approvingly at the decor.

Hammond bent over the cabinet. 'Whisky? Gin? Brandy? Or would you prefer a chilled wine?'

'Do I spot a Bourbon in there?' Lancey put his head on one side to look into the cabinet.

'Indeed – one unopened Jack Daniels,' Hammond replied, squinting at the label. He opened the fridge next to the cabinet, removed the ice tray, shook out a number of lumps and dropped them into two glasses.

'Thanks –' said Lancey taking the bottle and the glass to help himself. 'Y'know, finest Bourbon I ever tasted was with the Apostolic Delegate on Wednesday night,' he chuckled, pouring himself a large tot. 'Unmarked bottle too. Must have matured for years. Texture like cream. Beeeyootiful.' He sipped the Jack Daniels and shook his head. 'Great character,' he murmured.

'What, the Bourbon?' asked Hammond, raising his own glass of Chivas Regal.

'Hm? Oh, no, the Apostolic Delegate. Had to do the same

job for him I'm doing for you tonight.' Lancey smiled. 'He wanted me to stay on but I said I had to get back to New York. Actually I felt like a bit of hotel life,' he admitted pointing at the room with his glass. 'All that ritual – pheuw!'

Hammond laughed. 'You're a popular man.'

Lancey shrugged modestly. 'Not really. I handle all the jobs on the east coast, and any I like the sound of elsewhere. My partners do the *real* work.'

Hammond broke the foil on a packet of peanuts and scattered them into a dish. 'Remember those emeralds you looked at for me in Johannesburg last year?' he asked, passing the dish across.

'Sure – thanks!' said Lancey, taking a handful. 'Y'know I had a problem thinking up a design for the ones you let me buy,' he added, crunching peanuts thoughtfully, 'until the winter. Y'know what inspired me? A snow crystal. Bingo! Out came the design. What a necklace.' He kissed the tips of his fingers passionately. 'Went for a song at a hundred and fifty thousand bucks.' He shook his head sadly.

Hammond looked politely interested.

Lancey swilled the Bourbon inside his mouth. 'What happened to the other emeralds?'

'Oh. Most of them found buyers in Europe,' Hammond replied vaguely. 'But wait till you see the gems tonight. By the way – we have to dress as popcorn men to satisfy the supplier's silly fetish. I managed to get a couple of costumes for us,' he added breezily. 'We'll change in the car nearer to the stadium.'

Lancey chocked on a peanut. '*Popcorn* men?'

'Yes, popcorn men. Forgot to mention it the other evening – I'll just get them, they're on my bed.' He smiled broadly and walked into the adjoining room.

'What kind of a nut are we meeting?' asked Lancey shouting through the open door.

'Perfectly reputable, I'm told. Just a little high spirited, that's all. Heard about him from an immaculate source. One of my best clients in Zurich. On his recommendation alone I had no trouble whatsoever raising the necessary lolly.' Hammond reappeared carrying the two costumes over his arm. He held one out. 'Now, Bucky, I think this should fit you!'

* * *

Saxon Forth stood glued to the two-way mirror and chain

smoked. He'd just dispatched an affronted and grouchy Major Pink to Washington.

Next door, Sole sat numbly in front of twin TV screens. A four-course meal and a can of beer lay untouched beside his elbow.

Forth looked at him anxiously for any sign of a reaction to the screens. There wasn't one. He glanced at his watch. It was nearly seven.

Suddenly, Sole stood up and clenched his fists violently at one of the screens. A deeply tanned announcer gave the time check, and the latest results from the Grand Prix.

Forth rushed next door. He whirled Sole around by the shoulders.

Sole's lips moved repetitively, '*Merde*, popcorn *huit* popcorn *huit* popcorn *huit* popcorn *huit* . . .'

Forth shook him angrily. 'What the hell's popcorn wheat, popcorn wheat? What is it?' He struck him twice across the face.

Sole blinked and struggled out of Forth's grip. He looked at both screens. The TV coverage of the jumping event resumed. The video cameras panned obediently around the exterior of the stadium.

Sole sat down and stared at the screens.

Forth dropped to his haunches. 'C'mon Sole,' he said gently, 'tell me what popcorn wheat means eh? You want popcorn? Shall Uncle Saxon buy you some popcorn?'

'Pop-corn *huit* po-opcorn *huit* pop-pop . . .' Sole's voice tailed off.

A horse thudded past on one screen. Squad O cameras panned restlessly around the tiers.

Forth looked from the screens to Sole's face, to the screens and back to Sole's expressionless face. He sighed deeply and stood up, waited a few minutes, then turned and walked out.

He opened his office door slowly, saying 'Popcorn wheat, popcorn wheat' over and over. He punched a switch on the speaker. 'Simma – get some popcorn sent in. Sweet, salted, covered in horseshit or whatever the hell else it's wrapped in these days. Is Williams there?'

'Yes, he is,' said Simma's voice.

'Send him in.' Forth switched her off.

Williams put his head around the door.

'Williams,' Forth frowned, 'what does popcorn wheat mean

203

to you?'

'Popcorn *wheat*? There's no such thing!'

'Yea – but Dubois keeps saying it. "Merde popcorn wheat. Merde popcorn wheat." It's driving me crazy!'

'*He*'s saying it?' Williams turned to the mirror. 'Jesus, Saxon – he's speaking French. Popcorn *huit* means popcorn *eight* for Christ's sake!' Williams looked at him with disdain.

Forth snapped his fingers. 'Godamn. Of course! You're a genius. Stay with him. See if he says anything else.'

Williams looked at him and left the room.

Forth smashed a clenched fist into his open palm and cursed his stupidity. Sole's reaction linked up with the announcer giving the time signal on the TV. That had to be it. What other connection was there?

He snapped on his own two screens. Various horsemen were being presented with their medals. In the background, attendants ran around the arena scooping up manure.

The video cameras panned gradually up the inside of the mast, facing the stadium.

Forth switched himself through to the control room.

'Control,' said the chesty voice.

'Forth here. Get the boys to turn their cameras on *anything* they see marked "popcorn". Popcorn men. Popcorn signs. Ads. Popcorn stands. Vans. Anything.'

The speaker cleared its voice. 'Popcorn, eh?' it said slowly.

Forth flicked him off. He faced the video screen and waited for the message to filter through to the men on site. Then he switched the speaker through to the earphones of all Squad O officers and marksmen on site.

'Fellas,' he paused, 'keep your eyes on anything marked popcorn. Anything and everything. Look at the area you're covering. Is there anyone hanging around a popcorn board? Any guy buying popcorn or selling it, that looks suspicious? Is there any message pinned to a popcorn sign perhaps?'

He snapped them off and buzzed Simma.

'Mm hmmm?' she answered sleepily.

'I want a message flashed on the big score board in the main stadium. Start coding it through the computer: "Suspect action with popcorn link. Check nearest O point for details." Got it?'

'Suspect action with popcorn link. Check nearest O point for details. Right?'

'Right. Flash it half a dozen times, wait a few seconds, and resume flashing. Where's my popcorn?'

'I sent out for it. I'll bring it in soon as it appears.'

'Move.' Forth sat back. The score board was the quickest means of communicating with any Squad O or MPD or RCMP officer on site who wasn't wearing earphones.

He unbuttoned his shirt and stretched out for a cigar. Then he punched two buttons on the speaker to connect him with the helicopter waiting patiently in the car park at the back of the mast.

'Chopper stadium,' said a voice cheerfully.

'Forth. Start circling the arena. Drop balloons and streamers. Make everybody think it's part of the fun.'

'Right away.'

The speaker died.

Forth attacked his cigar with the Zippo. He rubbed his eyes and studied the video screen. Several cameras panned uncertainly around everything marked popcorn, from empty cartons rolling in the breeze to a fluttering flag to a massive sign, to several bored and tired looking popcorn sellers.

It was seven thirty-one.

Forth chewed his lip anxiously. He glanced at the TV screen. The closing ceremonies had just begun.

A line of colourfully dressed drum majorettes high stepped into the centre of the arena. The screen cleared. A twirling baton soared into the air. An arm stretched up and caught it masterfully. A line of happy faces turned towards the camera. The TV chopper swung into action. Gradually the majorettes fell back into perfectly rehearsed circles. They turned. The aerial shot of them showed five uncannily regular Olympic circles in the official colours of the participating continents. Turquoise blue for Europe. Yellow for Asia. Black for Africa. Green for Oceania. Red for America.

The band started to play the Greek national anthem. The crowd murmured emotionally.

Forth turned down the sound. He let his eyes flicker from one screen to the other. Quickly he checked the number to link him directly with Pete Taylor's earphones on the site. He pressed the appropriate buttons rapidly.

'Taylor,' said Forth slowly.

'Yuh – don't bother me! Check out those *legs*,' drooled the speaker.

205

'Taylor – I need those peepers fast. Some men were seen talking to a coupla fellas by a popcorn sign at the back of the stadium,' he lied. 'They've just walked down stand 7 and are sitting on row DE four rows from the back. If you move down two floors in the mast, you should be on eye level with them. Buzz me as soon as you're there. I'll get the fella two floors above you to move down. *Now.*'

The speaker grunted and died.

Forth glued his eyes to the screens and waited.

Athletes began filling the rings in the arena in groups of a hundred and fifty. Flag bearers marched slowly into the stadium.

The speaker hissed. 'I'm here,' said Taylor.

'Great.' Forth cleared his throat. 'Now move your telescopic sight along row DE, four rows from the back, until you see a group of six beefy gorillas.'

'Four rows down, eh?' The speaker whistled gently as he moved his sight along the row. 'Got it,' he said smartly.

'Okay. They're bunched like bananas, huh? But see if you can pick out a guy in the middle in a dark grey –'

'Light's falling here, Saxon,' said the speaker.

'Sure, sure.' Forth closed his eyes for a second and focused his memory to the faces in the group. He blinked rapidly, 'Okay, two big guys in one row, two others close up next to them. One guy in front. One behind. Right?'

'Check,' the speaker agreed.

'Look at the guy in the middle, with one gorilla behind, one in front...'

'Uh...' the speaker hesitated, 'I *think* I got him.'

'Describe him to me,' said Forth.

'Square glasses. Receding hair, uh –'

'That's him.' Forth checked his watch. Seven forty. 'Keep him in view, Pete. I'll come back to you. I want to check with the others.'

Forth switched him off. He wiped his brow with the back of his hand.

He buzzed Williams next door. 'Any reactions?'

'No,' said Williams, 'he's just generally very high.'

Forth nodded and turned him off. He leaned over to the TV screen and adjusted the sound. The band played the final strains of 'O Canada'. The rings parted. The Canadian Prime Minister, his wife, baby, and two older children walked into the arena and waved at the hysterical crowd.

Forth smiled emotionally.

He felt pleased with himself that he'd been able to organize everything to happen at the end of the Games. It gave the crowds their money's worth.

It also meant the Iranian police minister had a chance to see his kid win a gold medal. Forth was glad to give him the chance. And speak to the kid, too.

If a man had to die at least his last hours should be happy.

It was odd, Forth mused. The Left wanted Ramshid out of the way as much as the CIA did. Different reasons of course.

To the Left, he was the police-state butcher who killed and tortured hundreds of dissidents.

To the CIA, Ramshid was an efficient and ambitious minister who planned to overthrow the Shah and lead a military *junta* himself.

The CIA didn't want that kind of upheaval. Not at any price.

It was easier to replace a police minister than to repair a messy *coup*.

CHAPTER SEVENTEEN

A shower of balloons fell out of the sky.

Walter threw back his head to let them bounce off his face.

'C'mon,' said Joe the popcorn man impatiently, trying to give him a white overall.

Walter laughed and took it, pulling it on over his Greek coat.

'Boy,' said Joe eyeing him up and down. 'Sole didn't tell me you'd be stinking like a dead polecat!'

Walter flushed with embarrassment. 'I had to run most of the way from downtown,' he explained feebly.

Joe shrugged. 'Shall we wait for Sole?' he looked back hopefully at his van in the car park.

'No. He'll know where to find us.'

'Okay. I just hope he's left me his taxi.' Joe pointed at the gate leading to the back of the Velodrome. He passed Walter a special popcorn ID clip. 'Let me do all the talking,' he said nodding towards a security guard slouched against the fence.

Walter shouldered a tray of popcorn and hobbled obediently along the path.

'*Bonsoir*,' Joe said to the guard.

'*Bonsoir*,' said the guard, sucking something out of his tooth.

Walter smiled and nodded and showed his clip.

The guard opened the gate. He let them walk on a few paces, and lifted his hand to his mouth.

'Velodrome Gate E car park,' he said into the tiny mike taped to one finger, 'two guys just walked through. Their popcorn ID's checked out, but who sells popcorn when everything's closing down? One stinks like Christ knows what. Maybe nothing. Maybe something. Nobody sells popcorn stinking like that.'

'Thanks,' said a voice from the near-by Squad O base. It switched through to camera control. 'Base V. Two suspect popcorn sellers just entered Velodrome Gate E from the car park. Alerting O and MPD officers in immediate vicinity. See if your cameras can pick them up.'

208

'Right away,' replied the chesty voice from camera control. Seven fifty-three.

'Control to Forth.'

Forth responded quickly. 'Yes?'

'Switching a couple of cameras to the back of the Velodrome, sir. Two popcorn suspects just entered through Gate E.'

'Okay,' Forth sharpened the picture on the video screen and waited until the cameramen got to work. He pressed buttons on the speaker to link him with six squad O and MPD officers nearest the Velodrome. 'Forth. Listen you guys. No trigger-happy hot-shots, okay? Just move in close and observe.' He released the buttons.

He glanced at the video screen as a camera panned slowly along the back arch of the Velodrome. A man and a woman in track suits walked casually by. Something caught the corner of Forth's eye. He looked away from the screen. Williams waved his arms frantically on the other side of the mirror.

Forth leaped from his chair and rushed next door.

Sole was screaming at the screen. Forth looked hastily over his shoulder. All he could see were clusters of people dotted about the Velodrome, listening to the final ceremonies over loudspeakers.

Sole had seen Walter and Joe the popcorn man walk down the path at the back of the Velodrome, and pause at the fountains.

But on the other side of the building, out of sight to them and in full view of the camera, Sole saw a couple he recognized, in *track suits*.

Somewhere in his mind he knew they shouldn't be there. He knew they shouldn't be together.

One was Staki. The other was the Vatican courier, Mark Land.

Sole stopped screaming. His mouth tried desperately to form words of warning. His brain wouldn't let it. He picked up the tray of food and hurtled it at the screen. Glass exploded in all directions.

'Quick,' said Forth, *'take him into my office.'*

* * *

Walter recognized Hammond's back view. The popcorn outfit ended somewhere just under his knees. The man next to

209

him wore an outfit that bulged obscenely.

Walter choked back a laugh.

'What's so darned funny?' asked Joe crossly.

'Those guys! They look like Laurel and Hardy in reverse!' He turned around to try and control himself, and caught sight of Joe's expression. 'Why don't you go back to the van and wait for us? Start the engine?'

Joe nodded. 'Still no sign of Sole.'

'Nothing,' said Walter, trying not to think about Sole. 'He may be at the van,' he suggested.

'Guess so.' Joe pulled a face. 'He promised me he'd leave the taxi for me.' He started to walk away.

'He probably did,' said Walter tightly, moving closer to the comic pair.

An anthem blared out over the loudspeaker above. Walter winced, clapping his hands over his ears. He walked on until he was about three feet away from the pair.

'*Russian* anthem?' Lancey sounded horrified.

'Of course!' said Hammond.

'But why Russian?'

'I assume it's simply a polite way of looking ahead to Moscow's Olympics in 1980.'

'Oh ... guess it must be. Spotted your friend yet?'

'No, but he's extraordinarily punctual,' Hammond assured him.

'Okay,' said Lancey miserably, 'just hope I don't see anybody who knows me.'

'Come now Bucky, where's your spirit of adventure?' Hammond slapped him comfortingly on the back.

Bucky?

Walter froze. Hammond's gem expert was *Bucky Lancey*? It wasn't possible. It had to be a trap. Walter looked around, panic stricken.

A camera focused on him from the other side of the fence. Four men edged slowly towards him.

*   *   *

Simma burst into Saxon Forth's office carrying an armload of assorted popcorn bags.

'*Jesus*,' he bellowed in amazement. 'Get that crap next door. Is the new video in there yet?'

'*Yes*,' she said crossly, marching out of the room.

'Williams – take Dubois back and put him in front of the new screen. *Move him.* Show him that godamn popcorn and see if it jumps anything between his ears. *Move!*'

Williams helped Sole hastily out of the door.

As soon as the door closed behind them, Forth pressed the buttons to link him with Taylor's earphones. 'Taylor? You okay?'

'Sure. Just getting a little bored. Can't see any legs from here,' the speaker said sadly.

'C'mon Pete, c'mon. Still got that guy in square glasses in view?'

'Course.'

Forth turned up the sound on the TV screen.

'Ouch!' the speaker winced.

'Sorry – I'll come back to you.' He switched Taylor off, and concentrated on the TV.

The Russian Ambassador walked into the centre of the arena and shook hands with the Canadian Prime Minister. The Russian anthem played through its final bars.

It was seven fifty-eight.

Forth looked across at the video screen. It showed him nothing but an expanse of Velodrome. He looked back again at the TV. The Canadian Prime Minister began walking around the formation of the Olympic rings, patting heads, exchanging greetings, shaking hands. His two sons ran along behind, and his wife held their youngest child in her arms.

Forth tapped the top of his desk thoughtfully. He reconnected the speaker with Taylor. 'Pete,' he said flatly. 'Our suspect just talked. Those guys on the other side of your sight have been hired to assassinate the Prime Minister, and his family.'

'*Christ!*' hissed the speaker.

Forth paused, and watched as the Prime Minister moved to the next ring. 'I want you to shoot the guy with the square glasses first, then keep pumping at the gorillas.'

'When?' the speaker asked politely.

'When I tell you. I've warned the other marksmen, but hang well out so they see it's you. Otherwise you'll get your head blown off!'

The speaker chuckled.

Forth waited until the Prime Minister had moved to the

next ring, and was directly between Taylor, on one side, and Ramshid with his bodyguards, on the other. The Prime Minister did a mock curtsey and laughed with a group of South American athletes. His youngest child stretched out to kiss a triple gold medallist. His two other children ran around excitedly.

'Okay, Pete,' said Forth.

'Now?' the speaker asked.

'*Now.*'

Taylor rested his elbows on the window ledge. His hands squeaked on the Armalite M16. He looked down the sight at the Iranian police minister's head. He aimed and fired.

The Iranian's square glasses splintered. Blood spurted from his eye sockets. His hands went up, clutching the air. Taylor moved the M16 from left to right, spinning shots into the backs that crouched over the descending body of the Iranian.

Taylor shoved his shoulders through the window and aimed again. Six Squad O marksmen's rifles spat out from different points in the stadium and hit him simultaneously.

'It's me, Taylor,' he protested feebly. He slumped over the window. Blood streamed from his mouth and ears.

The crowds started screaming. People ran frantically in all directions. The Prime Minister's personal security officers fought to hustle his family through the dismembered Olympic rings of people, and out of the nearest exit.

Another round of bullets smacked successively into Taylor's lifeless body.

The impact jerked him upwards. He tumbled out of the window, landing head first on a concrete slab below.

Forth looked away from the screens. He began to prepare a statement for the press.

*   *   *

Walter heard the shots echo around the stadium. The men edging towards him froze for a split second. Walter ducked in terror under the side of the Velodrome and ran across the deserted cycling ring.

It was dusky inside. He kept close to the wall and came up on the side he believed was closest to Gate E.

But he misjudged. He came up facing the entrance to the swimming pool under the mast's fan tail.

212

He ran blindly, the sound of shots and screaming ringing in his ears.

He found himself running up a sloping ramp. It lead to the main foyer and shopping arcade linking the swimming pool, under the mast, with the main stadium.

People surged around him, trying desperately to find any exit out of the stadium.

Walter pushed his way through them to get to the elevators. The crowd cleared for an instant. He banged the buttons repeatedly with his fist, and pressed himself against the closed doors.

Somebody shouted out his name. 'Walter, *run*. It's a trap. *Run!*'

He jumped up to look over the heads of the crowds. It was *Staki's voice!*

The elevator doors opened behind him. He fell backwards. The doors closed and he started to move upwards.

Suddenly he was exposed to the dusk.

He glanced around in terror. The ascent of the panoramic elevator, up the parabolic spine of the mast, was intended to thrill him with the sights of Montreal.

He was trapped in a glass cage.

He looked down at the other elevator two storeys below. Both elevators were clearly lit.

Staki was in it. She was fighting violently with somebody.

Walter dropped to the elevator floor and tried to see who it was.

There was something familiar about the man's face.

'You bloody bitch, trying to double-cross us like that,' shouted the courier, banging Staki's head against the elevator. She tried to reach for the buttons. He wrenched her arm away and held the button for the top floor.

She fought back viciously. 'I'm not, you ape – for Christ's sake *listen* to me. Those men were trying to surround him, Hammond and Lancey. Did you want them to find the diamonds *and* the money?'

The courier sweated profusely. He let go of her.

She leaned back against the elevator. 'I *had* to warn him. How else would we get him?'

The courier looked up at the wildly gesticulating figure in the elevator above.

'Staki!' Walter screamed. 'Can you hear me? Stop your elevator on the tenth floor!' He pressed his flat palms against the transparent elevator wall and pointed upwards, praying she'd get the message.

The courier saw him. 'He's trying to say something.'

Staki turned around and looked up. She saw Walter's hands and tried to read his lips. 'He's saying meet him on the tenth floor.'

The courier twisted her arm behind her brutally. 'Nod, you stinking bitch. I'll make sure I get those diamonds. If you try to double-cross me I'll kill you.'

Staki nodded frantically. She tried desperately to pull out of the courier's grip.

'Don't bother,' he said. *'Borg and his bloody weakness for Chinese women!'* he shouted, kicking her to the floor 'I told him you'd be hopeless. I knew you'd lose your nerve. You could hardly touch *Mark Land* when we put him in the freezer!' He drew out his gun.

Walter watched, horrified. He beat his fists uselessly against the wall of the elevator. The man had blond hair and a beaked nose. Mark Land!

How was it possible? How had Staki found out in time to get to the site to warn him? If Hammond and Lancey were tied up with this impostor, why involve *him*?

He watched the lights flash the floors above his head. Two more to go.

*　　*　　*

A group of marksmen stood below. They watched the ascent of the two elevators. Other marksmen rushed to take up positions on each floor inside the mast. The helicopter flayed the air above them.

Police cars ringed the site. Car 46 screeched to a halt closest to the mast base. The driver pulled out his mike. 'Car 46 to Forth.'

'What's happening?' said Forth's voice through the plastic slats.

'Three suspects in elevators, sir. Marksmen taking up positions on the floors. Whole area sealed off.'

'Right. What about those other jokers by the Velodrome?'

214

asked Forth's voice.

'Constantin's questioning an English guy called Hammond now. He's trying to say they were playing a practical joke. Short guy with him tried to make a run for it. He's dead.'

'Uh huh.'

'Some practical joke,' continued the officer. 'They had bundles of beautiful crisp thousand dollar notes with them.'

'Uh huh?' said Forth flatly. 'Buzz me soon as those elevators stop.'

'Ten four.'

Forth looked at the video screen. Cameras traced the elevators' ascent. He reached for a cigar.

*   *   *

Walter's elevator purred to a halt. The doors parted slowly. He caught sight of the officers running towards him, pressed his back against the elevator wall, and jammed the 'door shut' button. He banged the button for the sixteenth floor.

The elevator obeyed immediately.

Forth pounced on the speaker. 'Car 46? Can't somebody stop those godamn elevators?'

'Uh, sir, nobody knows how to work the mechanism. We're trying to find the engineer now,' said the officer, flushing with embarrassment in the dark.

'What've you guys got for brains? Toenail parings?' Forth switched off in disgust.

Walter looked down at the other elevator. He pressed two hands to the floor, then one hand and a finger from the other hand.

The courier read him and pressed button sixteen. He turned savagely on Staki. 'When I took that job as Mark Land's assistant in London I wanted to switch the gems *my* way. But no. Borg thought your boyfriend was a better cover. Get him to switch the gems. Introduce him to Hammond. Kill them both and you kill the evidence. He didn't think you'd turn on us you filthy bitch.'

'I can't!' she screamed, beating him on the chest. 'He's been using my father's business as a front for his stinking drug trafficking – he *owns* us you stupid bastard, *owns us all*!'

215

The elevator doors parted. Walter shoved his way out through a number of waiters who clamoured to push into it. Running steps echoed around the chamber of the stairwell.

Walter fought his way past. He glanced up at the panel button above the other elevator. Floor fifteen.

The footsteps ran closer.

He turned, panicking for the stairs, clearing several at a time.

The elevator doors parted. Staki and the courier heard footsteps below and above. They ran towards the stairs.

Walter faced the restaurant. He looked around wildly. Long lines of tables awaited the mayoral reception. Row upon row of expensively prepared dishes stretched out endlessly before him.

A chef and two waiters emerged from the back. He ran at them, screaming to get out of the way. They disappeared hastily.

Staki and the courier heard him as they cleared the last few stairs.

Walter ran to the far side of the restaurant and through a door at the back. He jumped on to a spiral staircase. It led to the upper storey of the restaurant at the top of the mast.

He rushed into a room similar to the one below. A helicopter hovered outside the windows on the far side. A voice barked orders over a megaphone. Waiters crowded to push their way out of the doors to get to the elevators.

Walter dived under a table.

Staki and the courier appeared a few feet away from him. The helicopter spotted them and started firing. Glass splintered across the entire far end of the room. They dropped to the floor and started to crawl towards the back wall, out of the helicopter's sightline.

Walter watched them, too bewildered to believe they were together. 'Staki!' he shouted.

The courier swung his body around and fired, hitting the table leg inches from Walter's face. Walter lunged out with his feet, kicking the gun from the courier's hand.

Another pane of glass shattered violently behind them. Bullets spat into the floor.

The courier rose to his knees. Staki crawled behind a pillar. Bullets thudded into the courier's chest, missing her by a foot. The courier tried to get up. Bullets hailed around him. The top of his head spun across the tablecloths. He slumped to the floor.

Staki leaned weakly against the pillar. 'Walter – help me, help me.'

Walter crouched behind the table, as a third pane of glass burst into the restaurant.

A regiment of wine bottles exploded spraying glass and wine from one side of the restaurant to the other.

Walter lay flat on the floor behind the table and stretched out his hand. 'Staki. I'm behind you. Don't look towards the windows. Start edging back. Slowly. The chopper's looking for us.'

She obeyed. Suddenly she screamed out with pain as her hands pressed down on broken glass. Bullets spat around her.

Walter jumped and dragged her under the full length cloth of a carving table a foot away. The chopper's view was blocked by the pillar. Its propellor beat the air outside like the wings of a giant mosquito. Then it swung away to fly around the building to get a better view from the other side of the restaurant.

Staki's face poured with blood. Walter held her in his arms. He tried to staunch the flow from her forehead.

Her lips moved.

'Don't speak,' he said. 'I'll get you out of here.'

'I had to warn you,' she choked.

He shook his head and held his sleeve against her forehead, feeling the blood soak through to his arm. 'Staki. How did you find out?' he whispered.

She tried to say something.

'Staki? He bent his ear to her lips. '*Staki*,' he repeated. He took his arm away from her forehead. 'Oh God. Don't die. Don't leave me alone.' He held her body close to him.

A pane of glass burst over the table. Walter shuddered. He dropped her body.

The chopper moved to the next window.

Walter lifted the edge of the tablecloth. Arc lights suddenly lit up the interior of the restaurant from outside. The dusk was falling rapidly.

Walter reeled backwards. He stared blankly at Staki's body and the glazed, sightless eyes. He reached out and touched her hair. It was matted with blood. He blinked. This wasn't somebody he knew. It couldn't be.

217

He lifted up the edge of the tablecloth a second time. The arc lights darted around the far end of the restaurant.

He hesitated. Then something forced him to run. He zig-zagged from one pillar to the next, to get to the back door. Bullets zapped into the wall.

He moved from the door towards the spiral stairway. He gazed up it blankly.

The helicopter hovered, puzzled, outside the window. There was no sign of life in the restaurant. It pumped a token round of bullets through the last whole pane of sheet glass. Nothing moved. Arc lights flayed the interior.

Walter walked slowly up the spiral stairway. He could taste blood, smell it. His senses felt paralysed by it.

He paused. His feet moved backwards.

There was a trapdoor above him. A cupboard at the bottom of the stairs. He turned towards it. He opened it. It was filled with neatly stacked tablecloths and waiters' uniforms. Walter reached out for them like a man in a dream. He took a bundle and held it protectively against his chest.

He looked up at the trapdoor. He bolted up the stairs and began to beat it with his fists. It moved easily. He pushed it open, ran up a few more steps and found himself in a control room. He threw the bundle into it.

He hauled himself up, drew in his legs and replaced the trap door.

The small, neatly fitted room housed the mechanism that controlled the stadium canopy. The canopy could be lowered down, umbrella like, to seal the open stadium roof, in a matter of minutes.

Walter looked at his clothes. He stank with Staki's blood. He watched his hands tear off his coat and trousers. They reached for a tablecloth and bundled it inside the clothes.

Walter stared at the levers controlling the canopy. Instructions were pinned up in English and French.

He looked at the tablecloth bundled into his clothes, and gently did up the buttons on his coat. He ripped a hole in the trousers and hooked them on the coat buttons. He stood up and hugged his scarecrow.

He read through the instructions excitedly. *To release the canopy pull the right lever to open the flap on the outer wall.* He pulled it, then leaned forwards to fit the scarecrow into the gap, sliding the trousers legs around the canopy ropes, and tying them firmly.

Pull the left lever down the metal ropes to unfold the canopy.

He paused. His arms stretched out to the waiter's uniform. They dressed him slowly.

He pulled the left lever. The metal ropes tightened under his grip. The bundle disappeared.

Screams and shouts echoed up from below. The mechanism whined smoothly and powerfully.

Machine gun fire burst out wildly next to his ear.

He pulled up the trap door and dropped to the stairway. He ran to the bottom, and pushed open the door into the restaurant. It was filled with policemen and waiters kicking aside broken glass and splattered food, to get to the bodies. Walter sauntered by them.

'Hey!' somebody yelled. 'The third guy's just jumped out with the canopy!'

They fought one another to get to the windows. Walter walked towards the stairway next to the elevators. He pushed by a number of men in dark suits, walking importantly to the top floor.

The mast seemed to crawl with people. Policemen. Waiters. Athletes. Spectators. All shouting and running.

Walter moved blindly down the stairs, increasing his pace with each floor.

He ran down fourteen flights and staggered at the bottom. Ambulance men pumped the elevator buttons next to him. Men in white uniforms like his own ran across the foyer wheeling stretchers.

Walter reeled like a drunk man.

Nobody took the slightest bit of notice.

He walked along a covered ramp leading out of the foyer.

A series of rifle shots cracked against the outer wall.

Walter started to run. A door loomed ahead. He flew at it with his feet in mid air. It burst open and he skimmed into a tunnel of darkness.

He picked himself up off the rubber floor and ran blindly into the tunnel. Suddenly he felt a cool gust of air. He emerged into the night.

Walter blinked in amazement.

He'd run down the covered path leading to the Metro at Pie 1X.

Saxon Forth glanced up at Simma. She waited, notebook in hand, to take down the press statement.

He scratched the back of his neck and stared at the video screen.

Two ambulance men lifted Staki gently on to the stretcher, and flung a white cloth over her body. They strapped her down.

Two other ambulance men lifted the body of Peter Twenton Smith, alias Mark Land, alias Thomas Harbaker, and laid it gently on a stretcher.

A police officer searched about for the top of Smith's head.

'Okay Simma,' said Forth, turning from the screen. 'Headline: Squad O Forces prevent assassination attempt on Canadian Premier and family period marksman shot in shoot-out with assassins period two assassins shot dead trying to escape in the stadium period another shot trying to escape by the Velodrome period a fourth man is being held for questioning period he's English but no further details can be disclosed at this stage period assassins believed to be members of an international revolutionary front period Squad O forces received news of the proposed attack from their intelligence network minutes before the attack period three spectators only comma lost their lives in the shoot-out period Head of Squad O Saxon Forth said that the minimum of bloodshed was achieved through the efficient co-ordination of officers, policemen and marksmen guarding the site period.'

Forth paused. 'We'll issue another release about Ramshid's identity. When we identify him.' He smiled at her. 'Clean up my English, sweetheart.'

'I always do,' Simma replied, closing her notebook.

Forth bent over the speaker. 'Adams?'

'Yes sir?' he replied.

'Move Dubois. See he has some ID on him. Drive him to a block away from his home. Dump him.'

'Yes, sir.' The connection died.

Forth stretched out his hand and patted Simma's cheek. 'Thanks,' he said gratefully.

'What for?' she asked, shrugging.

He reached for his cigars.

* * *

Walter bolted towards the train waiting patiently by the platform.

Groups of people poured out of the tunnel and were sucked greedily into the train's open doors.

Walter ran to the end. He had to find an empty compartment. He jumped in just as the doors closed behind him.

The train started to move.

Walter looked at his reflection in the glass and began jeering insanely.

He caught sight of the white uniform. His eyes bulged at themselves in the glass.

White uniform?

He began to pat around it frantically.

His Greek civil war coat? Floating high above the Olympic stadium being pumped by bullets? All those diamonds bursting from the seams? Being scattered to oblivion?

Was he that stupid?

Then he saw his own expression. He pointed and burst out laughing. Nobody could look that silly. Nobody.

He tore off the waiter's jacket and trousers. He flung them against the ceiling of the moving train, let them fall into his arms, and hurled them along the floor against the train's direction.

He shouted with delight. It was like running up a down escalator as a kid.

He stood on the seats and swung wildly on the hand grips. He glanced at his nude reflection in the glass and spreadeagled himself across the corridor.

He crouched down and looked again at the window.

He could see somebody laughing and crying maniacally.

They took the roughest, toughest coppers in the force — and threw away the rule book.

THE CRIME COMMANDOES

Peter Cave 50p

CRANE was mean. He had a reputation for leaning on villains. One day he leaned too hard, and a suspect died. Crane was fired.

CORNISH was trouble. Bomb disposal was his business, but he was a walking timebomb himself. In the Army he made sergeant — twice. Both times he was busted back to private for insubordination.

LAKE had a soft voice, a friendly grin, and hands that could snap a man in two.

BABSLEY was police boxing champion until he discovered his Superintendent was taking bribes, and dealt out his own brand of justice.

JELLY was an Alsatian with a nose for explosives. Even he had been rejected as unmanageable by police dog trainers.

FOUR disgraced men and a half-mad dog — a compact, elite and deadly squad. Set up by the authorities, but having no official status. Coppers who followed no rule book; who carried machine guns instead of charge books. Using the methods of terrorists against the terrorists.

THE CRIME COMMANDOES.

Use the special order form at the end of this book

Apples Carstairs — the new avenger

THE BIG NEEDLE

Symon Myles   45p

The doorbell rang at dawn. Apples was in bed with
Annabel and Babs, as usual. Then came the news which
changed his lifestyle for good.
His daughter was dying.
And someone had to pay . . .

'Breathtaking pace . . . Chandleresque wisecracks,'
LONDON EVENING NEWS

THE BIG BLACK

Symon Myles   45p

The blackmail photo was fuzzy. But the man in the
compromising position was undoubtedly Apples.
Apples didn't give a damn.
Until he discovered he was not the only victim on the
blackmailer's list . . .

'Unputdownable' MERCURY

THE BIG HIT

Symon Myles   45p

Winston Divine was a star. He had success, fame and
money. So why was he running scared? He decided to
confide in an old friend — Apples Carstairs.
Winston died minutes later.
And Apples had to know why . . .

'Cool, sexy and violent. But good.'
LIVERPOOL DAILY POST

Use the special order form at the end of this book

Armchair bookshop

All good bookshops stock Everest titles. If you have any difficulty getting our books – or if you prefer to shop from home – please fill in this form.

————————